Christmas
from the
HEART

SHEILA ROBERTS

Christmas
from the
HEART

mira

mira

ISBN-13: 978-0-7783-6096-4

Christmas from the Heart

Recycling programs
for this product may
not exist in your area.

For questions and comments about the quality of this book, please contact us at CustomerService@Harlequin.com.

BookClubbish.com

Printed in U.S.A.

For Carol

Christmas from the HEART

1

From: Olivia Berg, Director, Christmas from the Heart
Date: 2-14-19
To: Ms. Marla Thompson, CSR Director, Hightower Enterprises
Subject: Holiday Joy

Dear Ms. Thompson,
Happy Valentine's Day to you! I'm following up our January newsletter with a special greeting as this is, of course, the month for love. Love for our sweethearts, our family and friends, and for those in need. As you could see from the newsletter, we put the money our loyal supporters donated to us to good use. So many families benefited from your generous donation to Christmas from the Heart last year and I just wanted to remind you that, even though the holidays seem far away they will be here before we know it. I hope we can count on Hightower Enterprises again this year. We have such a history together. Let's keep up the good work!
Warmly,
Olivia Berg

Christmas from the Heart
Giving from the heart makes all the difference

From: Marla Thompson, CSR Director, Hightower Enterprises
Date: 2-14-19
To: Ms. Olivia Berg, Director, Christmas from the Heart
Subject: Holiday Joy

Dear Ms. Berg,
Thanks for reaching out. Our fiscal year is just ending and I haven't yet received word as to how our charitable donations will be dispersed this year. I will keep you apprised.
Best,
Marla Thompson
CSR Director, Hightower Enterprises

From: Olivia Berg, Director, Christmas from the Heart
Date: 2-14-19
To: Ms. Marla Thompson, CSR Director, Hightower Enterprises
Subject: Holiday Joy

Thank you so much. Looking forward to hearing from you!
Olivia Berg
Christmas from the Heart
Giving from the heart makes all the difference

From: Olivia Berg, Director, Christmas from the Heart
Date: 5-1-19
To: Ms. Marla Thompson, CSR Director, Hightower Enterprises
Subject: Happy May Day!

Dear Ms. Thompson, just wanted to wish you a happy May Day. The flowers here in Pine River are now in full bloom, and our

organization has been busy helping people make their dreams bloom, as well. As you know, while our focus is primarily the holidays, Christmas from the Heart tries to help people all year round when needs arise. Of course, Christmas is our big thrust, and as there is no other organization working in this area, we are much needed. As are your kind contributions. I still haven't heard and I do hope we can count on you.
Warmly,
Olivia Berg
Christmas from the Heart
Giving from the heart makes all the difference

From: Olivia Berg, Director, Christmas from the Heart
Date: 5-5-19
To: Ms. Marla Thompson
Subject: Just checking

Reaching out again in case my last email went astray. I'm wondering if you have any news for me regarding Hightower's involvement with our cause for this coming year.
Thanks!
Olivia Berg
Christmas from the Heart
Giving from the heart makes all the difference

From: Marla Thompson, CSR Director, Hightower Enterprises
Date: 5-5-19
To: Ms. Olivia Berg
Subject: Just checking

Ms. Berg, sorry I haven't been able to get back to you sooner. I'm afraid I have some bad news for you. It appears that the company

is going to be scaling back on their charitable giving this year and funds have already been budgeted for other causes. I'm aware of the fact that in the past we've donated to your organization and I'm sorry I don't have better news for you. I do wish you all the best in your search for other funding.
Best,
Marla Thompson
CSR Director, Hightower Enterprises

From: Olivia Berg, Director, Christmas from the Heart
Date: 5-5-19
To: Ms. Marla Thompson
Subject: Just checking

There must be some sort of misunderstanding! Hightower has always donated to Christmas from the Heart. The company's founder, Elias Hightower, was my great-grandmother's first contributor, and he promised her that Hightower would always be there for this organization. This is a company tradition! Please speak to your director.
Hopefully,
Olivia Berg
Christmas from the Heart
Giving from the heart makes all the difference

From: Marla Thompson, CSR Director, Hightower Enterprises
Date: 5-5-19
To: Ms. Olivia Berg
Subject: Just checking

I'm sorry. The decision is out of my hands.
Marla Thompson
CSR Director, Hightower Enterprises

From: Olivia Berg, Director, Christmas from the Heart
Date: 5-5-19
To: Ms. Marla Thompson
Subject: Just checking

Then please tell me who I need to talk to. Who's your CFO?
Olivia Berg
Christmas from the Heart
Giving from the heart makes all the difference

From: Marla Thompson, CSR Director, Hightower Enterprises
Date: 5-5-19
To: Ms. Olivia Berg
Subject: Just checking

Our CFO is Guy Hightower, and his email is ghightower@hightowerenterprises.com
Good luck!
Marla Thompson
CSR Director, Hightower Enterprises

From: Olivia Berg, Director, Christmas from the Heart
Date: 5-5-19
To: Guy Hightower, CFO, Hightower Enterprises
Subject: Please reconsider

Dear Mr. Hightower, I understand from your corporate social resources director that Hightower isn't planning on making any donation to Christmas from the Heart this year. There must be some mistake! Surely you're aware of the long-standing relationship between your company and our organization. I'm sure I can count on you for some small amount.
Best,
Olivia Berg

Christmas from the Heart
Giving from the heart makes all the difference

Guy Hightower frowned when he saw the email from Olivia Berg in his in-box. Marla Thompson had been forwarding her emails to him, keeping him abreast of Olivia Berg's varied begging tactics, and had finally even come into his office, trying to dump the load of guilt the woman had laid on her from her shoulders to his.

"Don't open it," he told himself. He opened it anyway. Then he read it and swore.

Actually, he'd been swearing ever since meeting with his brothers to discuss the budget back in December. If either of them had listened to him three years ago, they wouldn't be having to pull the company belt so tight now. This was the problem with being the youngest. It didn't matter how many degrees you had, how smart you were or what your job title was. Big brothers never listened.

Hard to listen when you were going through your third divorce.

That was Mike's excuse. What was Bryan's? Oh yeah. He was a wuss. He always agreed with Mike, no matter what. And Mike hadn't wanted to change directions. Never mind that the company was struggling, keep on doing the same thing. The definition of insanity.

Sorry, Little Miss Christmas. Times were tough all over. Hightower had kept its commitment to the more visible causes and turned the little fish loose. And that was how it worked in the corporate world.

He typed his reply.

Dear Ms. Berg, I regret that Hightower can't help you this year. We've had to reassess our commitments to various causes. I'm sure you'll understand.

Then he signed off with the time-honored adios: Respect-fully, Guy Hightower.

And if she didn't understand, well, not his problem. He had his hands full trying to keep the family company afloat. Maybe now Mike would be ready to take his advice and diversify.

Olivia Berg—Livi to her family and friends—read the email from Guy Hightower a second time. Yes, the message was the same. Really? *Really?* Who was this man, Ebenezer Scrooge the Second?

She plowed her fingers through her hair, the birthstone ring Morris had given her for her birthday catching in the curls. She was so angry she barely noticed.

With a snarl, she began to type.

You should be ashamed. Your great-grandfather is probably turn-ing in his grave right now. What's the matter with you, anyway, you selfish bastard?

She pulled her fingers off the keyboard with a gasp. What was she thinking? Was this any way to get someone to con-tribute to her cause? And what kind of language was this? Her great-grandmother would be turning in her grave right now, along with Elias. Adelaide Brimwell had been a lady through and through. So had Livi's grandmother, Olivia, as well as Li-vi's mom.

The thought of her mother made her tear up. How she wished Mom was still around to advise her. They'd always planned that Livi would take over running the organization one day, but nei-ther had dreamed that day would come so soon. Her mother's heart attack had struck like lightning. Livi's brother had left town, moving to Seattle, which was just far enough south to keep the memories at bay. Livi had stayed put, holding on to

every single one, weaving them together into a lifeline to cling
to as she kept Christmas from the Heart afloat.

Oh, Mom. What should I do?

Try again came the answer.

Yes, her mother never gave up. She'd chased one potential
donor for two years before he finally came through. Livi still remembered the day her mom left the house, clad in a Mrs. Santa
costume she'd created—requisite white wig along with a frilly
white blouse and a red skirt topped with a red-striped apron.
She'd taken with her a batch of home-baked cookies nestled in
a red basket and returned home with a check for five hundred
dollars. The man had been a loyal contributor ever since. Livi
still took him cookies every year.

"Persistence pays," she told herself as she deleted what she'd
typed.

She started over.

I'm asking you to reconsider. Your company is our major donor,
and without you so many people will have little joy this Christmas.
Any amount you can give will be greatly appreciated.

There. He'd have to be a heartless monster not to respond
to that.

Guy trashed the guilt-inflicting email. What was he, Santa
Claus? He had his hands full keeping his company solvent.

But then, people like Olivia Berg never considered the fact
that a company might have needs of its own. What made them
feel so entitled to sit at the edge of the salt mine while a man
slaved away and then greet him with their hands out when he
emerged broken and bruised? Maybe some of those people always begging for money should get out there and actually *earn*

a living. Let them work their tails off, putting in seventy-hour weeks. *Sheesh.*

Anyway, the company had already met their good deed quota for the year. The only cause Guy was interested in now was Hightower Enterprises.

By the end of the workday, Guy Hightower still hadn't responded to Livi's last email. "You are a heartless monster," she grumbled, glaring at her empty email in-box.

"No word yet?" her part-time assistant, Bettina Thomas, asked as she shut down her computer.

Livi sighed and shook her head.

"That is so wrong," Bettina said in disgust.

It sure was. "They've been our major donor ever since my great-grandmother founded Christmas from the Heart. Without their contribution how will we put on the Christmas dinner at the community center? How many families won't have presents under the tree or Christmas stockings or a Christmas turkey?" There was no Salvation Army in Pine River, no Toys for Tots—none of the usual organizations serviced this area. There had been no need. Christmas from the Heart had it under control.

Until now.

"We've had to reassess our commitments," Livi quoted. The words left a bad taste in her mouth and she frowned. "It sounds like something your boyfriend says when he's dumping you."

"They are dumping us," Bettina pointed out. "But don't worry. We have time. We'll find someone else to come through."

"Not like Hightower. There must be something I can do," Livi mused.

"There is. Go home and eat chocolate."

And try not to think bad thoughts about Guy Hightower.

In all fairness, he probably didn't grasp the situation. She'd call him the next day and invite him to come to Pine River for a visit so she could let him see the need, show him a little of what Christmas from the Heart did for the community. She could take him to lunch, introduce him to some of the people in town, put a face—or better yet, several—to Christmas from the Heart. She'd top it all off by following in her mother's footsteps and baking him cookies. Then how could he help but catch the vision his great-grandfather and her great-grandmother had shared?

Yes, that would do it. Sometimes you had to be a little patient, give people a second chance.

2

Trying a more personal touch with Guy Hightower was the way to go, Olivia was sure of that, but getting past his secretary was proving to be a challenge. Maybe giving her name hadn't been such a good idea. The first time she called, Mr. Hightower was in a meeting. The second time she called, he was out. He was in another meeting on her third call, then unavailable on her fourth.

Finally, she asked, "Is there a good time to reach him?"

"I'm afraid Mr. Hightower is very busy," his secretary said evasively.

Livi suspected that Mr. Hightower was very busy avoiding her. "Tell him I'll only take a minute of his time," she pleaded.

"Can you hold please?"

"For as long as it takes," Olivia said sweetly.

Olivia Berg was never going to go away. She was going to keep on calling and calling, driving his secretary nuts, and Guy was beginning to suspect if he didn't talk to her she'd come to Seattle and camp out in the lobby of the Hightower Building until he would.

"Fine," he said irritably. "Put her through." *Get it over with.*

"Mr. Hightower, thank you so much for taking a moment to talk to me," she gushed as soon as he'd taken the call.

"I'm not sure we have much to talk about at this point, Ms. Berg," he said. "As I told you in my email—"

She cut him off, rushing on like a vacation time-share salesman. "I'm realizing that email isn't always the most effective way to communicate. I'd love to meet with you in person. I think if you could visit Pine River and see what Christmas from the Heart does—"

Like he had time to go charging up to her little town and get hassled in person. Now it was his turn to snip her off midsentence. "I'm sure you do a lot of good, but we can't help you this year."

"Mr. Hightower, we have such a history together."

He knew all about their history, probably more than she did.

"Surely you can manage something."

One thing Guy couldn't manage at this point was his temper. He'd just come from a very unpleasant meeting with his idiot brothers and he wanted to punch a wall. "Look—"

"Any amount would be helpful. People have so many needs during the holidays."

"I know they do but I can't help you."

"A big corporation like yours," she began.

Oh yeah. Play that card. *You're a big company so we'll hit you up and you should be proud that we are.* "I don't know how many ways to say this politely but the answer is no."

"You can't mean that," she coaxed. "Your company's been so good to us all these years."

And here came the guilt card. Wrong card to play. "I'm afraid I can."

"Again, please consider the history we have together," she pleaded.

"I'm sorry, but things change."

"Change isn't always good," she snapped. "You have no idea how many people depend on Christmas from the Heart."

"I've got people depending on me, too. Okay?"

"Well, of course. But surely…"

"I can't give you anything." His voice was rising, right along with his blood pressure.

"There's no need to yell," she said stiffly. "I'd just hoped you'd reconsider. We're not asking a lot."

"It's a lot if you don't have it."

"Hightower Enterprises is a big company. Really, Mr. Hightower—"

Now she was going to lecture him on what his company could and couldn't afford to give? Okay, that was it. "What don't you understand about the word *no*? Look, lady, I've been as polite as I can, but I'm not getting through, so we're done here. We can't give to every leech that latches onto us and that's that."

"Leech!" she repeated, her voice vibrating with shock. "Well, of all the rude…"

"Hey, if you want to talk about rude, I'm not the one bugging people so they can't get their work done. I'm not the one who can't take no for an answer. But believe it or not, that's what it is. So cut it out with the high-pressure crap 'cause I'm not giving you squat. Got that?" He didn't give her time to say whether she got it or not. He ended the call.

And then he suffered a major guilt attack. That had been cold. Ebenezer Scrooge couldn't have said it better.

He rubbed his aching forehead. What was the matter with him, anyway? People had needs. They lost jobs and not always because they'd done anything wrong. Sometimes you worked your butt off and things didn't work out.

For all he knew, things might not work out for his company

in spite of his long hours. But that was no excuse for being a jerk. Bad PR for the company, too.

He heaved a sigh and pulled his checkbook out of his desk drawer, then wrote a check for a couple hundred. There. Maybe that would make Olivia Christmas from the Heart happy.

Livi's heart soared when she went to the post office to collect the mail and saw the official Hightower Enterprises envelope. Yes! Guy Hightower had a heart after all. Or maybe he simply felt bad for the way he'd behaved over the phone. Either way, she'd happily take his company's contribution.

Of course, she thought as she slit open the envelope, it probably would be less this year. But, okay, they could make do with...

Two hundred dollars? She stared at the check. It wasn't a company check. It was a personal one, and this was it.

If any other person had donated a couple hundred bucks, she'd have been delighted. Many of their donors gave small amounts of twenty-five or fifty dollars. But those were people on modest incomes, struggling to make ends meet, not well-heeled CFOs.

"You...cheapskate," she growled. "I hope you get what's coming to you this Christmas—poison in your eggnog and a lump of coal where the sun don't shine."

She stormed down the street back to her office, which was nothing more than a small suite in the second story of an old Victorian that housed Tillie's Teapot, a tearoom that was a draw for both locals and people from neighboring towns. Tillie Henderson owned both the tearoom and the house. She was pushing ninety, and her two daughters, Jean and Annette, did most of the work now—cooking and managing the place, serving high tea, offering elegant lunches and Sunday brunches you had to make a reservation for a month in advance. Tillie herself still acted as hostess on the weekdays, though, and had the final say in the business decisions. She'd not only contributed to Christmas from the Heart over the years but had offered them office space at a bargain price. They shared the upper floor with an interior decorator and a writer who preferred to get out of the house to work. The interior decorator was rarely around, usually out staging houses for the local real estate companies, but the writer, Jillian George, was always in her office, and Livi could usually hear her in there toward the end of the day, reading aloud what she'd written earlier. Jillian wrote gory murder mysteries. If she was looking for someone to bump off, Livi had just the man.

She marched upstairs to Christmas from the Heart headquarters, sat down at her little desk and glared at her computer screen. Of course, she needed to acknowledge Guy Hightower's contribution. And she should be grateful. People gave to charities out of the goodness of their hearts and every gift helped the cause. But, in light of how much his company normally gave, this sure came off as stingy.

She opened her trusty refurbished laptop and began to type.

Dear Mr. Hightower. Thank you for your contribution.

No way was she going to call it generous.

We cheerfully accept all contributions, even small ones.

Heehee.

I do hope this Christmas you are blessed as generously as you've given.

Double heehee.
She hit Send with a smile.
"What are you looking so happy about?"
Livi looked up to see Kate Greer, her best friend and right-hand woman, leaning against the doorjamb. Kate was a genius

with money, and when she wasn't doing accounting for local businesses like Tillie's, she could be found giving her time to Christmas from the Heart, watching over their finances.

Like Livi, she had hit the big 3-0, but she had more to show for it—a fat diamond on her left hand and a wedding planned for the next spring. She even had money in savings. Built like a Barbie doll, she did Pilates three times a week and had recently splurged for a Botox touch-up.

Livi didn't make enough to have extra money for savings, much less face fix-ups. New shoes were a splurge. Anyway, even if she had the money, she wasn't sure she could bring herself to spend it on such luxuries when Christmas from the Heart needed life support.

"I'm not happy," Livi informed her friend. "I'm just indulging in a moment of petty, evil glee." She went on to explain about the latest development with Guy Hightower and her tongue-in-cheek response to his token contribution.

Kate frowned disapprovingly and shook her head. "Was that one of your smarter moves?"

The evil glee disappeared faster than cookies for Santa. "Well."

"You don't want to burn bridges. I get that you're frustrated, but it's not like you to be so undiplomatic. That's my job," she added with a smile, softening the scold.

"I know. It's just that this jerk has got me so mad. And talk about undiplomatic. Leeches? Really?"

"He might feel like that. Maybe they get hit up a lot. They don't have to give you anything," Kate reminded her.

"But they gave to other nonprofits," Livi protested. "After supporting us for generations. It's like…breaking a treaty. And a lot of people are going to suffer because of it. And to put us off for so long and then unceremoniously dump us." She shook her head. "That was sick and wrong."

"Corporate finances are complicated. The company may be struggling to meet their payroll."

"We're all struggling," Livi said irritably. She held up the check. "A personal check. He's probably trying to ease his conscience."

"So, let him. What do you care?"

Of course, her friend was right. A donation was a donation. But Guy Hightower's words still stung. "A leech," she muttered.

"Yeah, that's you. Some leech. That pittance you take can hardly be called a salary."

"I don't need much," Olivia said. "I get by." To supplement her income, she cleaned house for one of the town's more well-off women and picked up an occasional pet-sitting job when someone got the itch to travel. So what if she didn't have a lot of money in savings? So what if she was still living at home? That was helping her make ends meet and helping her father, as well.

"You're running around in consignment clothes and at some point you're going to have to replace that beater of yours. Plus you've put nothing into your retirement fund in the last six months, Miss Live-on-fumes-so-you-can-help-the-whole-world." This was the downside of having her friend for her accountant.

"I'm not going to be helping very many people this year," Livi said miserably.

"Things will work out somehow," Kate assured her.

"Yeah, well, it's finding the *somehow* that I'm worried about."

"Come on. Let's go downstairs and have lunch. We can drown your sorrows in some Earl Grey and we'll brainstorm ways to make up the difference."

Livi currently had a whopping thirty-two dollars in her checking account and three dollars and some change in her wallet. Much as she liked Tillie and her daughters and loved to support their business, she'd as soon go home and make herself a PB&J sandwich and save the money.

"I'm paying," Kate added, "so don't give me any excuses."

"I hate when you pay for lunch," Livi said.

"I know. How many times have we had this conversation—about a million? I can afford lunch at Tillie's and every time I buy lunch it saves you money, which means you have more to pour back into Christmas from the Heart. So, really, when I buy lunch I'm doing a good deed."

"You already do enough good deeds around here."

"So do you. Come on, let's go. I'm starving."

Lunch at Tillie's Teapot always made Livi feel better when she was having a bad day. So what was different about today? The smells were as wonderful, the herbed scones were delicious, the homemade quiche to die for and Tillie's lemon pound cake was always incredible. But nothing tasted as good as it should have. Guilt made a poor seasoning. Kate was right. Livi shouldn't have sent that email. Instead she should have sent a gushy, suck-up thank-you note. What was wrong with her, anyway?

That could be summed up in two words: Guy Hightower. The man was not bringing out the best in her. The sun was shining, the flowers were in bloom, people were coming and going, all smiling, and she wanted to jump in the river. She'd blown it. And when you were dealing with big money and big egos you couldn't afford to blow it. Who knew what damage her lack of graciousness had done?

Probably none, she finally decided. Guy Hightower was a jerk.

Guy put in an extra two miles on the treadmill at the gym, but it didn't help him run off his anger. Olivia Berg was a snotty ingrate. Christmas from the Heart. Yeah, right. She was all heart until you didn't come through, then look out. They were well rid of her and her tacky little charity. It would be a cold day in the Caribbean before she ever saw another penny of Hightower money.

Of course, he'd matched her sarcastic tone, firing back an email of his own:

And I hope you'll get just what you deserve. With your great people skills, you'll have no problem finding more sponsors for your cause.

As if he'd shown any great people skills in their encounter. He should have called her back and apologized, explained that he was under a lot of pressure. But then she'd have started in on him all over again.

He finished up at the gym, then went to his condo, where he showered, pulled a microbrew from the fridge and plopped onto his couch to glare at the killer view from his tenth-floor window. He supposed Olivia Berg would be scandalized if she saw where he lived. So he had a nice place? So, sue him. He'd waited ten years to buy this place, living with slob roommates and hoarding his money. He worked his butt off, had rarely taken a vacation since he'd stepped in as CFO. This place and his Maserati GranTurismo were his only extravagances, and he refused to feel guilty about either of them. Well, okay, so he and his brothers still had the place in Vail. But that was family owned so it didn't count. Not that anyone had any business to be counting.

A text came in from one of his old college buddies wanting to shoot some pool at their favorite sports bar.

"Oh yeah, now I remember. That's what you look like," teased Jackson when Guy walked up to him at the bar. "I was starting to forget."

Guy held up a hand. "I know, I know. Life's been crazy."

"Your life's been crazy ever since you put on the Hightower harness. Hale's Red Menace for my man," he said to the bartender, ordering Guy's favorite local amber ale. "On me." He gave Guy an assessing once-over. "You're already starting to look old."

"And you're starting to look like a loser," Guy shot back. "Forty hours a week. What's that gonna get you?"

"A life."

The bartender gave Guy his beer, and he and his friend clinked bottles. "Here's to having a life," Guy said. "Which I've got."

"Yeah, that's probably what Scrooge said," his friend scoffed.

Scrooge. Who'd invited him to this party? "He's my hero," Guy quipped, and then thought of Olivia Berg. She was convinced he was a Scrooge.

She was also a judgmental little pest. "Come on. I see a pool table calling our name," he said.

"Fifty bucks for a race to seven?" suggested Jackson.

"That all you can afford?" Guy taunted.

"Okay, a hundred. It'll be the easiest hundred I ever made. You're probably out of practice."

Jackson broke and Guy went next and a little voice at the back of his mind hissed, *You just wasted a hundred dollars betting on a pool game.*

I didn't waste it 'cause I'm not gonna have to pay it, Guy hissed back, and missed his first shot.

"Yep, out of practice," teased Jackson.

No, just distracted.

And Guy remained distracted for the rest of the evening, missing shots he could normally make with his eyes closed. In the end he wound up forking over a hundred bucks to his pal.

*You just wasted…*the voice began.

Shut up!

Guy paid for one last round of beers, then scrammed. He'd had enough of pool for one night and he'd definitely had enough of the voice.

On Saturday, he had a date with a woman he'd been seeing off and on. Partway through dinner she began hinting about a vacation cruise. Like he had time to take a cruise? Like they were that serious? His lack of enthusiasm disappointed her and her disappointment irked him, and before the night was over they were done. "This relationship is going nowhere," she'd said.

That had been fine with him. The last serious relationship he'd had was in college and that had definitely gone somewhere. Somewhere bad. Oh yeah, Miss Perfect had loved him until she found someone with more money, then she'd dumped him like so much junk stock.

When Guy had demanded to know what was so special about the loser she was leaving him for—the guy she'd been sneaking into her life—she'd pretended her choice had nothing to do with greedy, grasping finger syndrome. "He's sweet."

He sure wasn't good-looking or very well liked. So, sweet? Really? Yeah, she'd been looking beneath the surface. Of his bank account.

"What? And I'm not?" Guy had demanded. He'd been sweet. Obviously, not sweet enough. Guy had only offered skiing at Vail while Mr. Sweet had offered a visit to Paris with his family.

"Come on, Jordan," Guy had argued. "The guy's a tool."

"And he's already a millionaire thanks to the app he created," she'd shot back, showing her true colors.

"I guess you have to think about the future," he'd said. His jaw had been clenched so tightly he'd barely been able to get the words out.

At least she'd had the grace to blush. But that was as far as her conscience was prepared to go. She left him in the coffee shop, bleeding internally.

Heart operation without anesthetic. Guy hadn't known which was worse, the pain of rejection or the humiliation. Just when he'd thought things were getting serious between them.

He should have seen the signs—the texts that went unanswered, the canceled dates. He'd been the world's smartest business major and the world's dumbest boyfriend.

"Lesson learned," his mother had said when she'd pried the whole ugly tale out of him. "There are givers in this world and there are takers. Spend enough time with someone and you'll eventually learn which one she is."

"I don't know why I didn't see it," he'd said miserably. He should have. A third of Jordan's sentences had seemed to start with "Buy me," or "Let's," which usually also amounted to "Buy me," only he got to be included.

"Don't be in a hurry. Take your time," his mom had advised. "The right woman will come along when she's supposed to."

Or not.

Ever since, he'd preferred to keep things light. He was in no hurry to get serious, and seeing the love mess his older brother's life was confirmed the wisdom of that. Women dated Hightower men for one thing only: their money. It was all they really wanted. Even the so-called altruistic ones like Olivia Berg. When it came to money, in the end, nobody was altruistic.

3

Summer skipped by, bringing a parade of sunny days to Pine River, filled with picnics, coffee dates with girlfriends and hikes along the river with Morris. What it didn't bring was very many new contributors for Christmas from the Heart.

Livi had beaten every bush and climbed every money tree she could think of, with very little success. It seemed that many smaller companies were struggling, and this far into the year, large companies had already set their budgets.

In September she hosted a Saturday afternoon tea at Tillie's, inviting forty businesses from nearby towns and had a whopping attendance of twelve. After plying them with cookies and scones and giving a strong PowerPoint presentation, five wrote out checks for a small amount that would barely cover the cost of the tea. The others wished her well and told her to contact them next year.

She would. "If Christmas from the Heart is still around," she'd grumbled as she and Bettina and Kate sat at a table, drowning their disappointment in tea.

"You will be," Kate said, and helped herself to a leftover scone. There were plenty of leftovers. "You've just hit a bump in the road."

It felt more like a roadblock.

But not the end of the road. Livi was not going to let that happen.

And come Thanksgiving she was determined to be grateful for the people who did support the nonprofit. They wouldn't be able to do as much this year with a big chunk of their funding missing—there would be less food distributed and no gifts other than Christmas stockings—but they'd still do what they could.

"Thanksgiving already," Tillie said to her and Kate as she stopped by their table to see how they were enjoying their butternut bisque.

What was not to enjoy about butternut bisque? Or anything else to be found at Tillie's Teapot. As usual, the place was bursting with the aroma of freshly baked breads and cakes and cookies and filled with friends taking a break between shopping and errands to meet for lunch.

Tillie was a little bent over and her hands were gnarled with arthritis, but she still put on lipstick and lined her eyebrows brown every day—the deep brown an interesting contrast to her white hair—and wore dangly earrings. When the season called for it she wore festive sweaters a younger woman might have worn to an ugly sweater party. Today she was in a black one with pockets shaped like turkeys. This was paired with slacks so orange she should have been passing out sunglasses to her customers. It was a mystery to Livi how Tillie could have such a beautifully decorated tearoom and then dress so…interestingly. Maybe her daughters had taken control of decorating the place. Livi had never had the nerve to ask.

Tillie shook her head. "I don't know where the year has gone."

"It is going fast," Livi agreed.

Too fast. After the weekend, things would kick into high gear at the Christmas from the Heart office, with more to do and less to do it with. At least they still had supporters like Tillie.

"I imagine you're going to want to pick up our tea packets next week," Tillie said to Livi. In addition to donating money every year, Tillie and her daughters put together small net bags filled with a half a dozen tea bags and a few small chocolates that could be stuffed in stockings or put into gift baskets. There would be less food to give out and no gift baskets this year thanks to he who would not be named—only stockings, and Livi was hoping they finally had enough goodies coming in to fill them at least two-thirds full. The stockings were given out, one per household, and contents varied, depending on the family. She included candy canes, of course, and always a couple of mandarin oranges, which the local grocery stores donated, along with candy, much of which she purchased in grocery and drugstores at Halloween at 50 percent off and then saved for Christmas stockings. Families with small children always got a jar of bubbles in the stocking along with other small toys. She also made sure there were stockings for widows and widowers, and people with pets.

Stuffing five hundred stockings was a big undertaking, but Livi always set up an assembly line around her conference room table, and her crew of volunteers would work, chat and eat pizza donated to them from Little Italy, the best place in town for pizza. Actually, the only place in town for pizza.

First, though, there was Thanksgiving to prepare for, and after lunch Livi went home to bake pies—pumpkin and wild huckleberry made from the berries she had stored in the freezer. She and Kate had gone on a berry-picking binge in early September and she had enough berries stored for three pies. The little buggers were a pain to pick, so pies only got made for special occasions: Dad's birthday, the Fourth of July and Thanksgiving.

This year Livi's brother, David, was actually coming home for Thanksgiving. It would be their first one together since their mother died. Livi supposed the fact that he had a new wife made it easier for him to return for the holiday now. Terryl had filled much of the void.

Sometimes Livi wished there was someone who could fill that void for her. But really, who could take her mother's place? Mom had been her best friend. And her guide.

Without her mother, she often felt like she was going through life with a broken GPS, trying to take Christmas from the Heart in the right direction, trying to put her own life on track. She was almost through her thirties and she was still single, living in the same house where she grew up.

Of course, she didn't have to be single. Morris Bentley would marry her in a heartbeat. Morris had been in love with her since middle school. They'd attended their junior prom together in high school and had been on and off as a couple ever since. He was a sweet man, and she loved him, but she didn't LOVE him and he deserved more than friendship.

She wanted more for herself, too, even though she wasn't sure what more looked like. All she knew was that sometimes, in spite of her satisfying work and her good friends, her life seemed small. Like she was waiting for something big, some-one big. Someone who would make her pulse race when she looked at him.

It was silly, really. "There's nothing wrong with your life," she scolded herself as she walked the few blocks from her of-fice to her family home. "You have plenty to be thankful for."

How true it was. Compared to the struggling families she helped, to the lonely single moms trying to make ends meet and still spend time with their kids, she was downright wealthy and her life was great.

She got the pies done as well as the stuffing. Early in the morning, she'd stuff the bird and stick it in the oven. Then she'd put together a broccoli casserole, peel the potatoes and set the dining room table with Mom's Wedgwood dishes. Terryl and David would be bringing fruit salad and candied yams. The requisite sparkling cider was in the fridge, ready to be pulled out and poured into the good crystal that had been passed down from daughter to daughter for four generations. Everything would be festive.

She hoped her father would be able to drum up some small amount of enthusiasm for cutting the turkey. Ever since her mother's death he'd greeted Thanksgiving as an unwanted guest, one you had to be polite to while counting the hours until the intruder left.

He came home and found her putting the finishing touches on the dining table centerpiece, the same paper foldout turkey Mom had used for as long as Livi could remember. "Oh yes, Thanksgiving tomorrow," he said as if he'd forgotten all about it.

Livi was sure he was trying to. Her father had stayed in the same house where he and her mom had built a life together, but emotionally he'd been as gone as David, leaving for work at his insurance company every day and coming home every night to mindlessly eat whatever Livi fixed for him, then sit staring at the TV. Once upon a time, the whole family had sat around the table and shared their day's adventures. The kitchen table hadn't been used for anything but collecting junk mail since Mom died.

He nodded and managed a weak smile. "It'll be good to see David and Terryl."

"Leftover spaghetti for dinner," Livi said. "I didn't have time to make anything." They needed to eat it up anyway and make room in the fridge for new leftovers. Heaven knew, they'd have enough turkey left over to last them for a week.

"That's fine," Dad said. Then he kissed her on the cheek and vanished into the living room to turn on the news. If she wanted to see any more of him, she'd have to join him there. Which she probably would do. They didn't laugh like they used to, but it was companionable.

Later that night, when she went to bed with her laptop to stream some free episodes of *House Hunters International*, she reminded herself yet again that she had much for which to be thankful. And much to look forward to the next month. Christmas was her favorite holiday, and she'd fill the house with all her favorite decorations from her childhood—the well-worn, half-burned lantern-shaped candle from the fifties that had been her grandma's, the ceramic church and the nativity set Mom had made when she went through her ceramics phase, the nutcrackers her great-grandma had brought back from her visit to Germany. She'd even hang the mistletoe. Why not? May as well think positive.

Thanksgiving Day was almost perfect. The turkey turned out well, Terryl kept everyone laughing as she told about the year before when she'd decided to host her entire family for David's and her first Thanksgiving as husband and wife. The day's adventures included an underdone turkey and overdone pumpkin pie, and a grease fire on the stove that set off the smoke alarm and almost gave her grandma a heart attack.

"But I did master candied yams," she said.

"You sure did," Livi agreed. "These are great."

"They should be. She put a ton of Kahlua in them," David said.

"I know the way to my man's heart," she joked, and he grinned.

"Food will do it," Dad agreed, and, amazingly, he was also smiling.

And that made Livi happy. Maybe their family was finally starting to heal just a little. David certainly was. And he and Terryl were full of plans for the future. She'd just gotten a new job and they were looking at houses south of Seattle where prices were still high but not out of reach for a double-income couple.

"We're trying to get pregnant," Terryl confided to Livi as they put away leftovers. "It would make a great Christmas present for David."

"It would make a great Christmas present for all of us," Livi said. At the rate she was going maybe she'd never be a mother. At least she could enjoy being an aunt. She was suddenly aware of Terryl studying her. "What?" she said with a half smile.

"Just wondering if there's anyone special in your life yet, Livi."

Uh-oh. Had she sounded wistful? She shrugged. No big deal if her love life was about as exciting as a documentary on the history of mold. "Not really. I don't have time," she added, not wanting to sound like a love loser.

Except, in a way, she was. That was what happened when you held out for bells, whistles and fireworks. She'd felt all that for Morris when they were kids, when she thought she was into monster trucks and going to the Monroe County Fair to watch the demolition derby, but the fireworks had fizzled once she went away to college and stepped into the bigger world of learning.

Leaving home to attend the University of Washington had been her biggest adventure—lectures, classes, a huge library, the University Bookstore. All that hustle and bustle in the U District and a coffee shop on every corner. When she didn't have her nose in a textbook, she was getting high on dancing, flirting, then falling in love with the man of her dreams. Then falling out of love when she realized she didn't have enough in common with whoever that latest man of her dreams was. Livi wanted to do great things. It seemed like all the boys she met were just that—boys. They were cute all right, but their interests seemed limited to getting her into bed and playing video games.

She sighed. No one had really been right and in the end she'd come home alone. Maybe she was meant to be alone.

"Define *special*," she hedged.

"Someone other than Morris?" guessed Terryl.

Livi cringed. Terryl made her sound like a romantic snob. There was nothing wrong with Morris. So what if he wasn't a bookworm? That didn't make him stupid. And so what if he didn't want to see the world? The center of both their worlds was in Pine River.

Still. "I guess I just want more." Okay, she was a romantic snob.

"Hold out for it, then. I know we're all told there's no Prince Charming out there, but I don't buy it. I found mine."

"My brother, who is the world's biggest slob? Oh, you are besotted," Livi teased.

"Love overlooks the other person's flaws. Even though he farts in his sleep, I do love him," Terryl joked. "He's the best thing that ever happened to me," she added, suddenly serious.

"He is a good man," Livi agreed. "He worked on my first car and taught me how to change the oil, and before Morris came along, scared off every boy who came near me, even though I was two years older and could take care of myself. It made me crazy then, but looking back, I think it was sweet of him to want to protect me. And let me tell you, he succeeded. Nobody wanted to mess with the star of the Pine River wrestling team."

"What a good brother," cooed Terryl.

"He was." He'd also been a good son, helping out at Christmas from the Heart right along with Livi, mowing the lawn without being asked, helping their dad clean the garage. "And he still is."

"He's a great husband, too," Terryl said. "I'd almost given up on finding anyone worth putting up with until the day he came along. There I was at Starbucks and there he was, helping some old lady mop up her spilled coffee, and I knew he was a keeper."

It was such a sweet story. Terryl had hurried over to help, then teasingly asked if he'd stick around in case she, too, spilled her coffee. He'd stuck around and they'd been married within six months.

"Wait for your Prince Charming," Terryl said. "He'll show up. You're too amazing a woman to settle for anything less."

Amazing. Right.

Morris stopped by Friday night for leftovers and to play Pandemic, a board game that involved all the players working together to save the world from disease and death. He was a good team player, always willing to go along with whatever strategy David proposed.

"Sounds good to me," he'd say.

Anything anyone in her family ever suggested sounded good to Morris. He'd been one of her biggest supporters when she'd had to step up and take over running Christmas from the Heart. He'd donated twice as much money to the nonprofit as a certain stingy CEO, and he probably earned only a quarter as much.

Livi should have been crazy in love with Morris. He was cute in a big, burly Teddy Bear sort of way. He certainly had a big heart. And it beat only for her.

What was her problem, anyway? Oh yeah, that wanting-more thing.

They played two games, trying to save the world and failing both times, so they gave up and watched an action-packed Tom Cruise movie.

"I love those movies," Terryl said as the ending credits rolled. "You know, he does all his own stunts."

"Big deal. I could do that stuff," David joked.

"I know, right?" Terryl said, elbowing him in the ribs.

"Well, maybe some of 'em."

"It's okay, babe. You're my Tom Cruise," Terryl said, and gave him a kiss.

He gave her one right back.

"Gettin' kind of steamy in here," Morris said. "Do you two need to go upstairs?"

"Yeah, I think we do," David said. He pulled his wife up from the couch. "We got better things to do than sit around and talk."

Better things. Livi would have liked to have better things to do, too.

So, from the way he looked at her, would Morris.

"I should turn in," she said.

"I guess that means I'm leaving."

"I guess so," she said. "Anyway, you have to work tomorrow, right?"

"Yeah. Wanna get pizza after I get off?"

Lately it seemed she and Morris were drifting into the habit of spending more time together, and that was problematic. The more time they spent together the more it could feel like they were edging toward becoming a couple. At least to Morris. Of course, she enjoyed his company, but she couldn't let them wander too far down the road toward couplehood.

"Thanks for the offer," she said, "but I've got too much going on tomorrow." She had to make turkey soup and do laundry. And decorate. That could take… Okay she'd be done by evening. But she did have a mystery novel to finish.

She hoped Morris didn't ask her what all she had to do.

He didn't, and he hid his disappointment quickly, but she'd still seen it in his eyes, had seen that quick frown. Poor Morris. He wanted his princess as much as she wanted her prince.

"That was fun tonight, though," she said in an effort to make them both feel better.

"Yeah, it was," he said, resigned to his fate of being dateless on a Saturday night.

Well, so was she.

She walked him to the door, said a platonic good-night and then went back into the living room, picked up her phone and plopped on the couch to scroll through her Facebook feeds.

The last thing she was in a hurry to do was go upstairs, pass her brother's old bedroom, and hear him and Terryl in there doing "other things."

The next day, after her brother and sister-in-law had left, after the laundry was done and the soup was made, Livi pulled out the decorations, happy to have some time to reminisce. She set up the nativity set that came out every year, setting it out on the fireplace mantel along with red ribbon and fir boughs and then hung the stockings her mother had made for her and Dad and David. They were starting to look a little worn but Livi didn't care. It showed they'd been well used and enjoyed.

As she dug the ceramic church from the box of decorations, she could almost see her mother setting it on the dining room table, nestling it in a bed of cotton snow and surrounding it with vintage candles shaped like choirboys that Livi's grandmother had collected in the fifties.

"The light of the world," Mom would murmur. "Don't ever forget that, darling. And you be sure to keep your light shining."

"I'm trying, Mom," she whispered.

She hung the framed movie poster for *It's a Wonderful Life* that she and David had given their mother one Christmas. It had been Mom's favorite movie. Then she set out candles, Santas and angels, and hung the ornaments on the tree her father had set up, each one evoking a special memory. There was her "Baby's First Christmas" ornament. And the angel someone gave her mother after Grandma died. There were the last two of the Italian blown glass ornaments Grandma had given her mother and father for their first Christmas.

By now Terryl and David had probably bought their tree. She'd mentioned planning to get one on the way home Friday and then decorate it Saturday afternoon. Of course, David would help her trim it. He'd been well trained. Their family had always trimmed the tree together.

Now it was something Livi did alone. She longed for that

someone special to help her decorate, someone she could create
Christmas memories with.

Finally, the house was all dressed up for Christmas. Almost.
The only thing left was the mistletoe, a glitter-dusted silk sprig
atop an acrylic jewel. She held it up and looked at it, debating.
It seemed pointless to hang it.

In the end she did, simply because she couldn't bring herself
not to. And as she did she made a wish. *Bring me a Prince Charming this Christmas, Santa.*

Guy drove home from the slopes, tired but rested. A day of
snowboarding had been exactly what he needed to recharge
his batteries.

Normally after spending Turkey Day with the bros he'd have
gone to see his mother. But this year Mom had been on a cruise
with her second husband.

He didn't begrudge her that. She deserved to enjoy herself
and he was glad to see her happy.

Widowhood hadn't agreed with her. When Dad died she'd lost
her sparkle and her smile had shrunk right along with her dress
size. She remained interested in what her boys were doing but
had little enough to say about herself when any of them called
to check on her. She sold the house and downsized not only her
living quarters but her life.

"Mom, you should get out and do something," Guy had told
her once.

"Do what?"

"I don't know. Something."

"I have plenty to do, dear. I see the grandchildren. I have
my friends."

But you don't have a life. "How often do you do things with
them?" Guy had persisted.

"Often enough."

Whatever that meant.

"She's fine," Mike had said, waving away Guy's concerns. "She's got all of us to keep her busy."

Babysitting. Big whoop.

"Let her live her life the way she wants."

So Guy had, even when she finally found Del.

That had been two years ago. His brothers had been suspicious, certain the man was a fortune hunter out to get Mom's money. But it turned out Del had plenty of his own. Which was a good thing because Mom liked to live in style. These days she drove a new Range Rover, went to New York to shop and take in a musical, and took a cruise at least once a year with her new husband.

"I'm planning on you coming for Christmas, though," she'd said to Guy when he'd learned of her plans. "I promise not to make fruitcake."

And so it had been decided.

"I gotta do Christmas with the in-laws," Bryan had said. "I'll go down for New Year's."

"You can represent all of us," Mike had said. Mike still looked on Del as an interloper—who knew what Freud would say about that?—and refused to go down, saying, "I'll take her to Cabo in January."

That was just as well. Mike wouldn't exactly be good company. It wasn't happy holidays with him lately. It had been hard listening to him trash his soon-to-be ex while he drank himself into a stupor at Bryan's, where they'd gathered for Thanksgiving.

"Don't ever get married, bro," he'd slurred as Guy drove him home. "Women'll break your heart and decimate your bank account." He waved a finger back and forth. "And don't think that you'll find the one exception. There is no such thing."

As if he needed his brother to tell him? He'd already learned that.

He was pulling into his garage when a text came through from Hudson, whom he'd met earlier in the month at a fund-

raising event for the Seattle Art Museum, one of the few charities
Hightower still supported. She was divorced, in her late thirties
and claimed to be an avid skier. They hadn't hit the slopes together yet, but had met for coffee a couple of times. It had been
all he could squeeze in. Still, he kind of liked her, so some time
on the slopes in the future was a definite possibility.

Come save me. I have leftover pumpkin cheesecake tempting
me, she texted.

Couldn't have a girl falling into temptation. At least not
cheesecake temptation. Be there in an hour, he texted back.

He hadn't been to her place yet, so she gave him her address
to put in his GPS.

He stored his snowboard, cleaned up, grabbed a bottle of wine
and then made his way to her house in West Seattle.

"Nice place," he said as she let him in. Nice-looking woman,
too. Her hair was dark and long. Tight jeans and a sweater
showed off a great body. The woman had a rack on her.

"It'll do for now. I'm going to do some serious renovation in
the new year."

"A fixer-upper, huh?"

"Yeah, right now it's a bit of a dog, but the bones are good.
I never really liked it—Sean inherited it from his grandmother
when she died and we'd been renting it out—but when he offered it as part of the divorce settlement I figured why not. I
think I can turn a nice profit once I've renovated it."

Sean's grandma's old house and now it was Hudson's little
moneymaker. Mike's bitter warning popped up in Guy's mind
like a road sign. *Warning. Dangerous Curves Ahead.*

Suddenly Guy wasn't so interested in cheesecake. He stayed
awhile, listened while she went into detail about how she was
going to replace the old brick mantel with something new and
sleek—what would old Sean's grandma have thought of that?—
and redo the entire kitchen, then he suddenly remembered some

work that had to get done before he went into the office the next morning.

"No. Really?" A full lower lip went out in a sexy pout. "I was thinking we could spend a little more time getting to know each other better." They'd been sitting on the couch, and now she set her glass of wine on the coffee table and leaned in toward him. He caught a whiff of perfume.

Too late. Hearing about the spoils she'd gotten in the divorce had been a buzzkill. Mike was right. Women were all alike.

4

Livi looked at the figures on her computer screen and plowed her fingers through her hair. "We may as well change our name from Christmas from the Heart to Christmas from Half a Heart."

"It's not that bad," said Bettina.

But it was and they both knew it. "We're only going to be able to do half as much this year as we did last year. We're hobbled!"

"We'll still be giving people more help and encouragement than they'd get if we weren't in business."

"Business," Livi said in disgust. "Don't bring that word anywhere near our organization. It only makes me think of Hightower. Oooh, I hope that horrible man is plagued with nightmares this Christmas, that he sees ghosts even scarier than the ones Scrooge saw."

"Livi," Bettina said gently, "you need to let this go. He made a business decision. It was nothing personal."

"All business is personal," Livi retorted. She heaved a sigh. "But you're right. I need to let it go."

So what if the man had called her a leech? She knew she wasn't a leech. She was working hard to help people get through tough times, have hope, feel better about themselves. What was Guy Hightower doing?

"I don't know why I bother to give you reports if you're going to ignore my advice," Guy said in irritation.

He was sitting in his brother's office in the Hightower Building. Hightower Enterprises spread out over the entire top floor. Mike's corner office had the best view, the Seattle waterfront. The average person would see the fancy building, the plush business office environs and think Bill Gates had nothing on the Hightowers. But the company wasn't nearly as healthy as it looked. Still, Guy had hopes that they could turn things around if they were careful and shifted their focus in a new direction. If his brother would listen to him.

It was a long shot. Mike wasn't the best at listening. Maybe that went with being the eldest. When they were growing up, he'd been good at watching out for Bryan and Guy on the slopes, giving them pointers on how to improve their basketball game or impress girls. And, of course, he'd been good at bossing them around. Theoretically, he should have been good at running a company. He wasn't.

He looked the part of a successful businessman though—expensive haircuts and custom-tailored suits from Beckett & Robb. A watch that one of their middle-management employees would have to spend six months' worth of paychecks on.

Not that Guy begrudged him his fancy trimmings. He just wanted him to live up to the image. Really, when you were on a sinking ship who cared what was on your wrist?

"I'm not ignoring your advice," Mike insisted. "You're right. We need to diversify. But we can't do that until we get rid of some of the deadweight, and right now there's not a rush to buy what we've got to sell."

No surprise there. Guy had lobbied strongly for dumping some of their less profitable businesses, for hiring more tech support for others and growing their online presence in order to compete with giants like Amazon. But they'd dragged their feet too long, and many of the businesses the company owned were struggling, shrinking their profit margins. The retail spaces in their mini mall were only half-filled and two of their commercial real estate projects were in trouble.

"We wouldn't be in this mess if you'd listened to me three years ago," Guy said, not for the first time.

"Well, I didn't. And quit harping on it. My God, you sound like Bethany."

"Maybe if you'd listened to her once in a while, too, you guys wouldn't be splitting now."

Mike's eyes narrowed. "Do you have anything useful to say?"

"Yeah. It's all there in the report, so how about you actually read it? If we put my plan into action we might still be able to pull out of this tailspin."

The narrow stink-eye stare vanished. "Yeah?"

"Yeah."

"If that happens, little bro, you can count on a raise. Hell, we all can." That was Mike, always looking for the quick payoff.

"No, we can put the money back into the company," Guy corrected him.

What a mistake it had been to put Mike in charge. He was incapable of seeing the big picture.

Not for the first time, Guy thought about defecting from the family business. Anyplace else he'd be pulling in twice what he was now. And speaking of pulling, working with his brothers was pulling him down. But it was hard to break loose from the generational beast that was Hightower Enterprises.

In all fairness, that same beast had allowed Guy to attend prep school and an Ivy League college. It had allowed him to live in the family home on Lake Washington and enjoy a summer place on Hood Canal. It had given him ski trips to Aspen and Whistler and European vacations. It had bought the family place in Vail. It had defined his life growing up and it defined who he was as an adult. So, while he resented the beast he continued to serve it. He supposed he always would.

Some people might not think him very noble. Some people might think of him as a greedy businessman, a corporate slave. But then some people might be suffering from class envy. *Some people* might not get the big picture, see the jobs his company provided. If they did, then they'd be grateful for whatever donations they got for their pet charities.

December had now officially arrived, and with it came all the busyness of the season, doubled for Livi. In addition to baking cookies to freeze for later and finishing up the last of her shopping—which she vowed to get an early start on every year and never did—came all the to-dos associated with Christmas from the Heart.

The first Friday in the month she sat with Bettina, going over their checklist.

"We don't have as many entries in the fruitcake competition this year," Bettina reported.

"It's still early. They have until next week to sign up," Livi said. "Remember, we usually get several coming in at the last minute. Where are we with our donations for the silent auction?"

Bettina consulted her notes. "For gift baskets, so far we have one from the Candy Shoppe, Tillie's, of course, The Bath Shop, Robinson's Hardware, and a gift basket full of Tupperware from Trudy Olsen, and one from Jillian George with a collection of her books as well as chocolate and champagne."

"That one's always popular. What about Calories Don't

Count? I talked with Carol last month and she said she was going to do something."

"She is. This year instead of a baked goodies basket she's doing a giant holiday-themed cake."

"Ooh, we'll have to give that a spotlight location on the auction table. I've got gift cards from Little Italy, certificates for a free massage from Wellness Massage, a free styling and cut from Babes, and a free lube job from Pine River Automotive. And The Sportsman is offering two hundred dollars' worth of merchandise."

"Jimmy called while you were out and said Family Tree will donate a fifty-dollar gift card."

Fifty dollars to spend at the town's favorite local restaurant would also be a popular item. "Good," Livi said. "I'm glad they came through. And Jimmy finally committed to being one of our fruitcake judges, so now we've got our three." In addition to the restaurateur they also had Tillie and Carol Klaussen, who owned Calories Don't Count. Livi hoped they'd get their usual large turnout for the event. It was their biggest fund-raiser, and heaven knew they needed the money.

They moved on to discuss the community Christmas Day dinner. "We're not going to be able to buy as much food this year," Livi said with a sigh. "Thanks to the company that shall not be named," she added with a frown. "But at least we're good on the Christmas stockings." Some of the dollar stores in larger towns and cities had come through, and between their contributions and other donations, Christmas from the Heart would be giving away nice, full stockings. "Have you had a chance to see who's coming to help stuff them?"

"Yep," said Bettina. "We've got you, me, Kate, Jean and Annette."

Her faithful crew. Those women had been good friends to both her and her organization over the years.

Livi's cell phone summoned her. It was Morris, making sure

they were still on for picking up donations the following day. They had gotten a toy store in a neighboring town to contribute and had to hit that as well as several supermarkets that were giving them a deal on frozen turkeys, which she and Morris would take straight to the spare chest freezer in Tillie's kitchen that she let them use. Closer to Christmas they'd get transferred to the walk-in cooler to thaw for the big day.

This year, though, there were less than half as many turkeys in the freezer. Livi tried not to think about the ramifications of that.

She had managed to save enough money from her salary to purchase a couple of extra birds, along with some hams to reserve for the community Christmas dinner, which would serve much of the senior population as well as anyone who was homeless or struggling financially. Everyone who could paid a dollar to get in and brought an item for the food bank, which was ironic in a way, since many of the diners shopped at the food bank for their groceries. Nonetheless, the donation had become a tradition, not because the organization wanted to bilk people in need but because, over the years, they'd discovered that people liked being able to contribute something, even if it was a small amount. It felt more like hands together than a handout. In addition to paying their dollar, some people would bring small plates of home-baked cookies as well, which helped with the party atmosphere.

"I'll pick you up at one," he said.

"Great." She appreciated Morris's time. She especially appreciated the use of Morris's truck. "You want to stay for dinner after?" It was the least she could do considering he was giving up a Saturday to help her. Not that he considered it a sacrifice. He took advantage of any excuse she offered for them to hang out together.

"Sure," he said, sounding as if she'd just asked him if he'd like a chance to win free beer for life. As much as he did to help, he deserved free beer for life.

The rest of Livi's day went by in a holiday rush, and she went home tired but satisfied. She threw together a vegetable soup and warmed up some French bread for dinner and left it at that. Dad wouldn't care. He was barely aware of what he ate anyway.

"Smells good," he said when he came into the kitchen that night.

"It's just soup and French bread," she warned him.

"That'll be fine. I'm not that hungry."

He hadn't been that hungry ever since Mom died, and his pants hung loosely on him. Livi suspected that if she wasn't there cooking for him he wouldn't eat at all. He'd simply fade away. He'd been trying to, but Livi refused to let him. He still had his kids; they were still a family. Yes, Mom was gone, which was horrible, but the rest of them were still here, and surely they were here for a reason. That meant no giving up on life. No fading allowed.

"How was your day?" she asked.

"All right," he said. "How about you, Snowflake?"

Snowflake, the nickname he'd given her when she was a child. She could still remember him carrying her outside one snowy night and them catching snowflakes on their tongues. "No two are alike," he'd explained. "Each one is unique, special. Just like you, my little snowflake."

She loved that about her father. He had a gift for making people feel special. He hadn't used it much lately, though. Hadn't done much of anything in the last three years. Her father was on autopilot.

"We had a busy day," she told him.

"Uh-huh," he said absently. He picked up the junk mail from the kitchen table. "I'll be in the other room if you need me."

She watched him go and was half tempted to say, "I need you right now. I need you to be here, really be here." Instead, she got busy dishing up their meal.

★ ★ ★

Morris, unlike Livi's father, was very present, and happy to put in hours driving her around in his truck to pick up various items from their donors. "I didn't have anything else going," he said with a shrug when she thanked him.

True. Morris didn't have much going on. He liked working as an auto technician at Bob's Auto Repair, had always enjoyed messing around with cars. And he liked sports. In fact, he was fanatical about sports. His house was a regular Seahawks 12th Man shrine. But his interests stopped there. Morris wasn't into movies unless something was blowing up. Unlike Livi, he wasn't a big reader, and he had no desire to travel. "People are the same wherever you go," he'd say when she'd try to encourage him to expand his horizons.

"The same but different," she'd argue. "People speak different languages, eat different food, have different histories, and build different houses and monuments. Don't you ever want to see the Eiffel Tower?"

"Saw it in Vegas when the baseball team went there for play-offs."

An imitation Eiffel Tower had been enough for Morris. It wasn't enough for Livi, though. She enjoyed a good Super Bowl party—the people and the food, not the game—and she loved Pine River, but sometimes she wanted to talk about more than how the game should have been played differently or whose dog had gotten loose or what someone had paid for his car. Was she ever going to get to do that? Was she ever going to see the Eiffel Tower?

"Where'd you go?"

"What?"

"You're in the truck but you're not here," said Morris.

"I was just thinking about all the things I've got to do," she lied.

"I can help you, you know."

Maybe there were men out there more fascinating than Morris, more cultured and suave and exciting, but there probably weren't any out there more generous. She smiled at him. "You're such a sweetie."

He frowned. "Yeah, that's me, Mr. Sweetie. Maybe someday you won't just say stuff like that."

"What do you mean?"

He kept his gaze on the road. "I mean, maybe you'll really give me a chance instead of empty compliments."

"That wasn't empty," she protested. "I meant it."

He heaved a sigh that signaled she wasn't getting his point. "Yeah, I know."

Fortunately, they were pulling into their first store, so the conversation ended. Morris was smart enough not to pick it up again after they'd loaded the donation into the back of the truck. But their easy camaraderie didn't feel quite so easy after that.

Things got more awkward when they finally returned to the house. "Where's the mistletoe?" he asked as they hung up their coats in the hall closet. "You always have it up by now."

Stuck in love limbo, she'd wound up taking it down. There was no one in Pine River she wanted to kiss, so what was the point?

"I haven't put it up yet," she fibbed.

Morris gave a grunt and followed her into the living room, where her father sat in his recliner, watching CNN. "Hi, Mr. B," he said, and took his usual seat on the end of the couch.

"Hi, Morris. How's it going?" her father asked. Dad had always liked Morris, and in the past, when Dad was taking an active part in life, they'd enjoyed many Monday postgame armchair quarterbacking sessions, discussing whatever football game they'd watched on the weekend. Often, Morris had joined Dad and David to watch a Sunday afternoon game. He was practically family, and Livi suspected her father had been almost as disappointed as Morris when she'd finally broken up with him for good.

There wasn't much discussion today, but that didn't bother Morris. He picked up the newspaper's sports section and began to read.

Livi left them to their comfortable silence and went into the kitchen to check the roast she had cooking in the Crock-Pot. Calm, harmonious, comfortable—that would be life with Morris if she changed her mind. It wouldn't be such a bad life. And at least it would be a life.

He stayed for dinner and would have been content to stay later and watch a movie, but Livi sent him on his way, claiming she had a ton of paperwork to do.

"Are you sure?" he said. "We could all watch a movie."

"You kids go ahead," said Dad. "I think I'll go upstairs and read awhile."

That left Morris looking positively eager. "Come on, Liv," he urged. "You worked all day."

"All right." She gave up, "What do you want to watch?"

"I found something really cool on Netflix."

"A Christmas movie?" Livi was always up for a Christmas movie.

"Not exactly. But it's supposed to be good. It's about…"

"Cars?" she guessed, hoping she was wrong.

"Uh, maybe we better find something else."

"Good idea." Then she felt guilty. "You don't mind too much, do you?"

"I guess not. Maybe I can find something that's not too sappy," he added, showing how enthused he was over the change in programming.

"I'll make popcorn."

And so they settled in with popcorn and hot chocolate, sitting side by side like the good friends they were.

Until, halfway through the movie, Morris tried the time-honored tactic of stretching and then repositioning his arm over her shoulders. She gave him a stern look and he made a face and removed his arm. Then he pouted his way through the rest of the movie.

"You take me for granted," he informed her after it was over. "You know, I won't wait forever, Liv."

That would be fine by her. Then she wouldn't have to feel bad for not appreciating him as he deserved. "I'm not asking you to. You should see other people."

"Here?"

"There are single women in this town, you know."

He shrugged.

"Or go online or...something."

He frowned. "I'd never find anybody like you. We could have a good life, you know."

"I know," she said softly. Honestly, what was wrong with her that she had this Belle complex? She was no Disney princess. Why did she think she was so special?

Oh yeah. The snowflake thing. *Thanks, Dad.*

"Well, then?" he prompted.

"You know I care about you, but I just don't think of you that way anymore."

He put an arm back around her. "I could change your mind. Go get that mistletoe. In fact, who needs it?"

He was going for the lips, but she was too quick for him. She slipped out of his arms and stood up. "It's getting late."

"You can say that again," he grumped. "Maybe I will check out one of those online sites."

"A good idea," she said agreeably, which didn't make him smile. "Come on, now," she coaxed. "Don't be mad. We've got a good friendship. Why spoil it?"

"Because it could be more."

If it was going to be more, surely it would have become more years ago, when she came home from college. "Let's be happy with what we've got," she said.

Now, there was a concept. She should apply that to her own life. Maybe Morris was right. Maybe she should put that mistletoe back up and take whatever kisses she could get.

He heaved a heavy sigh. "All right, fine. I give up. For tonight," he added with a smile to say there were no hard feelings. And no giving up.

She linked her arm through his and walked him to the door. "You're a good man, Morris Bentley."

"And someday you're gonna realize that," he said.

"I already do or I wouldn't have said it," she assured him.

At the door, he kissed her on the cheek. It was sweet and it made her happy. But it didn't set off any fireworks. "See you in church," he said, and trotted off to his truck.

Yes, she would. And whenever she needed a strong back to help with deliveries. In a way, she wished she could get back those old high school hormone-high fireworks she'd once felt with Morris. It would make life so much easier.

Not that he was making life difficult. He was as friendly as ever when she saw him at church the next day, there with his mom, wearing his usual jeans and casual shirt. He was well muscled and had dimples when he smiled. He was certainly cute enough to easily find a replacement for Livi. If only he would.

"I wish I could find someone for Morris," she said to her crew of volunteers as they stood around her conference table, stuffing Christmas stockings full of goodies the next week.

Bettina was present, happy to have time away from her fussy six-month-old, who was teething. Kate was also there, as well as Tillie's daughters, Jean and Annette. Large cardboard cartons filled every bit of available space in the room. Some of them were stacked in corners, already packed with stockings to be delivered later in the month. Leftover pizza from Little Italy sat on a chair and the whole office smelled like an Italian restaurant.

"Don't look at me," Kate said. "Been there, done that. I should never have let you set us up. It's been over a year and the poor guy still blushes every time he sees me."

"It had to be a little embarrassing getting caught calling you Livi while you were going at it," said Bettina.

"Thank God nobody'd lost their clothes yet." Kate shook her head. "There's nothing worse than being a Livi stand-in."

"Sorry," Livi muttered. "I thought you two would be a match."

"There's more to a relationship than liking football," Kate informed her. "Although, I must say my new 12th man is awesome. And the sex...touchdown!"

"TMI," Jean said, making a face. At sixty, she was the oldest one present, but with her energy and sense of humor, the younger women tended to forget the age difference.

"Hey, just because you haven't had sex since dirt was brown," teased Annette, who was four years younger and on her third husband.

"Sex? What's that?" Jean cracked. Jean had been widowed at fifty. Her husband had been the love of her life and she had no desire to try to replace what she'd had with him, no matter how much she joked about her non-love life.

"Maybe we should match you up with Morris, Jean," Kate teased. "You've always wanted a boy toy—admit it."

"May as well, since it's plain Kate's not going to share her new man," Annette said with a wink. "Seriously, I'm happy for you, kiddo," she said to Kate. "Every woman deserves to find her someone special. Sometimes it takes a while," she added, "but it's worth the wait."

"Tom sure was," Kate said. "Who knew I'd meet the man of my dreams at the grocery store? Let me tell you, I never felt so hot in the frozen foods aisle."

"Tom is a great guy," Bettina said. "Danny says he's a wonderful principal. Everyone loves him."

Kate's expression turned dreamy. "*I* sure do. He's the best, and I will forever be grateful to Pine River Middle School for needing a new principal."

"You never know when or where that certain someone will show up," said Annette. "I met Joe when I was looking for a contractor to enclose my back porch."

"And I met my Hank at my cousin's wedding," said Tillie. "He was one of the groomsmen. Not the most handsome man in the room, but there was something about his smile. I knew from the moment I saw him that he was the one. And that's how it happens," she said to Livi. "When you least expect it, the right person comes into your life. It will happen for Morris. And for you."

Livi had her doubts about that. If her Prince Charming was going to come riding into Pine River he'd have done so by then.

"You don't need to worry about me," she said. "I'm fine."

"You don't want to go through life alone," Jean told her.

No, she didn't. The thought was rather depressing.

"But she doesn't want to settle, either," Kate argued. "Don't settle," she said sternly.

"There's not a lot to pick from here in Pine River," pointed out Bettina.

"Well, we'll just have to ask Santa to bring someone to town," Annette said with a smile. "Are you listening, Santa? Bring our girl someone handsome and brilliant and…"

"Rich," added Kate. "She needs someone rich who can donate a big chunk of change to Christmas from the Heart."

"There's more to life than money," said Bettina, whose husband, Danny, was barely beginning his teaching career. They weren't exactly swimming in money but they were crazy in love.

Crazy in love, that was what Livi wanted.

"Yeah, but it's just as easy to love a rich man as it is a poor man," Kate argued.

"Okay, rich," said Annette. "Let's add that to the list. Anything else, Livi?"

"Kind and generous," Livi said firmly. Scrooges need not apply.

"Okay, there you have it, Santa," Annette said, her eyes raised to the ceiling. "That's what Livi wants. Get those elves busy."

Ah, if only.

Santa Claus Is
Coming to Town

5

December 25 already? How had that happened? When Livi had gone to bed it had only been December 8. Now here she was at the teller window in Pine River First National, wearing red footie pajamas with panty hose pulled over her head and a Santa hat, pointing a squirt gun at Mrs. Whittier, the teller.

"Give me everything you've got," she snarled.

But instead of giving her money, Mrs. Whittier leaned over and bopped her on the head with a giant candy cane. "I certainly will not," Mrs. Whittier snapped. "Shame on you, Olivia."

"I need money," Livi wailed, rubbing her head.

"You have no one to blame but yourself. You haven't managed well and now you're paying the price. And I'm calling the police!"

Livi sped from the bank, losing her Santa hat in the process. Out she ran, slipping and sliding in the snow, to her getaway car, a vintage Mustang painted chartreuse. There stood her driver, the Grinch, leaning against the passenger side.

"Did you get the money?" he asked.

"No," she said, and began to cry.

"I knew you wouldn't. You're such a loser," he said, and marched around to the driver's side.

"Never mind. We'll go rob the candy store." She grabbed the door handle only to find it locked.

The Grinch got in behind the wheel.

"Open the door," she commanded.

"No can do," came his muffled voice from inside the car. "You're a loser and I don't hang out with losers." Then he gunned the car and drove away, dousing her with a rooster tail of snow.

She tried to chase him down the street but she slipped and fell, landing face-first. Now here came the police in red cars decorated with colored lights and jingle bells. The cops turned out to be Santa and his elves.

They jumped out of their patrol cars and surrounded her, pointing candy canes at her even bigger than the one Mrs. Whittier had wielded. A crowd was gathering.

She knelt there in the snow in front of everyone, covering her panty hose–contorted face with her hands and crying, "I'm sorry."

"You should be," said someone in the crowd. "You're ruining Christmas for us."

"Get her," yelled someone else.

Then, suddenly, something cold and hard whacked her in the shoulder. It was followed by another something cold and hard. And wet. Splat. Right on her head. Snowballs. The crowd was pelting her with snowballs.

"Somebody help me," she cried.

And there came the chartreuse Mustang, pulling up next to her. The Grinch leaned over and opened the door. "Get in!"

She dived in and they fishtailed off down the street, then

bolted for the mountains, racing up the highway deep into the Cascades.

"You redeemed yourself back there," the Grinch told her. He turned on the car radio and his "You're a Mean One, Mr. Grinch" theme song began to play.

"Everyone hates me."

"Yeah, ain't it great?"

Next thing she knew they were in front of a giant, dowdy-looking gray castle. The sky had turned dark.

"You'll be safe here," the Grinch said, and got out of the car.

Still wearing the panty hose on her head, she slouched behind him up the dark, snowy walk and into the castle. Its giant hallway was lit by one single candle standing on a small table. Several portraits hung on the wall: Ebenezer Scrooge, Lord Voldemort, the Grinch himself and...her?

Her host turned to her and smiled his green, Grinchy smile. "You let down a lot of people."

"I know," she said, and hung her head.

"You made a lot of people mad."

She sniffled and wiped away a tear.

"You're my kind of girl."

"What?" She looked up to see him reaching a green hairy hand toward her cheek. She swatted it away. "Stop that! And what are you so happy about?"

"What do you mean what am I so happy about? You wrecked Christmas for a lot of people. You've got potential."

"Wait a minute. What's going on here? This is all wrong. You're supposed to be a changed...whatever you are. You didn't steal Christmas after all."

"Urban legend, baby," he said with a smirk. "Come on, now, don't be coy. You and I are soul mates. I'm the man you've been waiting for all your life."

"You so are not!" she said, taking a step back.

"Sure I am. We failures have to stick together."

"I'm not a failure!" she cried. "I'm not!"

Livi was still crying, "I'm not a failure!" when she woke up. She pushed her hair out of her face and took several deep breaths. What a horrible dream. So this was what her subconscious thought of her.

It was no worse than her conscious thought.

She remembered one of the times her mother had brought her along when she was calling on Christmas from the Heart supporters. Livi had been eleven at the time, still young enough not to be embarrassed by the fact that her mother was wearing her Mrs. Santa outfit, honored to be included in such an important errand.

They'd stopped by the bank to collect a check from Mr. Hunter, the bank manager, and Mrs. Whittier had called a greeting when they walked in. Mom had stepped over to her teller window to say hello, Livi trailing along.

"I see you have a Mrs. Santa's helper with you today," Mrs. Whittier had said, smiling at Livi.

"Oh yes. She's my right-hand girl," Mom had replied, placing a hand on Livi's shoulder. Livi could still catch a whiff of her mother's hand lotion—Chantilly, her favorite scent. Her mother had painted her fingernails red to match her outfit. She'd painted Livi's nails red, too, and given her a Santa hat to wear. Livi considered it a badge of honor.

Livi may have only been eleven but she already knew how important it was to help others. Her mother didn't dress in a sexy superheroine star-spangled outfit or use bullet deflecting armbands, but in Livi's eyes she was just as heroic in her frilly blouse, red skirt and red-striped apron.

They'd moved on to where Mr. Hunter's desk sat and collected a check from him. "Someday I'll probably be presenting a check to you, won't I?" Mr. Hunter had said to Livi.

"You sure will," she'd said, feeling both proud and important.

She sure didn't feel that way lately. "Mom, I'm so sorry," she whispered. "I'm trying my best. I really am."

Don't give up, came a quiet whisper at the back of her mind. *Do your best and let God take care of the rest.*

Was she doing her best? It was still early in the morning, with the sun poking at the darkness with orange fingers. She got out of bed and padded over to her closet. There hung Mom's old Mrs. Santa costume, like a superhero cape, waiting to be activated.

Livi had kept it because she couldn't bear to part with it, but she'd never worn it. It somehow hadn't felt right for her to put it on. Suddenly, it felt like the thing to do, felt like if she just donned that frilly blouse and settled the white wig on her head, tied on the ruffled red-striped apron, something magical would happen. She took it out and laid it on the bed. If she'd gone to see Guy Hightower wearing this, would she have been able to melt his heart?

If she wore it now, whose heart could she melt? Surely someone's. A visual reminder of Christmas was sure to inspire people to be generous.

After her father had left for work, she showered and put on the Mrs. Santa superheroine outfit. She studied herself in the mirror hanging on her closet door. She had the same green eyes and curly hair as her mother had and was about the same size. A strong resemblance.

"You look so much like your mother," people often said.

Except she wasn't her mother.

Still, it was worth a try.

She dug out the little red wool jacket her mother had loved to wear and slipped it on. Then pulled on her boots and winter gloves and went out the door. Mr. Hunter had already donated to the cause. Maybe she could get him to pull some strings and help a little more.

The only thing about the bank that had changed since she

was a little girl was the number of employees. And their age.
Now, instead of two tellers and one bank manager, Pine River
First National boasted three tellers, a manager and a loan offi-
cer. The only teller still there from years ago was Mrs. Whittier.

"Oh my goodness, would you look at this," she greeted Livi.
"I thought for a moment it was your mother walking in here."

There were no other customers in the bank, so Livi felt free to
stroll over to the teller's window. "How are you, Mrs. Whittier?"

"Ready to retire. I have nine months and two days left, but
who's counting?"

Hard to imagine coming into the bank and not seeing that
familiar face. With the exception of a few more wrinkles and
a little more sagging skin at the neck, Mrs. Whittier looked
pretty much the same, still a little chunky, still sporting brown
hair. If she had gray hairs anywhere on her head she was keeping them well hidden.

"Are you here to collect a check for Christmas from the
Heart?" asked Mrs. Whittier.

"I'd sure like to. Of course, the bank has already been very
generous, but we're in a bit of a bind this year and I'm hoping
Mr. Hunter can find a little more to donate."

She looked to where Mr. Hunter sat at his desk in the far corner. He was a tall man starting into his sixties with salt-and-pep-
per hair and a clean-shaven chin. If you looked up *bank manager*
in the dictionary you'd see Mr. Hunter. Right then you'd see
Mr. Hunter spotting her and picking up his phone, getting suddenly busy on a call. That could be a coincidence.

"It can't hurt to try," Mrs. Whittier said, but she sounded du-
bious about Livi's success in getting a second helping of money.
"I'll tell him you're here to see him," she added in case Mr.
Hunter couldn't see that for himself.

She watched as Mrs. Whittier approached his desk. She saw
the subtle shake of his head. *No, no, tell her I'm busy.*

Then she saw Mrs. Whittier nod and give him the kind of

look her mother used to give her and David when they misbe-haved. *You will too see this young woman.*

With a resigned expression, he ended his imaginary call, got up from his desk and walked across the bank lobby to greet Livi, hand extended. "Olivia, it's nice to see you. And what brings you out on this cold day?" As if her outfit didn't tell him exactly what had brought her out. Maybe she shouldn't have worn it. It took away the advantage of a surprise attack.

"I'm doing Santa's business, Mr. Hunter."

"And we all appreciate how much you do," he said.

It was the perfect opening. "Thank you, and the bank was very generous this year, very supportive."

"We believe in helping our community." He glanced at his watch. Livi knew what would come next. *Now, if you'll excuse me.*

"And you have been a tremendous help, which is why I stopped by today. We lost a major donor this year and we've been trying desperately to make up the difference for months. I'm afraid it's been tough sledding for Santa," she added lightly.

He cleared his throat. "Well, yes, I can imagine. Here at Pine River First National we certainly understand about budgets." Then, before she could say anything, he said, "And I'm sure you understand that, as a financial institution, we must stick to ours."

"Of course," she said. "I thought perhaps you might have a little something left over that you need to spend before the end of the year."

"I'm afraid we don't, Olivia. I'd love to help you, but we've already disbursed all the money earmarked for charitable do-nations."

"I was hoping maybe there was a little bit left somewhere. You know, like when you pull up the sofa cushions and find some loose change."

He shook his head slowly. "Banks don't have loose change. And we have a board of directors we're accountable to."

"Of course," she murmured. *Don't cry. Don't. Cry.* She dropped her gaze to her magical Mrs. Santa apron. It looked like its superpowers only worked for her mother.

"But here." He reached into his back pocket and pulled out his wallet. Fished out a hundred-dollar bill. "Let me personally give a little something to the cause."

She managed a teary smile and a nod and then a choked thank-you.

"You're doing a fine job, Olivia. Your mother would be proud."

Again, she nodded and thanked him, then started for the door.

"Livi, wait," called Mrs. Whittier, and motioned her over.

She made her way to where the older woman stood and was conscious of the two other tellers watching her, looking sympathetic. Embarrassment heated her cheeks.

Mrs. Whittier held out a wad of bills. "We all chipped in. It's not much but maybe it will help."

That warmth spread to her heart. People really want to help. "Every contribution is important," Livi said. She'd write poor, embarrassed Mr. Hunter a special thank-you note as soon as she got to her office. And Mrs. Whittier and the other tellers, as well. "Do you want a donation receipt?"

"No. We're good," said one of the tellers, and Mrs. Whittier and the third teller nodded their agreement.

"Thank you."

"No, thank you for all you're doing. Don't get discouraged, Olivia. You may not be able to do everything this year that you did last year, but you'll still be making a difference."

"Thanks to people like you," Livi said gratefully.

Once she was out of the bank she unfolded the wad of bills Mrs. Whittier had given her. Two twenties and a ten. Plus what Mr. Hunter had contributed. It was more than she'd had when she went in and she could be grateful for that.

"Livi," said a surprised—no, make that shocked voice.

She turned to see her father, stopped on the snowy sidewalk, staring at her, his face pale. Her, dressed in Mom's Mrs. Santa outfit. It had to feel like seeing the Ghost of Christmas from the Heart Past.

She hurried over and gave him a kiss.

"Isn't that…" He couldn't finish the sentence.

"I'm out trying to get some last-minute donations," she explained. "I thought Mom's old Mrs. Santa costume would bring me luck."

"You look so much like your mother in it," he said, his voice wistful. He looked like he was going to cry.

"I didn't think how you might feel seeing me in it," she said. "I'm sorry."

"Don't be, Snowflake," he said, and gave her a smile and a hug. "If your mother was here right now she'd be so proud."

If her mother was there she'd be able to advise Livi. Better yet, she'd have managed to find another big donor to replace Hightower.

"Whatever you got, I'll match it," he said.

Her father already gave a lot to Christmas from the Heart. Unlike *some* people who ran big corporations, he didn't have a lot of money. "No, Daddy. You give enough already."

"No such thing as giving enough," he said. "You let me know tonight and I'll write you a check."

Shades of when she was a Camp Fire Girl. When it came time to sell those Camp Fire mints her father had always been her biggest customer.

"You're the best dad in the whole world," she said, and hugged him.

"And I've got the best daughter in the world."

A woman started to pass them and smiled, said to Livi, "Your outfit is adorable."

"Thanks," Livi said. "Mrs. Santa's out today collecting money for Christmas from the Heart."

"We're new to town," the woman said. "Someone was just telling me about that organization."

"My daughter runs it," said Livi's dad. "Christmas from the Heart helps a lot of people this time of year."

The woman opened her purse. "I'd like to donate something." She handed Livi a twenty. "Keep up the good work."

"I will," Olivia said. And darn it, she would. And every ten- and twenty-and hundred-dollar bill helped.

But she sure could still use a Christmas miracle.

Guy was feeling good when he squealed out of the Hightower Building in his Maserati at six-thirty in the evening. His brothers were finally listening to him and he had hopes that come the new year the company's future would be looking more positive.

"You're right, bro," Mike had said when the three of them had met that morning. "We've been dragging our feet too long."

No kidding. They'd been trying to outrun a tornado with fifty-pound weights tied to their ankles.

"Good ideas and I think we need to implement them. What do you say, Bry?"

"I say let's go for it," said Bryan the yes-man. Bryan was a typical middle child, a peacemaker and this moment of peaceful accord erased the lines between his eyebrows almost instantly.

As for Guy, Mike's words were music to his ears—the steady beat of progress and above it, like bells, the tinkling of fresh money into the Hightower coffers in the new year once they'd unloaded some of their deadweight. Ca-ching!

This called for a celebration. A one-man celebration, but oh well. He alone understood what an accomplishment it was to start steering their ship out of the shallows toward deeper, safer waters. So he and himself would toast to that tonight with his favorite microbrew and a nice, thick steak. Medium rare, with enough pink to be tender but not so rare that the cow would jump off the plate and kick him.

He turned on the car radio and cranked up Panic! at the Disco's song "High Hopes." That was what Guy had, and he was nodding his head along with the music and smiling as he pulled into the Safeway parking lot to pick up that steak and some salad in a bag.

Until he saw the man in the parka with the bell standing next to the red kettle. Right in front of the door. It seemed like every time he saw a Salvation Army worker his conscience felt an uncomfortable poke. This time was no exception. Here it came again. Poke. Poke, poke, poke!

He told his conscience to cut it out. He had nothing to feel guilty about, no matter what a certain someone at a certain penny-ante nonprofit thought.

To prove it, he took a ten from his wallet. Then he got out of his car and strode to the grocery store entrance. He stopped in front of the red kettle and folded it to fit in the slot, making sure the dude saw the ten first. *See? I'm no hard-hearted bastard.*

Only a ten? With what you make that's supposed to be a big deal?

His conscience was getting way too chatty lately, and it sounded a lot like Olivia Berg. *It's a big enough deal*, he informed it, especially since he'd been dropping tens into red kettles all month long.

Penance, came the uninvited observation.

He didn't need to make an act of penance for anything. He'd been right to turn down Christmas from the Heart, and that was that. And if he ever again heard from Olivia Berg the leech, he'd tell her.

6

By December 20 Livi was nearly ready for Christmas. The presents for her family and friends weren't much but they were from the heart. And that was what counted, right? She'd found some fancy soaps for her girlfriends and gotten Morris a calendar featuring cars. She'd found some pretty yarn at The Thrifty Owl, a secondhand shop, she'd discovered in a nearby— and slightly more prosperous—town, and she'd had enough to knit a scarf for Terryl. She'd gotten her brother some silly socks and his favorite old-fashioned Christmas candy, and everything was wrapped and under the tree.

David and Terryl would be coming up for Christmas Eve, then leaving after breakfast in the morning to drive to her parents' for a big family dinner. Livi would spend the afternoon at the community hall, serving dinner to those in need. Come evening, it would be just her and her father trying to fan the flames of Christmas cheer. She'd found a game she thought they could play together but she wasn't holding her breath on that happening. There'd been no family games since Mom died. She hoped her father would at least like the crossword puzzle book she'd bought him. He used to be fond of them. He could be again.

She'd baked candy cane cookies, holiday brownies and snowballs and delivered them to the neighbors. She'd also given Morris a plate of treats, slipping on a few pieces of the fudge she'd made for the Christmas movie marathon she was indulging in with Kate and Bettina. Kate had insisted they all needed a break and so they were binging on some of their favorite Hallmark offerings—*The Nine Lives of Christmas* and *Marry Me at Christmas*, then planning to finish up with *A Christmas Carol*.

Her father, knowing he was being invaded by women, made himself scarce after dinner, retreating to the den, which housed a second TV. "You have fun with the girls, Snowflake," he'd said, and vanished.

She didn't blame him. He'd never been one for romantic movies even when Mom was alive. Now they were anathema to him, and she knew he'd never watch *A Christmas Carol* again.

Kate was the first to arrive, and came bearing chocolate chip mint ice cream, hot fudge sauce and a can of whipped cream. "Remember, calories don't count when they're shared with friends," she said, quoting the sign that hung in Carol Klaussen's bakery.

"If that's true then how come I always gain ten pounds at Christmas?" Livi retorted.

"You're too busy working and not spending enough time with your girlfriends."

"I've had more time this year," Livi said. "I must be more organized." Or maybe she had less to do now that she had less money to work with.

Thinking about that put her in a grumpy mood, and, although she tried to hide it from her friends, it came out when they came to the end of *A Christmas Carol*.

"I know, I just love happy endings, too," Bettina said, misreading the tears in Livi's eyes.

"I'm not sure she's thinking about Tiny Tim and the new and improved Scrooge," Kate said, taking in Livi's scowl.

"I'm not," Livi said hotly. "I'm thinking about a modern-day Scrooge and all the people who will be doing without because he couldn't part with a few extra dollars this year." She was having to make some heartbreaking decisions when it came to providing food to people. There simply wasn't enough to go around.

"His company turned you down, not him personally," Kate reminded her.

"Letting it go, remember?" put in Bettina.

"He is his company," Livi insisted. "And I have let it go. But he'd better hope we never meet in person."

"And what would you do if you did meet him?" Kate teased. "Poke him in the eye with a sprig of holly? Tie him to a chair with a string of Christmas lights and make him listen to 'Holly, Jolly Christmas' until he went crazy?"

"Maybe I'd kidnap him and drive him around on Christmas Day to visit the homes of people who won't be having such a good Christmas thanks to his stinginess."

"Like the Ghost of Christmas Present," said Bettina.

"Something like that." Except in real life, heartless people in high positions rarely got to see how their stinginess trickled down to others.

"We can't help you there," Kate said. "But..." She reached into the shopping bag she'd brought and pulled out a large, wrapped box. "I do have something for you for stress release. Open it."

Livi unwrapped the box to find her friend had brought her a dartboard. She raised both eyebrows. "Darts?"

"Whoa," Bettina said. "Are you forgetting what happened last time we played darts at Bruno's?"

Livi groaned. "Please don't remind me." She had completely

missed the dartboard on every throw, and after her last throw punctured Steve Nixon's behind she'd been banned from playing.

"This is for your office."

"Oh yes, Tillie would love me putting holes in the wall."

"Or the privacy of your own bedroom," Kate said. "Take it out."

Livi did and saw that her friend had superimposed a picture of a man who looked to be somewhere in his early fifties over the circle of colors."

"Who's that?" asked Bettina.

"It's Michael Hightower, the president of Hightower Enterprises. I tried to find a picture of Guy Hightower but couldn't."

"Hard to get a good picture under a rock," Livi muttered.

"Anyway, now you have something to take your aggression out on."

Livi thanked her and promised to make use of the present, although she'd have preferred to take her frustrations out on the man himself. He was so lucky she didn't know where he lived.

Just what Guy wanted to do, drag himself all the way up to Arlington, Washington, to Aunt Cathy's dairy farm before heading to his mom and stepdad's so he could pick up his great-great-grandmother's Limoges chocolate pot.

"It's a family heirloom," Mom had explained, "and we don't trust FedEx or UPS to get it to me in one piece."

"Oh, come on, Mom," he'd pleaded. "They're insured."

"Insured doesn't mean they can replace it if it gets broken," his mom had insisted. "And besides, you haven't visited your aunt Cathy in ages and she wants to see you."

Unlike his mother, his aunt had chosen country life over the city. Her dairy farmer husband wasn't as rich as Guy's dad had been, but the man had done okay for himself. Still, the sisters had definitely moved in different circles. Going to see Aunt

Cathy and Uncle Art had been a novelty when they were kids. Once they grew up and got busy with their own lives, it was more of a nuisance.

It was especially a nuisance now because instead of taking the fastest route to Idaho over I-90, he was stuck detouring over Highway 2. Beautiful country but a time suck nonetheless.

Of course, when he got there Aunt Cathy had insisted he stay for lunch. Uncle Art wanted to show him the improvements around the place. By the time they were done, the afternoon was slipping away and his foot was itching to hit the gas pedal on his Maserati.

A few lazy snowflakes arrived to set him free. "You'd better get on the road before the weather gets bad," said his aunt.

As if he didn't know how to drive in the snow. But Aunt Cathy was a worrier.

"Now, be careful with this," she cautioned as she handed him the box with the prized chocolate pot in it. "Some things are irreplaceable."

"Don't worry, I'll take good care of it," he assured her. To prove it, he drove down the driveway at the pace of a cow meandering across the meadow. He'd wait until he hit the highway to open up the throttle, then he'd let this baby go for it. He wasn't so sure about how much he'd enjoy spending time with the stepfamily, but he was sure he'd enjoy the drive to Mom's place.

The car gave a squeal as he turned onto the highway, the same squeal he'd heard a couple weeks earlier. He hadn't thought much of it at the time, but he did this time. He'd have to take the Maserati back in to the dealership when he returned home. When it came to high-end machines like this one, a man couldn't let things slide. Meanwhile, open road lay ahead and he pressed down on the accelerator and went for it.

The scenery on Highway 2 was travel magazine–worthy. Guy had seen enough of the world to know heaven when he saw it, and Western Washington with its lush trees, sparkling waters and mountains was, indeed, heaven. Not a bad detour if you had to take one.

He roared through Monroe, then Sultan and Skyway, racing past forests and rivers, pastures and barns. The snow was really starting to come down. He'd have to stop and chain up once he reached the pass.

Three miles past Gold Bar his steering lost power, turning the car from a smooth driving, purring tiger to a rhino. He checked the dash and saw his alternator light was on. What was this? He pulled over, got out and opened the hood and looked under it to discover that his serpentine belt had broken. No notice, sudden as a heart attack.

Except for that squeal. He'd heard it earlier, too, but hadn't paid attention.

He had no choice but to pay attention now. Guy may not have been an expert on cars but he did know that without that belt, he was going nowhere.

Frowning, he pulled his cell phone out of his North Face jacket. He hoped he wouldn't have to wait long for his towing service to get to him. Who knew where they could tow him. Would he find a garage anywhere that would have a belt for an Italian sports car?

No cell reception. Oh yeah, it just got better and better.

"Great," he muttered. He'd just had this baby tuned up a couple months back. He shouldn't be stuck here in the middle of nowhere. Why had he paid extra at the foreign car dealership for all those maintenance checks if they weren't going to check and maintain everything?

There was nothing for it. He'd have to walk back to town and find a phone.

He slammed the hood shut, pulled his boots out of the trunk and put them on, still frowning. He liked snow, he was fit enough to walk ten miles if he had to. He just didn't want to. He wanted to reach his destination. Thanks to whatever gremlins had hopped in his engine along the way, that probably wasn't happening today.

He was just starting his trudge to town when an older-model Honda Civic passed him and then stopped. It backed up and the passenger side window slid down. "Looks like you've got car troubles. Would you like a lift?" offered the driver.

Hadn't this woman's dad ever told her never to pick up strangers? If she was his sister he'd sure rip her a new one for stopping to let some man in her car, even in a blizzard. She had green eyes, curly hair the color of honey and plump, little kiss-me lips. Any crazy would climb right in and do who knew what to her.

Guy wasn't crazy, but he was pissed, and in no mood to make polite conversation.

"That's okay, I'm fine," he said, and continued to trudge on.

Freezing his ass off. Okay, maybe he was crazy.

Except, pissed as he was, he'd generate more than enough steam to keep warm.

She sure was cute, though.

She coasted along beside him, backward. "Not that you don't look fit enough to walk, but it's a ways in either direction. Cell phone reception can be spotty."

He'd already discovered that.

"Maybe you're afraid of girls?" she teased.

Not this girl. She had a smile like a magnet. Did he really want to walk back to Gold Bar?

He got in. "Thanks. I appreciate the lift."

"Where are you headed?"

"Idaho. Christmas with the family." Stepfamily.

"Oh my. You took the long way."

"I had to stop in Arlington and pick up something for my mom."

She nodded and smiled, obviously impressed by what a good son he was. Was this woman always so trusting?

He felt compelled to ask, "You don't always go around picking up strangers, do you?"

"Oh no." She smiled. Man, those lips.

"That's good. 'Cause you never know what kind of crazies are out there."

"You didn't look like one."

"Ted Bundy probably didn't, either. Ever hear of him?" Okay, that sounded creepy.

Her smile faltered momentarily.

"I promise I'm not a serial killer," he said in an effort to uncreep himself.

The smile returned full force. "I didn't think so. I'm a good judge of character."

"Yeah?" Suddenly he was feeling a little less pissed.

"Oh yes," she said with a nod that made the curls bounce.

He was a sucker for curly hair. You hardly ever saw women with real curly hair anymore. Why was that?

"And what makes you such a good judge of character?" he teased. She smelled like peppermint. He wondered if this little cutie was taken. Hard to tell since she was wearing gloves. There had to be a ring on that left hand. She looked about thirty, and by their thirties hotties like this one were never single. Or if they were, they came with baggage.

"I deal with a lot of people. You get so you know."

"Yeah? What do you do?" Coffee shop waitress, perhaps? Judging by the car she was driving, nothing that paid much.

"I run a nonprofit."

Oh no. One of those. A person out to help others—using someone else's money, of course. The memory of his unpleasant encounter with Olivia Berg arrived on the scene, irritating as jock itch. He could feel his jaw tightening.

This woman isn't Olivia Berg. Don't take your irritation out on her. "What's the name of your organization?" he asked, the very image of diplomatic courtesy.

"Christmas from the Heart."

"Christmas from…?" Oh no. This wasn't happening. This was some sick dream.

"Have you heard of it?"

"Uh, yeah." The last thing he wanted was to be captive in a car with this woman. "Hey, any place you can drop me where there's a phone will be great." *In fact, let me get out of this car right here, right now.*

"I can do better than that. We're not far from Pine River, where I live," she said. "We've got a garage there and Morris Bentley is an excellent mechanic. They can tow your car and have it fixed in no time."

The sooner the better.

"My name's Olivia Berg. My friends call me Livi."

He would not qualify for friendship once she learned who he was. As far as this woman was concerned, he was the devil incarnate.

She gave him an encouraging glance. *And your name is?*

Oh boy. He could feel the sweat sneaking out of his pores. He'd been perfectly justified in cutting loose her little charity. He had no cause to feel guilty. None. But there she was smiling at him like they were on the road to friendship. Little Olivia Berg, the great judge of character. And here he was, feeling like Scrooge in front of a firing squad. With no blindfold.

Even though he had nothing to be ashamed of he couldn't seem to spit out his name. *Lie.*

"Joe." *Yeah, Joe. Good, old everyman Joe.*

Her expression asked, *Joe What?*

Joe… Joe… Why was this woman so pushy?

A truck rolled past, sending up a rooster tail of snow. "Ford," he added. "Joe Ford."

"Nice to meet you, Joe."

She wouldn't be saying that if she knew who he was. But she wouldn't. He'd get his car fixed, get on his way and get back to his life. So it really didn't matter if he was wussing out and not telling little Livi Christmas his real name. She didn't need to know.

"Where are you from, Joe?"

"Seattle."

"Seattle is such a pretty city," she said. "I went to the University of Washington and loved it. My parents took me to dinner at the top of the Space Needle when I turned twenty-one."

She spoke with reverence, like she'd visited the Vatican. "It's a cool city," he agreed.

"It's sure fun to visit. I remember the first time I went to the Pike Place Market and saw those guys at the fish store tossing the fish back and forth. That was so cool."

"It's a real tourist attraction."

"I love tourist attractions," she said with a vigorous nod, making those honey-colored curls bounce again. "I hope before I die I can see a whole bunch of them. I'd love to see the Eiffel Tower and Big Ben and go for a gondola ride in Venice. Have you traveled a lot?"

He'd been there, done all of that. "Yeah," he said. "But some of the best places to see are right here in the US. It's hard to beat the Grand Canyon or California's wine country or skiing in Vail."

"I can imagine," she said wistfully. Obviously, Livi Berg didn't get around much. Too busy making hardworking businessmen feel guilty.

They were pulling into town now, a dot on the map cuddled by trees—fir, cedar, maple and the pine trees that had given the place its name. The downtown was a collection of ancient buildings spiffed up with cedar garlands stretched across their windows and red bows on the lampposts. A lot of trucks. Men in jeans and flannel shirts. Women hurrying along bundled in coats and boots, a couple towing small children behind them. Guy was no expert in fashion but he could tell that nobody here was keeping up. Even his chauffeur, cute as she was, wore a coat that screamed secondhand. Obviously, she wasn't living high on the money her charity brought in.

As if reading his thoughts, she said, "Most people here live simple lives. And our local economy hasn't caught up with Seattle."

Whose had? With Microsoft and Amazon providing thousands of jobs, the city was on fire. It had been growing ever since it made one of those best-places-to-live lists and condos and apartments had sprung up everywhere like mushrooms in the rainy city. Small houses in old neighborhoods were now worth a fortune. New, sleek buildings had gone up downtown and the freeways had gotten clogged. Pulling down the old Viaduct and replacing it with an underground tunnel had made everyone feel safer but so far it hadn't eliminated traffic. The city bulged and bustled and glistened, and for the kings and queens of the hill the pace was fast.

In contrast, this place looked like a movie set from the fifties.

They passed a bakery with trays of various cookies and a frothy-looking wedding cake on display in its window. Weddings. Look what all three of Mike's had led to, divorce and child support. Guy would have liked to have had a kid or two but to have a kid you had to stick it out with a woman. Fast relationships, easily begun and easily terminated were more Guy's speed so, realistically, kids were probably out of the picture.

They slid past the rest of the downtown—a hardware store, a bank, a couple of churches and a couple of restaurants. The post office had a wreath on its door. And there on the corner was the lone gas station and next to it Bob's Auto Repair.

"Thanks for the lift," he said, once she stopped the car. He was more than ready to get out. The smell of her perfume and his unease didn't mix well.

She opened her door as he opened his. "I'll introduce you."

Like he needed an introduction to a car mechanic? He started to tell her that wasn't necessary but she was already moving toward the door. Little Miss Helpful.

With her walking in front of him, he couldn't help but notice that Little Miss Helpful had nice legs, all wrapped in tight denim. And a cute butt peeking out from under her red coat.

Never mind her butt, he scolded himself, and followed her in.

The office area was small with a counter and a couple of chairs. Between those chairs an ancient end table held a stack of car and hunting magazines. A tiny tree sat on the counter decorated with car ornaments, probably the work of the owner's wife. The smell of motor oil drifted out to them.

And so did a man in the traditional grease-smudged mechanic's uniform who came in from the car bay to greet them. He was husky and had arms like tree trunks, the kind of guy who probably didn't need a jack to lift a car. He was wiping his hands with a rag and wearing the necessary greet-the-customer smile. At the sight of Little Miss Helpful the wattage on that smile turned up. Well, who could blame him?

"Hey, Livi," he said.

If there'd been any doubt about how the man felt toward this woman, his tone of voice cleared it up. This was a man in love. So, were they a duo?

"Hi, Morris," she said easily. Casually, the way you'd speak to a friend.

Livi Berg was not a woman in love. In like, yeah, but not love. Poor schlub.

"This is Joe Ford," she said. "I found him stranded on the highway a few miles back. His car's broken."

"Serpentine belt," Guy said, figuring he needed to speak for himself.

Livi inserted herself back into the conversation. "Can you tow his car in?"

Morris was looking him over, probably wondering what kind of car he drove, just how friendly he'd gotten with Livi on the

ride in and how soon he could get out of town. *Don't worry.
I'm not staying.*

"I need to get back on the road as soon as possible," Guy said,
part explanation, part assurance. "Trying to get to Idaho for
Christmas." *See? Urgent need here.*

"Kind of a roundabout way," the dude said suspiciously. As if
Guy had planned to break down outside his town and waylay
the woman of his dreams.

"He had to make a detour to Arlington," explained Little
Miss Helpful.

Morris Bentley nodded, taking that in. "What kind of wheels
you driving?"

"Maserati GranTurismo."

Two eyebrows rose. "Yeah?"

"Can you tow me in?"

"Sure. Can't get you fixed right away, though. We'll have to
special order that belt."

No surprise there, but it still didn't make Guy happy. "How
long will that take?"

"We can order it today. Have it by Monday, Tuesday at the
latest."

Tuesday? "Tuesday's Christmas Eve," Guy pointed out.

"We'll get you on the road as fast as we can."

Stuck in this town for the weekend. Yeah, that would be fun.

But he'd have to make the best. He had his laptop and he'd
just downloaded the latest John Grisham novel onto his phone.
He'd survive.

"Is there a motel in town?" he asked.

"The River's Bend is nice," said Livi. "It's just outside of town.
I'll be happy to give you a lift."

Morris, the car repairman, didn't look happy about her offer.
Don't worry, bud. She's cute but I'm not interested. The girl was
sweet as sugar icing on a cake. But he'd had a glimpse of what
was under that icing. This was a woman who always had to get

her way. And he was willing to bet she had a temper. He could only imagine the fit she'd thrown in her office when he'd turned down her donation request. The faux polite email he'd received in response to his personal donation had been laced with vitriol and had spoken volumes about what lay behind that pretty mask.

"I'll just hitch a ride with the tow truck," he said. "I need to get my computer and duffel bag anyway."

"Oh, Morris can drop that by," she said breezily. "Can't you, Morris?"

Morris's brows dipped in sync with his mouth. Guy caught the look she shot him. *Just do it.* Oh yeah, this dude was one whipped puppy.

"You don't need to," Guy said in an effort to save him.

"It's no big deal," the mechanic said with a shrug of his boulder-sized shoulders.

"Okay. Thanks. And how about a loaner?"

Morris was shaking his head before Guy could even finish his sentence. "Sorry, they're all being used."

It took superhuman strength for Guy not to start turning the air blue.

"I really don't mind driving you to the motel," said Livi.

It was either take her offer or walk. Morris looked like the only place he wanted to drive Guy was off a cliff.

"Thanks," Guy said to her. Then to the mechanic, "What do I owe you?"

Morris quoted a price and Guy reached for his wallet and his charge card.

Whoa, don't be doing that. The last thing he wanted was to pay for something in front of Olivia Berg as Guy Hightower, Scrooge of Seattle. He pulled out a hundred-dollar bill and told Bentley to keep the change. The man deserved some kind of compensation for his trouble, and Guy was betting there wouldn't be any coming from Little Miss Helpful. Not the kind Bentley wanted, anyway.

He took the money, looking torn between gratitude and resentment.

"Morris always goes the extra mile," Livi explained as she led Guy back out to her car.

He did for her, obviously. Some men had no cojones.

Livi hoped she wasn't coming across as pushy. She really was trying to help the stranger.

But she was trying to help Christmas from the Heart, as well. She was no fool and she knew a potential donor when she saw one. Fancy car, expensive clothes, and now whipping out hundred-dollar bills like they were ones. The man had some money. Maybe he worked for a big corporation or owned a small business. Maybe he had connections. Whatever the case, she intended to find out. And get a donation.

Heaven knew they needed it. Her poor nonprofit was running on fumes. She thought of Joe Ford's Maserati stuck by the side of the road. That was Christmas from the Heart if they didn't find some new contributors. This man's car breaking down right outside of town was a gift, no doubt about it.

"You never did tell me. What do you do for a living, Joe?" she asked.

Shit, here it came. He'd known it would only be a matter of time until she hit him up for money. "I…" What to say? He could almost smell smoke as the wheels spun in his brain. He wasn't good at improvising. *Stay somewhat close to the truth*, he advised himself. "My family has a small company."

Livi Berg would probably beg to differ. She saw Hightower Enterprises as a corporate giant. But size was a subjective thing.

"What does your company do?"

He could practically see her salivating. "A lot of things."

Thank God she didn't push it. "It's a lot of work owning your own company."

"It's probably a lot of work running a nonprofit," he said, trying to shift the attention away from himself. Except did he really want to hear about her nonprofit?

"It is," she said. "But it's so satisfying. I love being able to help people in need."

No kidding. He never would have guessed. It probably made her feel superior to everyone else.

"My great-grandmother actually started Christmas from the Heart," she went on. "And the women in my family have run it ever since. Many of our donors have been with us since the beginning." The words, barely out of her mouth, pulled it down at the corners.

Guy braced himself for what was about to come next.

Sure enough. "Sadly, we lost one of our major contributors this year. I'm afraid many families won't have a very merry Christmas because of it."

"The business might have had to make some cutbacks. It happens, you know."

She shook her head vehemently. "Not this business. They're a giant."

That had been wrestling with giant problems. "Aren't there are other charities that can pick up the slack?" She wasn't the only nonprofit in the world. In fact, no matter how highly she thought of herself and her organization, there were plenty of others. He knew, because Hightower got requests from all of them.

"Not around here." She sighed. "I have put in a few calls though and I'm hoping we'll get some help. But there are always so many needs this time of year, you know."

She made it sound like a question. "Yeah, there are. And I'm sure the company that had to cut you loose is doing its part to help meet some somewhere."

She said nothing to that but her smile stayed away.

It was dusk when they pulled up in front of a one-level relic from the sixties perched alongside the Skykomish River. The parking lot was filled with cars and potholes that even the snow couldn't hide. "A lot of people come here for cross-country skiing and snowshoeing," she explained as she eased the car around the worst of the holes to where the office was located. A neon No Vacancy sign greeted them from the window.

"Oh dear," she murmured.

"Is there any other place in town?" he asked.

She started to shake her head, then her face lit up. "Actually, there is."

"Think they'll have room?"

"I know they will."

Back out they went, dodging potholes, then she turned her car on the road toward town once more. He hadn't seen any place when they'd driven in. Maybe there was a bed-and-breakfast somewhere. Or maybe she knew someone on Airbnb.

Sure enough, once back in the heart of town they turned away from the main street and drove into the residential district, passing old Victorians, simple cottages and Craftsman-style homes all nestled together. Many of them looked thirsty for paint but almost all of them had lights strung along their roofline or a wreath on the door. One had a collection of inflatable figures on the lawn, and the residents were in the process of bringing them to life. A Santa sprang up and waved at Guy. Another house had a refrigerator sitting on the front porch.

"That's Grandma Bell," Livi explained. "She's a bit of a hoarder. Her son's coming later this week to haul that old fridge away."

What to say to that? *Nothing*, Guy decided.

A couple of driveways held new cars, but most of what he saw were older models. Pine River was an old, tired town in need of a facelift and trying to make do with cheap makeup, all the while hoping some company would come along and want to start a relationship.

As if reading his mind, Livi said, "I know it doesn't look like

CHRISTMAS FROM THE HEART

much but the people here are great. And they really pull together."

"So, do all the houses look about like this?" That probably sounded snobby.

"Most of the homes are older," she said. "We've got a small development to the east that has newer houses. They're nice," she added, "but they don't have character like a lot of these."

They probably didn't have energy inefficient windows or asbestos paint, either.

"Here we are," she said, pulling up in front of a blue Victorian with gingerbread trim painted white. Icicle lights hung from the roofline and there was a wreath on the front door. Unlike some of the other houses he'd seen, this one had been well maintained.

"Is this a bed-and-breakfast?" he asked as they went up the front walk.

"It is now."

"I don't understand."

"This is my family's home."

He was staying with Livi Berg? Oh no. Hell, no.

7

Livi opened the front door but Guy's feet remained frozen on the front porch. "I can't stay here."

"It's no trouble, really. It's just Dad and me and we've got a guest room."

Probably something all girlie that doubled as a sewing room. Livi Berg looked like the type who sewed. Or quilted. Or whatever. She probably baked, too. A vision of frosted sugar cookies danced into Guy's head and he pushed it firmly away.

"There must be someplace else," he said. She looked hurt and he realized he sounded churlish. "I mean…" *I don't want to stay with you and your dad and hear about your stupid charity and feel like a shit when I have no reason to feel like a shit.* Gremlins. Gremlins had sneaked into his car engine and done this to him.

"It's no bother," she said, misreading him completely. "In fact, it would be nice."

Not for him.

She stood in the doorway in her red coat and jeans with boots with fake fur trim and tassels, looking like she was posing for some family-friendly magazine ad. Beyond her, a cozy living room with a worn couch, a recliner and a fireplace beckoned. The mantel was decorated with greenery and a small nativity set. A Christmas tree stood in one corner with presents under it. There was no Christmas tree in his condo. He and his brothers had stopped bothering with presents for each other years ago. He ordered stuff online for the nephews and nieces and had it shipped.

Now she was raising an eyebrow expectantly.

Well, crap. It was either here with Little Miss Helpful and her dad or sleep out in the snow. He stepped through the door and his heart rate skyrocketed like a man in the woods, knowing a grizzly bear lurked somewhere ahead.

Morris Bentley knew a player when he saw one, and with his fancy car and hundred-dollar bills, this stranger had *player* written all over him. He was average looking, probably still in his thirties, medium height with brown hair. Well, okay, maybe a little better looking than average. But not that much. Fit enough, but Morris was bigger and could take him easily. Not that Livi had bothered to compare. The wheels said it all, and so had the look she'd given Morris telling him to butt out. He knew she'd be all over moneybags Joe Ford like magnetic slime.

Morris's jaw clenched as he rumbled Bob's tow truck down the road. He didn't like this turn of events, not one bit. Livi had been desperate for new donors ever since that shit at Hightower Enterprises left her hanging, and desperate women sometimes did desperate things. Like getting involved with rich guys who were better at making promises than keeping them. This newcomer looked exotic, and Livi, with her talk of gondolas and Eiffel Towers, craved exotic. She was always binging on that TV show where people looked for houses in far-flung corners of the world.

Why she did was a mystery to Morris. There was nothing wrong with where they lived or the life they had. If she could just get that through her head, they could be so happy together.

It didn't take him long to spot the stranded sports car, its body slowly getting buried in snow. Red, of course. As he hooked the thing up to his winch he put in his request to Santa. *Bring that belt fast.* The sooner he got this car up and running, the sooner he could get the newcomer out of town.

He towed the rich-boy toy back to the garage and got it into the work bay. His fellow mechanic, Lenny, left the truck he'd been working on to check out the Maserati. "Oh man," he said reverently. "There's something you don't see every day. Man, what I'd give to own a beauty like this."

Morris had to admit, the car was a work of art, sleek and shiny, and he could only imagine how beautifully it handled. But… "What would you do with a car like this in Pine River?"

"To hell with Pine River. I'd drive to LA, find me a movie star babe and live it up."

Lenny, with his scrawny bod and scruffy face, wasn't exactly the stuff movie star babes' dreams were made of, but Morris didn't say that. It wasn't cool to mess with a man's fantasy.

"Yeah, I wouldn't mind getting a chance to drive something like this," he admitted.

"That'll never happen, not on what we make," Lenny said, returning to Earth.

Morris shrugged. "I'm okay with what I got." He had his truck and the 1971 orange Dodge Charger that had been his dad's. Really, what more did a man need? Fancy foreign jobs like this were nothing but flash for people with cash.

He lifted the hood to confirm that the belt was, indeed, the problem.

"Look at that," Lenny said.

"Don't be droolin' on the engine," Morris teased.

"Man, I'd love to see the dude who owns this. Sorry I missed him when Livi brought him in."

"He's nothing special," Morris said. "Puts his pants on one leg at a time, just like us."

"Yeah, but I bet he wears better pants."

Who cared what he wore?

The rich boy had been right. The belt was, indeed, shot. If only the guy drove the kind of car normal people drove, Morris would have had the belt he needed in stock. He'd have gotten that clown back on the road within the hour.

He left Lenny drooling and went back in the office and ordered the belt. Then he called Livi to find out where she'd dumped the guy so he could deliver his duffel bag.

"Actually, he's staying here," she said, cheerful as an elf.

"He's staying with you?" The tool hadn't wasted any time. How had he managed that?

"There isn't anyplace else. River Bend was full up."

There had to be someplace.

"How perfect is that?" she said, and chortled.

"I don't like it," Morris said.

"What do you mean?"

"That kind of guy chews up women and spits 'em out."

"Oh, honestly," she said in disgust.

"He's a user."

"He is not. You don't know anything about him," she argued.

"Yes, I do. I know he's got money." Morris may not have earned a fancy college degree but he was no dope. He knew about men like Joe Ford. People sucked up to them and they took advantage of it. Livi was already sucking up and this guy would be more than happy to take advantage of her.

"That hardly makes him a bad man," she said. "In fact, it makes him a real godsend."

"Money isn't everything," Morris said irritably.

"It is when you need it. Morris, this is a blessing in disguise, a Christmas bonus. He'll be staying right here with Dad and me and I'll have plenty of opportunities to show him everything Christmas from the Heart does for our community. I'm sure he'll give us a donation."

"Guys like that are takers, not givers," Morris said.

"Morris, you can't judge a book by its cover."

Oh yes, he could. And he could judge a man by his choice of wheels. A muscle car said, "I'm as buff as my ride." A Prius said, "I care about the environment…and getting good gas mileage." A truck grunted, "I haul my stuff to the dump myself." Motorcycles sang, "Born to be wild," even when they were driven by retired dentists. But a sports car, that said, "I've got money and I don't care if you give me a speeding ticket 'cause I can afford it. I take what I want, and whatever I want I deserve." A man like that didn't deserve Livi—that was for sure.

Saying all that to her would be a waste of breath so Morris tried a different argument. "You judged that book by his cover. You think because he's rich he's gonna be generous."

"A lot of rich people are."

"A lot of 'em aren't. Or have you forgotten Guy Hightower?"

"Of course I haven't. And that's another reason to get to know this man. He might be willing to step in and fill the gaping hole in our funding."

"Well, you be careful around him," Morris cautioned. "A rich playboy like that wouldn't think nothing of breaking your heart."

"You're sweet to worry about me, but there's no need. Just bring over his things."

"All right," Morris said. "I'll bring 'em."

But he made no promise not to worry. He was worried. Joe Ford was trouble and Livi couldn't see it and Morris had no idea how to get through to her. This was going to be like trying to guard the henhouse with two broken legs, two broken arms and no gun.

★ ★ ★

If Joe Ford had any intention of breaking Livi's heart or even a passing interest in the rest of her, Livi thought, he sure wasn't showing it. He'd seemed interested when he first got into her car, and that flirty smile of his had sent a jolt through her that about set her bra on fire. But something had shifted. She could still feel the electric current zipping between them like a downed wire, but he was skirting as far around that wire as possible.

He'd looked at David's bedroom, which was now the guest room, and nodded approval. Then, after she'd shown him the bathroom and where the towels were, he'd thanked her and strode purposefully back to the room and shut the door. A clear message that he wasn't looking for new friends.

How frustrating! A handsome, charming stranger—rich stranger—was here in town under her very roof and instead of being sociable, he was hiding in his room.

Maybe he was shy. Except he'd seemed anything but shy when she first met him. Maybe he thought there was something between her and Morris. Yes, that was probably it. She'd have to make sure he knew there was nothing there but friendship.

Morris appeared shortly after she'd gone downstairs to think of a way to lure her houseguest out of his room. He was carrying a duffel bag and a laptop case.

He looked past Livi into the living room. "Where is he?"

"Upstairs, in the guest room."

Morris nodded. "Good. Maybe he'll stay there."

She frowned at him and took the duffel bag.

"I guess he doesn't want to hang out. So how about you and me do something tonight?"

"I can't. I have to make dinner for Dad. And you know I've got a ton of things to do to get ready for the fruitcake competition tomorrow." Actually, most everything was done but she did need to check in with her judges, and Bettina was swinging by to drop off a couple of last-minute entries she'd been given.

"Okay." Morris pointed a finger at her. "Just don't go getting all starry-eyed over Mr. Money Man."

She made a face. "Honestly, Morris. How shallow do you think I am?"

"You're not shallow at all. But I know you'd do anything for Christmas from the Heart. And he's got a sports car. That doesn't work," Morris added.

As if there was some symbolism in that.

She snagged the laptop case. "Thanks for bringing these by."

"You're welcome," he said grudgingly, then turned and slouched down the porch.

Of course Morris was jealous. But darn it all, they weren't a couple so he had no right to be. And she had no need to feel guilty for being attracted to a good-looking man.

She would have been attracted to Joe Ford even if he didn't have a penny. There'd been something about his smile when he first got into her car that made her want to know more about him. His current unease made him a fascinating mystery. A mystery she was determined to solve.

She took his overnight bag and computer upstairs and knocked on the bedroom door. He'd shed his coat and shoes and met her wearing a gray cashmere sweater with his jeans. Oh, but he filled out that sweater beautifully. He wasn't as husky as Morris. He was toned but slimmer. And polished-looking. Elegant.

He caught her checking him out and her cheeks flamed. "My friend Morris brought your things," she said. *Friend. As in just friends.*

"Thanks," he said, and took them from her.

"You're welcome to hang out in our living room if you want," she offered.

"That's okay. I have some things I need to do." He held up the laptop case as proof.

"Of course. I just wanted you to know you didn't have to stay stuck in here."

"I don't feel stuck. It's a nice room." His smile had lost its flirty vibe.

Okay, there would be no luring him out until dinner. "Whatever works for you," she said cheerfully. "Dinner's at six."

"You don't have to feed me," he protested.

"I know. But you don't want to starve. It's nothing fancy, just meat loaf and baked potatoes."

"Sounds good."

"It is," she said. "Not to brag or anything, but I make a mean meat loaf."

"I look forward to trying it."

And then there was nothing left to say other than, "See you later. Just come on down to the kitchen."

"Will do."

"Okay," she said, and backed away, giving him a little wave as she left.

He acknowledged it with a nod and shut the door.

Once downstairs she hurried to the kitchen to bake some cookies. Cookies melted hearts and sweetened the sourest of temperaments. Cookies put people in happy moods. And after having his car break down and his trip delayed, poor Joe Ford could probably use some cheering up.

Okay, and buttering up. There was a hidden agenda behind her baking binge. But so what? It was a worthy agenda.

She was pulling out the makings for gumdrop cookies when her father came into the kitchen in search of coffee. "Did I hear someone at the door?"

"Yes. We've got somebody staying with us."

Dad's brows knit. "We do?"

"His name is Joe Ford and his car broke down. I gave him a lift into town."

Her father looked horrified. "You picked up a stranger? Livi, what were you thinking?"

"I was thinking he had a long way to walk in the snow. And I was thinking about the story of the Good Samaritan," she added.

"That was a parable," Dad said firmly. "And now he's staying with us? How did you go from giving him a lift to bringing him here?"

"There's not room at River's Bend."

Her father still looked far from happy.

"It's okay, Dad. He's not going to rob us."

"How do you know?"

"Because he was driving a fancy car. He's a businessman. A rich businessman," she couldn't help adding.

Now Dad got it. But he looked at her disapprovingly. "I hope that's not the reason for this kindness."

"Of course not." Well, it wasn't the only reason. "I didn't know a thing about him when I stopped to pick him up. Anyway, he's on his way to see his family for Christmas and he's stuck here until Morris can get the part for his car, and he's eating dinner with us."

"Then we'll do our best to make him feel welcome," Dad said, his stern expression slipping away.

He almost sounded like his old self, the man who used to welcome company with a smile and a hearty handshake. Maybe this stranger dropping into their lives so unexpectedly was exactly what they both needed.

"I'm going to get over there later than I thought," Guy said to his mother.

She sounded suspicious. "Why?"

"My car crapped out on me. I'm stuck in a little town off Highway 2."

"Oh no. We've all been looking forward to seeing you."

He doubted that. His mom, yes, but the rest of the crew... What did they care about a newly inherited family member?

"You'll make it for Christmas, though, won't you?"

"I should. It depends on how long it takes to get the part."

"Oh, Guy," she said in disgust as if he'd planned for this to happen. "If you'd only get a dependable American-made car. Or taken the plane."

"There is no plane anymore. Remember?" They'd ditched their Beechcraft G36 Bonanza a year ago at Guy's insistence. Mike had mourned it like a lost lover.

"Well, then you should have flown business class."

"You're forgetting I had to go pick up a chocolate pot."

"Now I wish I'd never asked you to pick it up. Oh, darling, I am sorry. If it wasn't for me you could have flown and been here by now."

"No worries," he said. He'd actually preferred to drive. He enjoyed driving his fancy baby, and he liked having the time alone to clear his head, listen to music or an audiobook.

"I've been looking forward to having you with us," she said again.

And he'd been up for seeing his mom. They'd always been close, but he didn't see her or talk to her as much now that she was remarried.

Not that he begrudged his mom her new life. With her sons so busy working long hours, not to mention marrying and divorcing and remarrying, she'd gotten little enough family time. Guy had felt guilty about not doing more with her and had been almost relieved when she'd met Del and hit Restart on her life. They'd met at a swanky benefit dinner and she'd gotten swept along on the euphoria of new love and carried off to Lake Coeur d'Alene where Del had a little lodge with six bedrooms, four bathrooms and six thousand square feet.

Guy was sure when he finally did arrive he'd find a twelve-foot tree in the living room and the mantel on the stone fireplace would be swathed in fir and pine and decorated with Mercury glass vases and candles. Del's daughters Lizbeth and Melianna would be present, Lizbeth with her bratty kid and Melianna probably with the latest two-second love of her life. Not that he could talk. His relationships didn't last much longer. But the trip would be worth it to see his mom and get some of that short-bread she'd promised to make him. So no matter what, he'd be there. Late, but better late than never. Maybe he'd luck out and miss seeing the stepsisters.

"Don't worry, Mom. I'll get there," he assured her. There was nothing in this town to keep him hanging around.

"How about me?" whispered the vision of a curly-haired little doll with kiss-me lips.

"Nope," he told it. A woman like that would never understand him. And he didn't need someone in his life to be his judge and jury. He opened his laptop and caught up on some work.

He was finishing his last email when she knocked on the bedroom door. "Dinner's ready."

Simple words. They made him think of his life as a little kid. They'd had a gardener and a housekeeper but Mom had claimed the kitchen for herself. During the school year, when the family was home, she'd insisted on cooking dinner during the week. Weekends were for eating out and catered affairs, but weekdays were for stuffed pork tenderloins, seafood Alfredo and, her sons' favorite, pizza with her homemade crust. She could outbake the best French pastry chef and her chocolate eclairs had been the stuff dreams were made of. As her sons got older and busy with sports, she'd found it harder to gather her family for meals, but it hadn't stopped her from trying. Sometimes, when he wasn't stuck at the office, Dad had even joined them. That was rare.

So was making it to any of Guy's lacrosse games or tennis matches. Dad had been up to his clogged arteries in the rat race. And now his sons were following in his footsteps, doing what had to be done to keep the Hightower legacy going.

"I'll be right there," he called to his hostess. He sent the email, shut the laptop, then slipped on his Ferragamos and went downstairs. The aroma of cooked meat and onions drew him past a small formal dining room, where a ceramic church and a bunch of corny-looking candles sat on an empty table, to the kitchen, which was warm and cozy. An ancient red Formica table occupied one corner and was set for three with white plates and red napkins.

Livi was setting a couple of bottles of salad dressing on the table. She wore the same long-sleeved green top she'd worn when she brought his things up to him. It brought out the green in her eyes and accentuated her curves.

A man in his early sixties already sat at the table. He gave Guy a polite smile and stood to shake hands. "I'm Andrew Berg. Welcome to our home."

"Joe Ford," Guy said, stumbling over his new name.

"Good to meet you, Joe."

"Thanks for opening your home," Guy said.

"Can't let someone be homeless at Christmas," said Mr. Berg as Olivia set a platter with slices of the promised meat loaf on the table. It looked like sliced dog food. With mushrooms.

Meat loaf. His mom had never made it and they'd never eaten it in any of the restaurants the family had frequented. It wasn't steak, that was for sure. But it smelled good and his stomach, deciding not to be picky, rumbled. A bowl with baked potatoes sat next to the meat dish as well as a tossed salad. He was smelling something else, though, something that said *bakery*. He looked to the counter and caught sight of what looked like oatmeal cookies sitting on a cooling rack.

"That's dessert," Livi told him with a dimpled smile.

"Looks good," Guy said.

"It is. Livi's a wonderful cook," her father said. "So, let's say grace before this gets cold."

Grace? People still did that?

They did in the Berg household. Heads were bowed and Mr. Berg offered up a short prayer, which he ended with an "Amen."

"Amen," his daughter echoed.

"Amen," Guy said, the word feeling foreign on his tongue. It had been way too long since he'd heard that word.

"Coffee?" Livi asked him.

"Sure."

"Do you take anything in it?"

"Sugar." If she knew who he was, she'd have put arsenic in it.

"Tell us a little about yourself," Mr. Berg said, as he passed Guy the platter of sliced dog food.

"Not much to tell," Guy said. "I live in Seattle." Livi handed him a mug of coffee and he thanked her, all the while casting about in his mind for a topic other than himself to introduce into the conversation.

"Livi went to school there, at the University of Washington, my old alma mater. You a Seahawks fan?"

"I am." His family had a full season suite at CenturyLink Field. The airplane had been a line item they could cut. That suite was a necessity. All three brothers were football buffs and the company used the suite for business as much as for pleasure. Many deals had been made in that suite and many loans secured. And extended.

"Having a pretty good season this year," said Mr. Berg, and Guy agreed. Sports, always a safe topic.

Guy was about to take them further down that road when Mr. Berg said, "Sorry you've got car troubles. My daughter tells me you're on your way to see family."

"I was."

"It's important to be with the people you care about this time of year," Mr. Berg said, and a shadow crossed his face.

Guy knew that kind of pain. He'd felt it, seen it in his mom's face.

His host shook off the shadow. "What kind of business are you in, Joe?"

Oh boy. Now it was getting dicey. "Just a family business," Guy said. "How about you, Mr. Berg?"

"Call me Andrew. I'm in insurance."

"Ah. Maybe you could advise me. What's the best to have, term or whole life?"

That was all it took to divert Andrew Berg, thank God. Guy let him talk, nodding between bites of meat loaf—not bad stuff, actually—and asking questions to keep him talking.

He was expounding the advantages of term insurance for a young man when the doorbell rang. "That's Bettina," said Olivia. "She's dropping off some last-minute entries for the fruit-cake competition."

"Have her join us for dessert," said Mr. Berg as Olivia got up.

"Good idea," she said, and disappeared.

A moment later she was back with a petite woman around her age, slim with olive skin and long dark hair, following her. The woman was dressed casually, with a parka over a sweatshirt, jeans and boots, and she carried a small cardboard box.

"This is my assistant, Bettina Thomas. Bettina, this is Joe Ford. He's staying with us for a couple of days."

Bettina was looking at him assessingly, so Guy explained, "My car died outside of town and the Bergs have taken me in."

"Ah," she said with a nod. But that assessing look remained. He knew what she was thinking as sure as if there was a bubble over her head. *Single?*

Yes. Permanently so.

"It's nice to meet you," she said. "Welcome to Pine River. If you have to be stranded there's no better place."

Guy could think of about a hundred better but he smiled and nodded.

"Sit down," Mr. Berg offered as Livi set a plate of cookies on the table. "Livi made gumdrop cookies."

"Just for a minute," Bettina said, helping herself to one. "I've got to get home."

"The demands of motherhood," Mr. Berg said, nodding wisely.

"I've got to admit, nobody tells you when you announce that you're pregnant what you're getting into. I feel like I haven't slept in a hundred years."

"I think it's time for Aunt Livi to come babysit so you can have a nap," Livi said, passing the plate of cookies to Guy.

He took one and bit into it. Olivia Berg knew how to bake. She was obviously a good friend and liked kids. Guy would have been into getting to know her a lot better. If she hadn't been Olivia Berg.

"Maybe, after we get through the holidays. Speaking of, I have bad news," Bettina said, looking suddenly pained.

"Oh no. What?" asked Livi.

"We've lost one of our fruitcake judges. Jimmy just called. He's come down with the flu."

From the expression on Livi's face the end of the world must have come. "Oh no," she groaned, driving her fingers into those honey-colored curls.

Bettina helped herself to another cookie and passed the plate to Andrew Berg. "Oh yes. He said he tried to call you but you weren't answering your phone."

"I left it in my purse," said Livi.

"Well, we're one judge short for tomorrow."

"We have to have three in case of a tie."

"You could do it," Bettina said.

Livi shook her head. "That wouldn't look right. Anyway, you know I'll be too busy overseeing everything."

"How about Mr. Berg?" Bettina suggested, looking at Livi's father.

"Oh no," he said. "I'm the organizer's dad. That wouldn't look right, either."

"Who are we going to get at the last minute?" Livi fretted. "All the other good bakers in town are entered in the contest." Then her gaze settled on Guy.

So did her assistant's.

He held up both hands. "Oh no. Not me. I'm a stranger. Nobody here even knows me."

"Which makes you perfect for the job," Livi said happily. "You'd be completely unbiased. I know it's a terrible imposition."

It sure was. This woman had no boundaries.

Obviously, since she'd offered a total stranger a room in her house and was now feeding him dinner. Guilt jabbed Guy's conscience.

"It is a fun event," she added, "and a big fund-raiser for Christmas from the Heart."

Naturally, it had to be for frickin' Christmas from the Heart.

"It really is a fun party," Bettina added, as chipper and enthusiastic as her boss. "Everyone in town comes. We have hot cider and cocoa and Christmas cookies and soft pretzels and corn dogs. And live music."

Corn dogs. Oh yeah, there was an incentive.

"So, what do you say?" Livi asked.

I say let me out of here. Guy smiled weakly. Both women were looking at him, holding their breath. He was trapped. "I guess. But I don't like fruitcake." Big understatement. Fruitcake was even grosser than corn dogs.

"So much the better," Livi said gleefully. "The entrants will have to work really hard to please you."

"This will be interesting," Bettina predicted.

No, this was going to be torture.

8

Livi rewarded Guy's altruism with cookies and eggnog ice cream. Her assistant made predictions of all the fun he'd have, took a cookie for the road and left him to the ministrations of the Bergs.

"How much fruitcake does a judge have to eat?" he asked.

"Only a bite. And we'll have sherbet to cleanse your palate."

He'd have preferred whiskey but he doubted he'd find that anywhere at the fruitcake competition.

"I really appreciate you agreeing to help us," Livi gushed, and her dad smiled approvingly. "It is a popular fund-raiser."

"And well supported," put in her father. "This is a tight-knit community. People here help each other."

"If that's the case, why do you even need Christmas from the Heart?" Guy asked.

Livi looked at him as if he'd suggested they didn't need oxygen.

"It's not a wealthy community," Mr. Berg said. "Most of our

residents are blue-collar workers commuting to warehouse jobs in Monroe or construction projects wherever they can find them. Some people work up at the ski resorts. Many are unemployed. And we have our share of seniors on a limited income and single moms trying to make ends meet on minimum-wage jobs. Christmas from the Heart fills the gap."

"Sounds like you could use some light industry out here," Guy mused.

"Or another Amazon," Livi said. "Meanwhile, we do the best we can to help our residents and the people in the surrounding towns who are struggling."

"The fruitcake competition is a big hit, partly because people have a chance to contribute no matter what their income," Mr. Berg explained. "It was all Livi's idea," he added, beaming with pride at his daughter.

"The grand prize winner gets a two-hundred-and-fifty-dollar gift card from the grocery store and runners-up each get a fifty-dollar one. In addition to that we have an elf central booth where people can barter services and goods for the new year. So, a handyman may trade a Saturday afternoon of work for a meal baked by one of our seniors. Last year a retired schoolteacher traded a summer of free child care with one of our single moms in exchange for the mom and her daughter weeding her vegetable garden and helping with canning."

"How do you raise money for your nonprofit in all this?" Guy wanted to know.

"Vendors pay for booths, and we have a silent auction. All our local businesses offer goods and services and that usually brings in a nice chunk of money. We also have a giant wooden Christmas box where people put cash donations. Everyone who donates gets a pin that says *I gave from the heart*. They have a different design each year and people collect them."

Oh yeah, sounded like a real collectible. Right up there with baseball cards and vintage comic books. Guy nodded politely.

"Many of the local businesses write checks and donate them at this," added Mr. Berg. "Livi writes their name on a big dry-erase board."

There was an honor.

They chatted a while longer, both father and daughter talking up the merits of the fruitcake torture event and of the nonprofit in general, then Mr. Berg thanked his daughter for the meal, kissed the top of her head and excused himself.

Guy was ready to scram, too, but his mother had trained him right, so he stayed and helped clear the table.

"I'm glad you were able to join us," Livi said as she loaded the dishwasher. "This was good for my father."

She bent to load a plate and Guy caught a tantalizing glimpse of cleavage. He stepped away from temptation and moved to the table for more dishes. "How so?"

"He hasn't been too social since my mother died. Having to put himself out a little for a stranger, well, for a moment he was almost his old self again."

Guy nodded. "I get that. It about killed my mom when my dad died." It had about killed him, too. "Sometimes you need something to pull you out of yourself."

"Or someone," Livi said.

He looked out the kitchen window at a backyard covered in snow. A couple of trees stood with bare branches. He wondered what kind of trees they were. Here in the country, where people lived more closely to the land, probably fruit trees. Guy had no complaints about his condo in the city, but there was something about a house and a backyard. A man could play soccer with his kids in a backyard. He could sit under a tree and drink a microbrew and watch the sunset.

But that wasn't his life. His life was about keeping a company in the black so other men could have jobs and afford to buy that house with the backyard and the fruit trees. And in the end, that did more to help people than donating to a rinky-dink charity.

Still, come the next day, he'd go to the fruitcake competition and help decide who deserved a grocery store gift card. And he'd put a hundred in the donation box and get a stupid button to prove that, like everyone else here in Whoville, he, too, had a heart.

They finished cleaning the kitchen and she offered him more coffee. The sensible part of him advised beating it to his room. There was no point in hanging out with this woman. They were two different people living two different lives. He was already going to be stuck with her the following day. It would be best to go up to his room and start that Grisham novel.

Before he could take his own sensible advice he heard himself saying, "Sure." What a dope.

She refilled the cookie plate and they settled back down at the kitchen table. He took another cookie. Just to be polite. "These are good," he said, holding it up like some idiot in a food commercial.

"Thanks. My mom and I used to make them together every Christmas. And gingerbread boys and sugar cookies, too, of course."

"The kind shaped like stars and trees with that frosting on them?"

Livi nodded.

"My mom used to make those. They were my dad's favorite. After he died she couldn't bring herself to do it."

"It's hard to carry on after you've lost someone," Livi said. "My mom was my best friend."

She looked like she was going to cry and Guy felt a sudden urge to put an arm around her shoulder. Her settled for "I'm sorry."

She gave him a wobbly smile. "I know I'll see her again in heaven though and that's a comfort."

"It's still hard for those of us left here on earth," Guy said. *Just a little bitter about his own loss? Yeah, maybe.*

"I imagine you miss your dad as much as I miss my mom."

"I do," he admitted. "But more than that I miss what we never got."

She looked at him quizzically.

"He was talking about retiring in another year, spending more time with the family," Guy explained. "He worked so hard at the business when we were kids that we didn't see much of him. He and my brothers and I talked about going to our place in Vail for some skiing. Dad hadn't been on the slopes in years and he was looking forward to getting back into it. He never got the chance."

"That's sad," she said softly.

Guy shrugged. "But that's life."

"I guess the bottom line is you have to live your life right now and not wait for that perfect time in the future to do those things you want to do." Her brows knit together.

Those knit brows spoke volumes. "Are you taking your own advice?"

"Well," she hedged.

"What is it you want to do?"

"I'd like to travel. I really want to see the Eiffel Tower."

"So, what's stopping you?"

"Money, for one thing."

"You can save for it."

"That could take a while on what I make," she said with a rueful smile.

Ah. The price of doing good. Her salary had to be pitiful. "Have you ever thought of getting a real job?"

The ill-considered words popped out of his mouth and lay between them like a toxic spill. Where had that come from? The gremlins, of course.

She stiffened. "I have a real job."

"I didn't mean that the way it sounded," he lied, and hoped she wouldn't ask him how he had meant it.

"My job may not be as prestigious as one in the corporate world and my nonprofit may not be big, but what we do is important and it's impacting people's lives."

Suddenly it wasn't so cozy in the kitchen. "Of course," he said.

What Guy did with his business was important, and it, too, impacted people's lives. His brain was working again, and it commanded him to keep that thought to himself. The last thing he needed was to get into a philosophical debate with Olivia Berg. Anyway, that could open the door to more prying questions about his business.

"And if I have to choose between ever seeing the Eiffel Tower and seeing people's lives changed for the better I'll pass on the Eiffel Tower," she continued.

"Yeah, absolutely," he agreed. "I guess I just thought maybe you could find a way to do both. You know, as opposed to either or." She didn't look at all mollified. He took a final gulp of his coffee, then stood, pointing in the direction of the doorway. "I've, uh, got some work to do. I think I'll just, uh... Thanks for the dinner," he finished, and scrammed.

What a fiasco. He should have listened to his practical self. Lingering in the kitchen with Little Miss Helpful had been a stupid choice. And he was stuck with her the next day, too. Fala-la and frickin' merry Christmas.

Livi poured the last of Joe Ford's coffee down the drain and stuck the mug in the dishwasher, all the while kicking herself for getting up on her high horse. Way to alienate a possible donor. More than just a donor, she had to admit. She liked Joe Ford, liked talking to him.

Rather, she had liked talking to him until she blew it. What had she been thinking, anyway?

She hadn't. His comment had hit a nerve and she'd simply reacted. And now he'd bolted. They'd been making such progress, too, sharing life experiences. Obviously, they had things in common. Well, not the skiing. Her brother had skied but she'd always been a little afraid of going fast downhill. Still, she liked to cross-country ski—something that was much more afford-able. Maybe Joe liked to cross-country, as well. He obviously enjoyed the outdoors. So did she. He'd lost a parent, so had she. He liked cookies. She did, too.

She leaned against the counter and chewed on her lower lip. He especially liked sugar cookies. She hadn't baked those since Mom died. Everything else she'd managed—the pies at Thanks-giving, the Christmas decorations, every other cookie. But the frosted sugar cookies, that was a different story.

She could still see herself as a little girl, perched at the edge of the kitchen table, helping her mother frost and decorate those cookies. The stars got yellow sprinkles, the Santas were trimmed with pink frosting, and the trees, the best of them all, those got a light green frosting and a gentle shake of multicolored sprin-kles—"Not too much dear, just enough to look pretty"—and a silver dragée at the top to stand in for a star. Livi always con-centrated so hard to make sure that tiny silver ball was placed exactly. "Oh, that's perfect," Mom would say, and it described both the cookie and their time together.

"I don't think I can do it, Mom," Livi said.

Not even for Christmas from the Heart? a voice seemed to whisper.

Livi took in a deep breath.

And to bring back a happy memory? To honor those special times and the life we enjoyed together? And to pass on a little of that happiness?

Passing on happiness, keeping her mother's memory alive—yes, she should make those sugar cookies. Livi took out the old blue mixing bowl that had been her grandmother's and then her mother's. She got out the eggs and butter and flour and sugar and got to work. Half an hour later the kitchen smelled just the way she remembered.

"I wish you were here in person," she said as she rolled out another batch of cookies. "But I'll settle for having you here in spirit."

And wouldn't it be fun if, someday, she had a little girl of her own to bake sugar cookies with?

Ding, ding, ding, said her biological clock. *I'm winding down so you'd better find a sperm donor soon.*

"Yeah, good luck with that," she muttered.

Did Joe Ford have a girlfriend?

And why was she even bothering to speculate about him? She'd be lucky if she even got so much as a dollar from Joe let alone any sperm donation after bitching out on him.

Don't think like that, she told herself. *You're making him sugar cookies. Sugar cookies make great olive branches.* So maybe she'd get a donation after all.

Of money. She'd probably have to settle for just money.

She finished with her baking and got the cookies frosted. And shed only a few tears in the process. She decided to take a few in to her father, who was hiding out in the den with a book.

"I thought I smelled something good," he said as she came in. "What have we here?" Then he caught sight of what was on the plate and his smile faltered.

"I think Mom would want us to keep enjoying them," she said, although looking at his expression she doubted he'd find any enjoyment in her offering.

He nodded and took the plate. "Thank you, Snowflake."

She twisted her fingers together. "Maybe I shouldn't have."

"Yes, you should have. It would have made your mother happy to see you making them."

"It would have made her happy to see you eating them," she said softly.

He nodded, but made no move to take one.

He looked like a man anxious for a solitary moment so she kissed his cheek and left him, shutting the pocket door behind her. It was barely closed when she heard a sob. This had not been one of her better ideas.

With a sigh, she returned to the kitchen. Oh well. They were done now. May as well take some up to Joe. She put some on another plate and went upstairs to deliver her cookies and maybe a little speech about how she really was a nice person and never got snappy, then knocked on the door.

It felt like the little drummer boy was banging around in her chest. This was going to go over about as well as the delivery to her father. She'd already given Joe cookies at dinner. This would come across as a desperate ploy for attention. But it was too late to slink away now that she'd knocked.

Joe opened the door looking wary. Until he saw the cookies. "Oh wow."

Success. She smiled. "Peace offering," she said as she handed over the plate.

"There's no need for that."

"I thought there was. I got a little snappy."

He shrugged. "We all do when we're stressed and over-worked."

"Which is why I guess I should be saving up for a vacation."

"All work and no play, they say."

"Oh, I fit in some play."

He leaned against the doorjamb and helped himself to a cookie. "Yeah?" He took a bite. "Oh man, that's good."

"Just like you remember?"

"Better. Only don't tell my mom." He took another bite. Chewed, swallowed.

And she stood there, not wanting to leave.

He didn't seem to want her to. "So, what do you do for fun around here?"

"I ski."

"Yeah?"

Okay, tell the whole truth. "Cross-country," she said.

He nodded, half approving. "Pretty country for that."

"I was never brave enough to try downhill," she confessed.

"You should try it. It gives you a real rush."

A real rush. When it came down to it, she didn't do much of anything that gave her a real rush.

"What else?"

What else? "There's a restaurant here in town that has a little dance floor. Morris and I go dancing sometimes." Oh no, that had been a misstep. "Not that there's anything between us," she hurried on. "We're just friends."

"One of you is just friends," Joe said. Joe had good powers of observation.

"We've known each other for years."

"But he's not cutting it."

"Morris is a nice man and a good friend."

"Like I said, he's not cutting it."

"He doesn't care if he ever sees the Eiffel Tower." Good grief. What was she saying? "Okay, how shallow does that make me sound?"

"It doesn't. You're obviously two different people who want different things out of life. No point being with somebody when it's not going to work."

Well, she and Morris did want the same basic things—a home and family. Did Joe Ford want a home and family?

"What else do you do for fun?" he prompted.

"Not much," she admitted. "My family used to play cards but Dad and I haven't done anything like that since we lost Mom."

"Cards, huh?"

Now he was looking at her speculatively.

Cookies and cards. Joe Ford could be lured back out of the guest room. She cast out a lure she was sure would work. "I'm unbeatable at progressive gin rummy."

A corner of his mouth quirked up and the little drummer boy

woke up and started on his drum again. That smile. Oh, that smile. It lit up his eyes. Lit her up pretty good, too.

"Yeah?" he said.

She raised her chin in challenge. "Yeah."

"Got some cards?"

"Of course."

"I'll be down in a few," he said.

"I don't believe in stroking egos," she warned.

"And I don't believe in chivalry," he shot back. "There are no friends in cards."

"Okay. But don't say I didn't warn you," she said, and sashayed off down the hall. Oh yes, she and Joe Ford were now well on their way to becoming friends. Could they possibly become more?

9

By the time Guy came down, his hostess had the cards out and hot chocolate poured into mugs. More cookies sat on the plate on the kitchen table. Greeting card perfect.

She smiled up at him as she shuffled the deck and taunted, "Prepare to lose."

"I don't lose at cards." He and his brothers used to play a lot of poker on those ski trips to Vail. He always came away with the pot.

She cocked an eyebrow. "Oh? Ever hear the expression pride goes before a fall?"

"Yeah, and I'm afraid you're gonna fall big-time," he said as he sat down. All those shiny curls, those pretty green eyes—someone else at this table was in danger of falling. Big-time.

She dealt three cards for the first round. "I almost feel sorry for you."

"You that confident, huh?" he teased. Her perfume reached

out with invisible fingers and tickled his nose. He wanted to play with a lock of her hair.

She looked at her hand and smiled. "I am."

She must have gotten a wild card. "Want to bet on it?"

She shook her head. "I don't think so."

"Ah, not so confident after all. I don't want that card, by the way," he said, passing on the four of diamonds on the discard pile.

"Oh, I am. But on the off chance that you got lucky I wouldn't have anything to pay you with. I've only got a couple of dollars in my purse. I don't want that, either," she said.

He drew and got a wild card, which gave him three of a kind. "So, wager something else."

"More cookies?"

"You already gave me cookies."

"Fudge?"

"Not that into fudge." Looking at Livi, he had something much better in mind.

"Okay, then what?"

"How about a kiss?"

Her eyes opened wide and her face flushed. "A kiss?" she repeated as if he'd just proposed she sleep with him.

Okay, that had been stupid. What could he say? He'd been under the influence of perfume.

He bluffed it out. "Hey, I like to gamble big."

"We hardly know each other," she protested.

Wasn't that the truth? If she knew he was Guy Hightower she'd spit in his face. But right now he was plain old Joe Ford, enjoying an evening with a pretty woman.

"We're getting to know each other," he pointed out. And he realized he wanted her to get to know him, to see that he was more than the stingy guardian of a company's treasure chest. "One kiss won't hurt. Unless there's someone else?"

"No, no." The words came out half assurance and half regret.

"Well, then?"

"What will you give me if I win?" she asked, her cheeks still flushed.

"If I lose, I'll make breakfast tomorrow. How's that?"

That was acceptable. Her smile returned. "Okay. We just happen to have plenty of eggs."

"Good," he said, then discarded and laid down his cards, faceup.

"You had a wild card," she accused.

"But not up my sleeve."

She frowned and drew. Then laid down. She'd had a wild card, too, but nothing else matched. Even when she played it on what he'd laid down, he still caught her with ten points.

"I'm looking forward to that kiss," he teased, bringing back her blush.

"It's only the first hand," she said. "You got lucky."

He'd like to get lucky with Little Miss Helpful. But that *really* wasn't in the cards. He'd have to settle for a kiss.

She won the next hand, going out with a run of four, but only caught him with a couple of points and the third hand went to him. "I hope you're a good kisser," he teased as he dealt the cards.

"I hope you're a good cook," she retorted.

"Not really, but I can handle eggs."

"You don't cook much?"

"No time, really," he said. "I put in pretty long hours."

She examined her cards. "No one in your life to cook for you?"

She was fishing. He hid a smile. "Nope. Back to that time thing."

"You have to make time for people somewhere in your life."

"I have people in my life. I've got my mom and two brothers, a couple of nephews and a niece, a stepdad and stepsisters, people I work with." His family was too busy to hang out outside of work. He rarely had time for his old college buddies. Most of his social life revolved around business.

It counted. "But really, when you're working sixty and seventy hours a week, it doesn't leave a lot of time for much of anything else."

"That's kind of sad," she said, and drew a card.

"Sad?"

"Well, it's good to have a job, but I'd think you'd want a little more balance in your life."

This from the woman who couldn't afford to take a vacation. "I don't just have a job. I have a company. I'm responsible for a lot of jobs."

"Of course," she murmured.

"You make it sound like it's a bad thing to be in business."

"Oh, it's not," she said quickly. "Without businesspeople there'd be no one to help organizations like mine," she said.

Damn straight.

"I guess I was just thinking that maybe there's a difference between you being in business and business being in you so much that the rest of your life gets shoved off into a corner."

She discarded and he picked it up. "It all goes together, Livi. I care about what I do as much as you do, and for good reason. Businesses give people jobs. Jobs equal security and happiness. Corporations get a bad rap, but when it comes right down to it, those corporations that give people a paycheck help them have a life." So much for not getting into a philosophical debate.

"It looks like you've got a pretty good life," she observed.

That hit a nerve. Yeah, he did. He had his condo and the family place in Vail. He had stocks and mutual funds and a nice 401K. But so what? His dad had worked hard and his father before him. Guy's brothers worked hard and so did he.

"Should I feel guilty because I'm doing well?"

"No, not at all. I don't begrudge anyone his success," she said, keeping her gaze on the card she'd just drawn.

"Are you sure?"

"Really," she insisted, sorting through the cards in her hand. "But isn't it wonderful when you're doing well to be able to help others do well, too?"

"I do that," he insisted. It was his turn. He drew and discarded. Well, crap. There went a wild card.

She beamed at him. "I'm glad to hear that. I think generosity is the best quality a person can have. And speaking of, thanks," she said, and scooped up his discard. And went down, leaving him stuck with twenty-five points. "I like my eggs over easy."

"Don't put your order in yet. The game's not over." And neither was this conversation.

"You know," he said casually, as they organized their hands, "it's easy for people to judge how other people manage their money but sometimes they don't have all the facts."

She frowned.

"You don't agree with that?" he prompted.

"I do in most cases. But some businesses…" She pressed her lips tightly together and picked up a card.

"The major donor you lost?"

"It was wrong. The company's founder was my great-grandmother's first donor. He supported Christmas from the Heart wholeheartedly."

Old Elias Hightower again. Guy frowned.

To hear Livi speak, you'd have thought his great-granddad was a saint. He may have looked like a saint to a lot of people, but the ones he'd cheated early in his life with shady business deals probably hadn't thought so.

By the time Livi's great-grandma had come along, Elias had managed to pass himself off as a solid family man and pillar of the community, all the while keeping his mistress hidden from the public eye. Family legend had it that Elias had tried to seduce Adelaide Brimwell, hoping to make her his new mistress. Adelaide had threatened to tell her husband, and the only way to shut her up was to make a hefty contribution to her charity. Elias forked over a sizable chunk and got to keep his false but good reputation and Adelaide found a champion for her cause. Thus began the relationship between the Hightowers and Christmas from the Heart.

"I'd say she pretty much blackmailed him," Guy's dad had once said when the subject of corporate responsibility came up. "But in her case the ends justified the means, and old Elias needed to pay for his sins anyway."

This was one bedtime story Olivia Berg had probably never heard.

"His company has been there for us ever since," Livi continued, warming to her subject.

Paying for Great-Granddad's sins.

"He's probably turning in his grave at the way they've abandoned us."

More likely he was turning in his grave over how his great-grandkids had managed to screw up managing the company since taking over. "The company could be having problems you don't know about."

She sighed. "I suppose. It was just the way the whole thing was handled. It was so...heartless. And I bet if their CFO had looked hard enough he could have found some money."

He probably could have. But instead he'd given their money to higher-profile nonprofits. Guy felt slightly ill. Cookies, hot chocolate and guilt didn't mix well together.

"I guess I'm sounding..." She stopped and gnawed that kissable lower lip.

"What?" Guy prompted.

"Entitled. And I shouldn't feel entitled to something that's given and not owed."

She had that right.

"But I am hugely disappointed. After so many years, being cut off, losing that funding—we were orphaned. And insulted, to boot. We're not leeches," she said with a scowl. "That was what the CFO called me. Picture that."

He was, and it made him wince. "Maybe he was having a bad day." *Or maybe he was being a jerk.* "They'll probably make up for it next year," he said, and vowed to do exactly that.

"That sure doesn't help us this year. Honestly, if I had that man here right now I'd..." She sputtered to a stop. "I'm sorry. I'm being completely unprofessional."

"It's okay," he assured her. "This isn't a business meeting."

"Still, you're right. I don't know what's going on at the company. For all I know the man's had to take a pay cut."

Not yet.

"He's probably got a family to feed."

Not even a cat.

"You never really know about people."

Thank God she didn't know about him. Guy was so rattled he missed picking up a card he needed.

On her turn, she drew and went down. "Ha! Gotcha," she crowed.

Yes, she did. She had him, hook, line and sinker, and he was flopping at her feet.

"So, let's quit talking about all those evil businessmen," he said as they started their next hand. "Tell me what you do for the holidays."

That put her in a happy mood again. "Well, on Christmas Eve day we'll be delivering Christmas stockings and turkeys to homes here in town and in Gold Bar and Skykomish."

Back to Christmas from the Heart again. The woman lived, ate and breathed it. Guy found himself envying her passion. In spite of the long hours he worked he didn't feel that kind of passion for his company.

"Then my brother and his wife will come up to spend the night," she continued, "which means as soon as those deliveries are made I'll be busy baking red velvet cake and heating ham for

Christmas Eve dinner. We always play a couple of games after dinner and then stay up late watching Christmas movies. Of course, my brother will still wake us up early to open presents."

"Yeah, I was always the one who did that."

"You're welcome to join us for dinner if you're still stranded here," she offered.

"Thanks."

If he hadn't promised his mom he'd be with her, he'd have loved to. He could easily envision Christmas in the Berg household—eggnog, presents, lit candles, and a smiling, happy family. It was the kind of holiday his mom had created for them growing up, only with more expensive presents. The kind of holiday he'd loved before his dad died and it all fell apart.

"You probably have your own Christmas traditions, too," she said.

"We did. When my dad was alive. Things changed after he died." And not for the better.

Guy had just gotten his MBA when his father had his heart attack, forcing his sons to shoulder burdens they weren't yet ready for. Mike had already been working at Hightower for four years, learning the business, and wife number one was spending his money as fast as he could make it. Their dad had been grooming him to take over the company but that was supposed to have been much further down the road. Bryan had gone to the Hightower salt mine right after college and he'd been there for two years and was still pretty much clueless and only mildly invested in his job. Then there'd been Guy, the boy genius, the third member of the young Hightower triumvirate that would someday control the family empire. He'd been in no hurry to come on board. He'd worked hard in school and wanted time off to play. There was time. The old man would be around forever.

Except it didn't turn out that way. Their father *was* an old man, seventeen years older than his wife and worn-out. He'd thrown a clot when he had the heart attack and that had left him paralyzed on one side and in rehab.

"We spent our last Christmas as a family at the rehab center." Guy remembered how the place had smelled—pine-scented cleaner trying to overpower the scent of urine. A little old lady had hobbled past him, leaning on a walker and grimacing. She wore a Santa hat on her head, probably stuck there by the woman who was with her and talking about the wonderful turkey dinner that would be served later.

Neither Bryan nor Guy had stuck around for turkey dinner. Bryan had stood around helplessly for twenty minutes while Dad sat in his wheelchair, unable to talk, and Mom tried to smile through the tears washing away her makeup, then he'd bolted. Guy hadn't lasted much longer. After some inane comment on how Dad would be out of that thing and back on top soon, he'd kissed Mom on the cheek, promised to take her out to eat the next day and then beat it, leaving Mike to eat turkey dinner with the aged and infirm. It went with being the oldest. Guy had gone back home and found Bryan there, making serious inroads into a bottle of Scotch. He'd joined his brother and they'd drunk their way through Christmas. His dad died two days later and they'd drunk their way through New Year's, too.

After that Mom dived into mourning, Mike stepped into shoes still too big for him and got his first divorce. Bryan got serious about work and tried to keep up. Guy joined the Hightower Empire, put his shoulder to the wheel and went to work.

As for Christmas? At first they tried to re-create what they'd had as a family, everyone gathering at Mom's, but sadness tarnished it. After the first Christmas without their dad, Bryan's wife had stepped into the role of holiday hostess, insisting everyone come to their house. That had really felt wrong. The Hightower version of the holiday eventually turned into skiing with the brothers when they were in between women or taking Mom out for dinner.

Guy doubted he'd find that greeting-card-perfect Christmas with his mom's new family. She was determined to try, but really, it was like trying to patch up something broken. You always knew it was cracked. You were always aware of the patch.

He hadn't realized he was frowning until Livi laid a hand on his and murmured, "I'm sorry, Joe."

He shrugged. "Stuff like that happens in every family." Then he remembered her mom. "I guess you already know that."

Her hand slid away and she looked at her cards, blinking back tears. "It's hard to lose people you care about. But it sure makes you appreciate the ones who are left all the more. And it's important to honor their memories and keep those special traditions alive."

Or maybe make new ones. Hard to make new traditions when you didn't have anyone special to make them with.

He got his head back in the card game. Christmases past were gone and out of reach. Better to stay here in the present, playing cards with a little cutie who, so far, thought he was a good man.

He didn't want to go too far into the future, either. Except maybe he could change it. Maybe he could change her opinion of him. His was changing toward her. Olivia Berg, he was coming to realize, was something special.

They played out a few hands, the score remaining close. Until the last hand. Oh yeah, luck was being a lady tonight. He stuck Livi with thirty points and that won the game for him.

She looked stunned. "I can't believe you beat me."

"Well, you know what they say. Pride goes before a fall," he teased.

She stuck out her lower lip. Oh yeah, he was ready for that kiss. "Hey now, no pouting just because I'm not making breakfast."

"You got lucky."

Oh, how he'd like to get lucky. "Okay, time to pay up."

Her cheeks turned pink again.

"I promise I'll make it painless," he murmured with a smile.

He leaned across the table and she did the same. Then he slipped a hand behind her neck and drew her to him. He could smell that peppermint perfume. Her hair was so soft. So were her lips and they tasted like hot chocolate. She sighed into the kiss and he let the moment stretch out, threading his fingers through her hair. Her hands slipped up to the nape of his neck, her fingers soft and warm against his skin.

He could have gone on like that all night, moving them away from the table and out onto that living room couch, deepening their kiss, pulling her close, enjoying the feel of her curves, inhaling her scent. But that wouldn't have been right. Even what he was doing was sure to put him on Santa's naughty list for life.

It had been worth it, though. He pulled back. "You're a good loser. And a good kisser," he added, making her cheeks turn pink. "Now, you have to have had other men tell you that," he said.

She shrugged.

"There's been no one special?"

"In college. And Morris and I once, when we were younger. But…" She sighed. "I don't know what I'm waiting for."

"The right one?" Someone who deserved her. Which instantly disqualified him.

"I guess. How about you?"

"I thought I was in love once. Turned out I was wrong."

Okay, they were wandering into chick territory. Next they'd be sharing their every heartbreak. He stood. "I've had enough sitting. How about a walk?"

She smiled up at him. "I love walking in the snow."

Of course she did. He sensed a holiday movie scene coming up.

Sure enough, the scene came to life when she turned on the Christmas lights and they stepped outside. Between her house and the neighbors, the street looked like a set on the Universal back lot. A light snow was falling to add to the already-thick white coat frosting yards and houses. Rooflines, bushes and trees all dripped with colored lights like jewels on a woman's neck.

The woman he was with needed no jewels. Her smile sparkled more than any diamond ever could.

"Mrs. Newton lives in this house," she said as they strolled past a little cottage with an ancient station wagon parked in the driveway. "She's on a fixed income but she gives a hundred dollars every year to Christmas from the Heart."

Guy remembered the check he'd sent off and felt squirmy.

The curtains of the place were open to show off a skinny artificial tree in the window. A fuzzy little dog perched on the couch caught sight of them, jumped up and put its paws on the window, and began barking, tail wagging.

"That's Juniper, her watchdog."

"More like watch rat," Guy said. If you were going to have a dog you should have a dog—a Lab or German shepherd or a golden retriever.

"I think he's cute," Livi said in Juniper's defense. "Do you have a dog?"

"I did when I was a kid."

It had broken his heart when their golden died. She'd been fifteen. "It was her time," Mom had said. "All living things die, but remember that doesn't mean they're gone from our hearts." *Small comfort.*

It had been the first time he'd experienced death. As time moved on he'd lost a set of grandparents in a car wreck and his other grandpa. And then Dad, and that had been the worst of all. His dad had been Guy's hero, tough in business, soft on his family. Having someone in your heart was a far cry from having that person with you.

"But no dog now?" Livi asked, bringing Guy back into the moment at hand.

"I'm not home enough to have one." No one special in his life, not even a dog. What did that say about him?

"We had a dachshund when I was growing up," Livi said. "I think I'd like to get a dog again at some point, maybe a cocka-poo."

He shook his head and said, "I'm sorely disappointed in you," which made her smile.

He liked making Olivia Berg smile. If only they'd met under different circumstances. Or earlier, before that disastrous phone conversation and the ensuing emails. He could have easily written a check for five times as much as what he'd sent her. Why hadn't he?

On they walked, her giving him the scoop on various neighbors. There were the Twitchams, who had been divorced and then remarried twice. Then there was the Williams family. "She's a single mom with three little boys. She'll be getting a stocking and a turkey from Christmas from the Heart," Livi said. "And she's planning to share her holiday meal with the little old man next door, who's fast becoming a surrogate grandfather for her children."

"Is there anyone in this town you don't know?" Guy asked.

Livi thought a moment, then said, "I don't think so. It's good to know your neighbors."

He didn't know any of his, but he said, "Yes, it is." And after agreeing on that important point it only seemed right to take her mittened hand in his.

She didn't pull away. Instead she smiled up at him. "I'm glad you got stranded here, Joe."

"So am I," he said, and wished he really was Joe Ford. Joe anybody.

Back at the house, after they'd hung up their coats, they sat in the living room, warming up with more hot chocolate and talking. Favorite books. He loved Grisham, so did she. She also loved Jane Austen, Agatha Christie and someone named Jillian George. Favorite movies. He wanted action. She wanted romance.

"But I did love all those Jack Reacher movies," she said. Of course she did. Jack Reacher, save-the-day hero. Favorite foods. Steak for him, cake for her. "I like to have my cake and eat it, too," she quipped.

Pretty, sweet, good sense of humor, kindhearted. Livi Berg was the whole package. Except everyone had their faults. What was hers?

That was easy. She was quick to judge. It had showed in that email she'd sent Guy and in the way she talked about him. Man, would she be happy to pass judgment on him, sentence him to a million years of hard labor in the North Pole. And here he was, playing cards with her, going for walks, even kissing the woman. He was out of his mind.

That was the only explanation for what he did when they got back to the house. At the foot of the stairs he put his arms around her and drew her to him. "I had a good time tonight."

She smiled up at him. "I did, too."

She wanted to be kissed and he wanted to kiss her, so of course he put his brain in lockdown and did exactly that.

And she kissed him back, her arms around his neck, her body pressed up snug against his deceitful heart.

"You only won one kiss," she teased after they'd come up for air.

"One for the road," he said, and then went upstairs. One for the road was right. If she found out who he was, he'd be hitting the road whether his car was fixed or not.

And he'd deserve it. Not so much because he'd pulled the plug on her nonprofit—he'd made the best decision he could at the time—but because of his cowardly deception. Here he was flirting with Olivia Berg, kissing her, staying at her house and eating her cookies and not telling her the truth.

He should have from the very beginning, should have said,

"This is who I am and if you think what I did was wrong convince me otherwise."

"What a tangled web we weave when first we practice to deceive." The poet was right and Guy had trapped himself in a sticky holiday web. How on earth was he going to get out of it?

10

Livi rarely wore makeup. There hadn't been much point living in the same town with the same people who'd known her all her life. But come Sunday morning the application of makeup suddenly felt vitally important and she found herself primping in front of the bathroom mirror before going downstairs to make breakfast. This had nothing to do with a certain handsome houseguest, she told herself. As the face of Christmas from the Heart she should look her best.

And her best involved lipstick and mascara. Except it had been so long since she'd used the mascara that it had dried in the tube and her lipstick was about as moist as chalk.

She settled for lip gloss.

"You are who you are," she told herself. And people either liked you for who you were or they didn't.

Joe Ford seemed to like her just fine so it was silly to try to change who she was. She only hoped he continued to because she certainly liked him. A lot. A whole lot.

★ ★ ★

Guy awoke to the aroma of bacon and coffee. He picked up his cell phone from the bedside table and checked the time. Eight-fifteen a.m. He normally slept in on Sundays. Most people slept in on Sundays.

But most people weren't Olivia Berg. He pulled on his jeans and a fresh sweater, and went down to the kitchen to find her at the stove in a red dress and boots, pulling a foil-lined sheet of bacon out of the oven. Her father was seated at the kitchen table, reading the Sunday paper, a mug of coffee in front of him.

He put it down at the sight of Guy and greeted him. He, too, was dressed for the day, wearing slacks and a red sweater pulled over a shirt and necktie. "Sit down, make yourself at home," he said.

"Would you like some coffee?" Livi offered as Guy took a seat at the table.

"Sure. Thanks."

"I'm glad you got up when you did," she said. "We're going to the early service at church. Another fifteen minutes and you'd have missed out."

Church. Oh yeah. That. When they were kids, his mom had made sure they all went.

"You're welcome to join us," Mr. Berg offered as his daughter set a mug of coffee in front of Guy.

"Uh, that's okay. I have some work to do." He already had a fruitcake competition looming. He didn't want to take his hypocritical self to church on top of that.

"Well, make yourself at home while we're gone," Livi said, and set a plate in front of him with bacon and scrambled eggs and toast.

This was all so homey and friendly and…uncomfortable. With each new kindness he felt increasingly undeserving and guilty. He was a fake, taking advantage of these people, and the knowledge was gnawing at his conscience. It was like being poked to death with a sprig of holly, being made to listen to "Jingle Bells" played at high speed over and over again. This was Christmas purgatory.

He was relieved when she said, "You won't see much of me for the next few hours. I have a lot to do to get ready for the event. And Dad has to be there to help set up tables and booths." The sense of relief ended when she added, "Morris will be coming by to pick you up." She put more bacon on his plate.

A cozy ride to fruitcake torture with the ex-boyfriend who still wanted to be the boyfriend. Oh yeah. Guy was all over that.

"I can walk," he said.

"But you don't know where it is," she said reasonably, and began putting things away in the refrigerator.

"I can look it up on my phone."

"It's no trouble for Morris. He'd be happy to."

Sure he would. And the Sugarplum Fairy couldn't dance.

Guy was about to insist on being allowed to get himself to the corny event when Mr. Berg said to his daughter, "We'd better finish getting ready or we're going to be late."

"Oh yes," she said, and set the pan in the sink.

Then both she and her father left Guy with his half-finished eggs and a second helping of bacon for which he'd lost his appetite. He frowned at his coffee mug. Scrooge, the ultimate bad boy businessman, had it easy compared to what Guy was going through. He'd only had to face ghosts.

"I wondered if you'd even make it today with everything you probably have to do," Tillie greeted Livi as she and her father walked into the narthex of the church.

"It is going to be a busy day," Livi admitted, "but I wanted to start it off right."

"You are such a dear girl," said Tillie. "Some young man is going to be lucky to get you." She looked speculatively over Livi's shoulder.

CHRISTMAS FROM THE HEART

Livi knew before she even turned around who had come in. Sure enough, there was Morris with his mom, who he picked up and squired to church every Sunday. Good old Morris. A dutiful son, a nice young man with a steady job. Everyone in town seemed to think he was the ideal man for her.

Certainly more of a match than a man who drove fancy foreign cars and threw around hundred-dollar bills. And played cards for kisses. Joe Ford may have had a plain name but there was nothing plain about him.

He's just passing through, she reminded herself. Men like him didn't stay in small towns. They went places and did things, the kind of things she only dreamed of doing. As for thinking they had anything in common, who was she kidding? That was like saying a thoroughbred racehorse and a donkey had things in common. *Yeah, four legs.*

Her father had already ducked into the sanctuary, not anxious to stand around and make small talk. Hardly surprising, considering he probably felt like a hunted animal with every single woman over the age of forty eyeballing him. Oh, the casseroles and cakes and pies that had showed up after Mom died. And the number of women needing life insurance or better car insurance had doubled in the last couple of years. Their machinations were in vain and always would be. Her father had loved only one woman and he had no desire to replace her.

Livi joined him in the sanctuary and a moment later Morris was slipping into the chair next to her, his mother on the other side of him.

"Good morning, Livi," said Mrs. Bentley. "Are you all ready for the fruitcake competition?"

Mrs. Bentley had won the previus year's competition and was hoping for a second win. Another reason Livi didn't want to be one of the judges. She didn't want anyone accusing her of playing favorites.

"We are," she said.

"I think the fruitcake this year is even better than my last year's one," Mrs. Bentley told her.

"You'll have a hard time beating my apricot fruitcake," said Mrs. Newton, who had slipped in next to her.

"I'm glad I'm not judging. I don't know how I'd be able to choose between the two of you," Livi said diplomatically.

"That was slick," Morris said to her after church as they made their way out the door. "You managed to make both Mrs. Newton and my mom feel like winners."

"They're both good bakers," she said.

"And you're a good BSer," he said.

"You have to be diplomatic when you run a nonprofit."

It would have been nice if she'd reminded herself of that before she sent her rude email to Guy Hightower. But oh well. He was history. The current event was Joe Ford. When he saw all the good things they did, maybe he could bring his company on board the next year as a major donor.

Speaking of... "Don't forget you're giving Joe a ride to the fruitcake festival."

"I can hardly wait," Morris grumbled. "I don't see why your dad can't bring him."

"Because Dad and Mr. Smith and Dr. Johnson are helping with setup. You know that. And it's enough that Joe's helping judge the fruitcakes. I don't want him to have to work before the event, as well. Anyway, you only have to bring him. I can take him home."

"Mom wants to get there early."

It was a feeble excuse and one Livi saw right through. Morris had not taken to the newcomer. But he was going to have to lay aside his feelings for the good of the cause.

"It still won't be as early as he'd have to be if he went with us," Livi said. "Dad and I are on our way over to the community hall right now." Morris still wasn't looking happy. She laid a hand on his arm. "Come on, Morris. Help me out here."

"I help out all the time," he said irritably.

"Yes, you do. And I appreciate it. You are one in a million," she said, and kissed his cheek.

"Okay, okay. You don't have to butter me up."

"I wasn't buttering. I was speaking the truth." Morris was a sweetie, and a good friend. He just wasn't a Joe Ford. And that was probably at the heart of his dislike for the man. "It's for Christmas from the Heart," she added. Lost dogs, food drives, little old ladies with car troubles—Morris was always there, whatever the need. And if she needed him to drive someone to a Christmas from the Heart event he couldn't tell her no.

"Yeah, yeah," he said, resigned to his fate. "But I don't like the guy."

"Morris, you're jealous," she accused.

"Okay, so maybe I am. But I got a feeling about him. Something ain't right."

"Well, I'd love to stand here and psychoanalyze him with you but I've got to get to the community hall. See you soon," she added.

Livi never really saw him. He was just good old Morris, the guy she'd dated once upon a time. Sometimes he wished Livi had never gone away to school.

But nobody in her right mind turned down a full scholarship. Still, going away changed her. She came back home not only knowing more but wanting more. Her great-grandparents had money but somewhere along the way that well had dried up, leaving her parents solidly middle-class. After college, though, she returned yearning for a life of glamour. She wanted to see the world, wanted to visit Jane Austen's home, walk on the moors where Cathy and Heathcliff had roamed. Morris had never been able to get into those books—"I am Heathcliff." What the hell? She'd wanted to see the Eiffel Tower and ski in the Alps. As if their own mountains weren't good enough?

She'd stayed in Pine River but she hankered for Seattle. Christmas from the Heart was the anchor that kept her in town. That, and her dad and her friends. Of which he was one.

What was it going to take to open Livi's eyes to the good life they could have together? He needed to find it fast, because this newcomer was stirring up all those old yearnings for glamour and excitement.

As if a good ball game or great sex couldn't be exciting enough. As if planning a wedding, having kids and watching them grow up wasn't good enough. He knew she wanted to be married, wanted a family. She could do all that with him. You didn't need to wander all over the world looking at stuff you could see on TV to have a good life.

"Morris, why are you frowning?" his mother asked after he'd settled her and her fruitcake in the car.

"I wasn't frowning."

"Yes, you were. You frowned all through lunch and you're still frowning. I swear, you frown after every encounter with Olivia Berg," she added.

His mom was way too observant. "I do not."

"Yes, you do." She shook her head. "You're wasting your time on her. She's not interested."

"Thanks, Mom," he growled.

"Well, it's true and you know it. If only your father was still alive to talk some sense into you."

A freak accident at work had taken his dad five years back and that had left Morris to watch over his mom and little sister. Sis had gotten married two years ago and moved to Oregon and now it was just Morris, picking Mom up for church on Sundays, eating lunch at her place afterward and taking her to Family Tree for dinner every Wednesday night for their midweek special.

Not that he minded watching out for his mom and spending time with her, but he missed his old man. And no matter what Mom thought, Dad would never try to talk him into giving up on Livi. Unlike Mom, who wanted Morris to hurry up and marry somebody so she could have grandkids, Dad understood true love. He'd waited patiently for Mom to come around through three years and one fiancé. Morris could wait.

"Why are we stopping at Olivia's?" she asked, when he pulled the car up in front of the Berg residence.

"They've got a guy staying with them and I have to give him a ride over to the community hall."

"Oh, honestly, Morris," Mom said in disgust. "Surely Livi could manage getting her own houseguest to the fruitcake competition."

"She and Mr. B had to get there early."

"So, who is this man?"

"Some rich dude whose car broke down and there wasn't any vacancies at River's Bend so they took him in. He's one of the fruitcake judges."

"One of the judges?" his mother said speculatively. That ended the complaining.

At least someone was looking forward to picking up the rich dude.

Morris Bentley arrived to pick up Guy at quarter to two, fifteen minutes before the big event was scheduled to begin. He was dressed in jeans, boots, and wore a Seahawks sports shirt under his jacket. There on the lapel was a pin that proudly proclaimed, "I gave from the heart." The one thing he wasn't wearing was a smile.

"Livi told me to pick you up," he said, and might as well have added, "I'd as soon throw you in the river."

Guy nodded. "Thanks." He felt Bentley's assessing gaze on him as they walked to Bentley's car, a vintage muscle car. The guy probably had a truck, too, like most of the men in town did. "Nice car," he said.

"It was my dad's," Bentley said. "Made in America." No foreign cars for Morris Bentley. "Got a truck, too," he added. *So take that.*

"Probably comes in handy," Guy said.

"I can haul a lot of wood." *Me and my blue ox, Babe.*

It was going to be a pissing contest all the way to the fruit-cake gross-out. Guy hoped they didn't have far to go.

A middle-aged woman with alarmingly black hair and a body like a linebacker sat in the front passenger seat, wearing a red wool coat and a scarf almost as black as her hair. She, unlike her son, was smiling.

"Hello," she greeted Guy as he climbed in the back. "You must be our new judge."

"Just for this time," Guy said. "I guess one of your regulars got sick and I'm filling in. I'm Guy… Joe Ford."

Bentley was in the car now and looking at Guy in the rear-view mirror, his eyes narrowed suspiciously. Great.

"It's nice to meet you, Joe. I'm Mary Bentley, Morris's mother. I have a fruitcake entered in the contest. Do you like fruitcake?"

Oh boy. "Who doesn't like fruitcake?" Guy hedged.

"A lot of people don't." She made it sound like a crime.

"That's 'cause they never had yours," Morris said to her.

Did he really believe that or was he lying? Either way, it made him a good son.

"This is quite the event," Mary Bentley informed Guy. "Everyone in town turns out."

"So I hear," he said.

"And it's for such a good cause. Christmas from the Heart helps so many people."

So he kept hearing. "Sounds like it."

Too bad he hadn't done some research into the organization before cutting them loose. But honestly, there was only so much money to go around, and, curse it all, it wasn't like Hightower hadn't given anything to anyone.

For their own ulterior motives. He looked out the window

at the houses they were passing. It sure wasn't the Highlands or Mercer Island. These people were struggling to find their footing in an ever-changing economy.

Well, everyone was struggling, even businesses that looked successful.

"Where are you from?" asked Mrs. Bentley.

"Seattle."

"I grew up in Seattle," she said. "It's certainly changed from when I was a girl. And not for the better," she added. "So over-populated and the freeways are a mess."

"It is a busy city," Guy said. Yeah, traffic wasn't good, but that didn't bother him. He liked the way the city had grown, liked the action.

"But I guess I've always been a small-town girl at heart," she continued.

"Nothing wrong with small towns," added her son.

And this small town was where he would live his whole life and be perfectly happy. He'd never think to take Livi Berg to Paris.

They pulled up in front of a large building with a metal roof that looked like a log cabin on steroids. It was massive and had an equally massive front porch running along its front. The community hall.

The event hadn't even started yet but already the parking lot was full—older-model cars, many with ski racks, a Prius or two, a ton of trucks with gun racks to remind him that he was in hunting country. Here was the heartbeat of the town. He could picture square dances and birthday parties taking place inside. Probably some anniversary parties and wedding receptions, too.

And fruitcake competitions.

Oh boy. Let the fun begin.

11

Livi was supervising the silent auction table when Joe Ford walked in. Even casually dressed he stood out from the crowd. A lot of men were present in jeans and sweaters and boots but his clothes plainly said, "I don't shop where the rest of you shop." He looked like he'd stepped out of the pages of *GQ*, and looking at him made her mouth water.

"Oh my gosh, is that the guy you were telling me about?" asked Kate, who was standing next to her.

"It is."

"You said he was good-looking but you didn't say hot enough to set this whole place on fire. I can't believe he doesn't have a girlfriend. He must be gay."

Livi remembered those two kisses they'd shared. "I don't think so."

"How do you know?"

Livi could feel a glow overtaking her cheeks that had nothing to do with the holidays.

Kate's eyes narrowed. "There's something you're not telling me."

It was too late to tell her now. Joe was fast approaching, Mrs. Bentley and a cranky-looking Morris flanking him.

"I'll tell you later," she said, and hurried forward to welcome him, the little drummer boy banging around in her chest.

The community hall was big, but once Guy got inside it seemed to shrink. Trussed up in tinsel and little white lights, the place was a holiday beehive, packed with people and thrumming with activity.

A quartet dressed like Dickens carolers stood in one corner singing "Deck the Halls," not that you could hear them that well above the various conversations taking place, the laughter and the excited kids running around whooping.

On the opposite side of the room, a guy in a cheap Santa suit sat on an ancient carved chair next to a huge Christmas tree taking present requests from kids who had yet to be turned loose. A chunky woman in an elf costume, probably his wife, was taking pictures.

People were lined up in front of a booth on another side of the hall, and Guy figured that was where everyone was bartering their services.

The silent auction items had been set up in another section of the hall, a long table spread with all manner of gift baskets and certificates. A crowd of happy fruitcake fans circled it, checking out the various offerings.

There were other booths as well, selling hot cider and cocoa, pretzels, corn dogs and popcorn and the aromas all mingled and danced on the air.

By the main door sat a giant box painted green with a huge red ribbon around it. Judging from the whiteboard set up next to it, already bearing names and numbers, that had to be the donation box. The woman he recognized as Livi's assistant was standing next to it, greeting people.

Livi's father and another man were down by the stage, the main attraction, setting up a final row of chairs for the audience. The front of the stage was festooned with cedar garlands while on the stage itself, off to one side stood a red cloth-draped table displaying the various fruitcakes that had been entered, a good dozen. A dozen fruitcakes to sample. What circle of hell did that qualify for? On the other side was the judges' table, complete with plates, forks, napkins and bottled water, as well as notepads and pencils and what looked like three-by-five notecards. A microphone had been set up in the center for whoever would be MC for the event.

And here came Olivia Berg. She looked like the spirit of Christmas in her clingy red dress, a Santa hat perched on her head. He wanted to reach out and tug on a lock of that curly hair. Instead, he stuffed his hands in his jacket pockets.

"Everything looks so festive," Mrs. Bentley said to her.

"I'm really proud of what a good job our decorating committee did this year, especially when we were on such a tight budget," Livi said.

That again. It always came down to money. Guy managed a weak smile.

Livi's smile was anything but weak. It was a hundred watts. This event was her baby and she was proud of it.

"Hi, Livi," called a little old man wearing slacks and tennis shoes and a tie populated with elves over a shirt that looked well-worn.

"Hi, Mr. Crandall. You're looking festive," she called back.

"'Tis the season." He finished with a wave and moved on.

Another man stopped by. "Just made my donation for this year," he told her.

"I knew we could count on you, Gerald," she said, and emphasized her gratitude with a friendly hug.

Livi Berg was good at what she did. Guy could picture her at a fund-raiser held someplace like the Four Seasons, schmoozing with five-hundred-dollar-a-plate diners. That was where she needed to be. She was picking up crumbs when she should be at the main table.

Well, she'd been at the Hightower table and look how much good that had done her. The generosity of these simple people and small business owners who were giving because they wanted to, not because they had to in order to maintain a good image, put him to shame.

"Are you all ready for your judging duties?" she asked Guy.

"I don't know. That's a lot of fruitcake."

"I could have done it," Morris said. "If you'd just asked me."

"Morris, your mom has a fruitcake entered. You'd be biased."

With his mother standing right next to him Morris wisely didn't argue with that. Instead, he said a sullen, "I'm gonna go help your dad set up chairs."

"And I'd better introduce you to the other judges," Livi said to Guy. "Will you excuse us, Mrs. Bentley?"

"Of course," Mrs. Bentley said, and wandered off in the direction of the silent auction table.

"This is quite a production," Guy said to Olivia as they made their way through the crowd.

"It is," she said. "This is our third year and it just keeps getting bigger and better. We've got people coming from as far away as Arlington now. Which is probably why the motel was full."

"For fruitcake," he said, shaking his head in disbelief.

"For prizes to be won," she said. "And the fun."

They got to the base of the stage, where two women stood chatting. One was ancient, stooped, with gnarled hands, wrinkles on top of wrinkles and white hair. She was wearing red slacks, a black sweater populated with penguins and a necklace of blinking Christmas lights. The woman next to her didn't look much older than Guy. She was slender, had straight brown hair, a nice face and an equally nice smile. If Livi hadn't come up beside her he'd have thought she was pretty good-looking. Next to Olivia Berg she faded to background.

"Joe, I'd like you to meet Tillie Henderson, who owns Tillie's Teapot," Livi said, motioning to the older woman. "It's the best tearoom for miles around."

Guy could already picture it—a chick-centric place with lace curtains and tables dressed up with fancy china like that Limoges chocolate pot sitting in his car. It sounded like the kind of place his mom would love.

"It's the only tearoom for miles around," Tillie said. She held out an arthritic hand for Guy to take. "Nice to meet you."

"Nice to meet you, too," he said. She reminded him of his grandma.

"And this is Carol Klaussen," Livi continued. "She owns Calories Don't Count, my favorite bakery."

The one they'd driven past. "I saw it. Looks like you've got lots of good stuff in there," he said.

"I do," she assured him.

"I don't know why you don't weigh two hundred pounds," Livi said to her. "I swear I gain a pound every time I come in."

"After a while the thrill wears off," Carol said. "Thanks for stepping in, Joe."

"I'm no expert like you two," he said. "I don't even like fruitcake." *So what am I doing here?* The gremlins, of course.

"All the better," said Carol. "If someone wins you over, it will be a real accomplishment."

"That's for sure," put in Tillie. "I'm a terrible one to judge because I never met a fruitcake I didn't like."

"I bet you've baked some good ones in your time," Guy told her.

She grinned. "Oh, he's a smooth one," she said to Livi.

They chatted a few more minutes, then Livi offered to take

Guy around the hall. "We have a few minutes before the judging begins."

Anything to postpone eating fruitcake. As they strolled past the men setting up the chairs Bentley shot Guy a look that threatened death and dismemberment if Guy moved in on Olivia. *Don't worry. She's all yours.*

Except she wasn't. Guy could see why Bentley was fixated on her, though. The more time Guy spent with her the more time he craved. He hadn't been so infatuated with a woman in years. Livi had the whole package—looks, intelligence and heart. If only he'd made a decent contribution to the cause.

It wasn't too late. He could write her a check that very day. She'd take it, of course.

But would it be enough to endear him to her? Nobody liked being duped.

They moved to the silent auction table, checking out the goods. "A lot of cool things here," he said.

"There sure are." She fingered a large basket of books. He saw a box of chocolates in there as well, and a bottle of cheap champagne.

"Isn't this one of those authors you said you like?"

"It is. I love a good mystery."

He sincerely hoped she didn't solve the mystery of who he was. Not yet, anyway. He wanted to tell her, wanted to end this farce, but he had to pick the perfect time and place to fess up.

"Jillian George actually has an office right next to mine."

"You must get a lot of free books then."

"Sometimes. I don't have most of these, certainly not in hardback."

"Who needs it in hardback when you can download something onto your phone or e-reader?"

She shrugged. "I still like the feel of a book in my hands."

"Having books on a device is a lot easier when you travel." Oh yeah. She couldn't afford to travel.

"Maybe someday I'll get one," she said with a chipper smile.

Guy found himself thinking how much fun it would be to show Olivia Berg more of the world. Starting with that Eiffel Tower she wanted to see.

"Hi, Livi," said a short redhead in jeans and an ugly Christmas sweater.

"Hi, Jenny," said Livi, and introduced Guy to Jenny Lind.

"This year's auction is even better than last year," Jenny said to Livi. "I'm so glad I've been saving up." She pointed to the gigantic cake shaped like a Christmas tree and decorated to the hilt with candies.

Saving to buy a fancy cake. Hightower Enterprises ordered everything from elaborate cakes to ice sculptures for their parties and never thought a thing about it.

"We're going to Family Tree after this to celebrate Gram's eightieth. I want to bring it for dessert. I sure hope I don't get outbid," Jenny said.

If she did, Guy vowed to buy the cake from whoever won it. As Jenny and Livi chatted, he quickly scrawled his fake name on the sheet in front of the author's gift basket. The bidding was up to thirty bucks. He bid a hundred. That should scare away the other bidders. A gift basket might make a good peace offering. He'd give Livi that, then promise her a check. And then what? He shied away from the then what.

They strolled around the room some more, checking out the food booths. She tried to convince him to buy a corn dog but he passed. He did insist on buying one for her, though, along with some hot cider.

They checked in to see how things were going at the booth where people were bartering. Lots of action there. Lots of good-natured teasing and laughter as people swapped goods and services, finding creative ways to stretch their money. Guy couldn't help but be impressed by the easy camaraderie. According to Livi a lot of these people were struggling financially, but no one appeared stressed or tense. Everyone was in high holiday spirits, the closeness of their community on display. These people had a connectedness that Guy envied.

He and Livi finally wound up at the giant gift box by the door, where Livi's assistant, Bettina, was presiding.

"Would you like to make a donation?" Bettina asked him.

The more points he racked up, the better. He pulled out a fifty and dropped it in the slot. All for a good cause.

Since when was impressing a woman a good cause? Okay, so he had ulterior motives. Either way, Christmas from the Heart was benefiting.

"That's very generous of you," Livi said. "Thank you so much."

He waved away her gratitude. "It's nothing." Boy, you could say that again.

Lenny and Morris were watching from the bartering booth where they'd both signed up to offer their usual oil change services. Lenny was hoping he'd score some home-baked meals. Between Livi and his mom, Morris had that covered. There wasn't much of anything he needed so he always simply offered his services.

"The rich dude is sure making an impression on Livi," Lenny observed. "I wonder how much dough he just put in the box. Livi looks ready to jump his bones."

"Hey," Morris said sharply. "Watch what you're saying."

"Sorry," Lenny muttered. "Looks like you've got serious competition."

"So he put something in the box. Big deal." Morris gave to Christmas from the Heart all the time.

"He's slick," Lenny went on. "How much you wanna bet those are designer jeans he's wearing?"

"Like Liv cares if some guy wears designer jeans?" Morris said with a snort.

"Women like rich guys," Lenny said with a shrug.

"Not Liv." Liv wasn't that shallow.

"You need to get a clue, man. This guy's got her engine revved."

"'Cause he's rich?" Morris sneered. "Liv doesn't care about fancy trimmings." But her nonprofit was her first love. And somebody coming along flashing cash was bound to turn her head.

"Maybe not, but it looks like they ain't hurtin'," said Lenny.

Lenny was right. Liv was smiling at the stranger like he was Santa Claus.

"Morris," said Mrs. Whittier, coming up to him. "I want to take advantage of your car expertise. What do you need in return?"

I need someone to get this slick turkey away from Liv. Sadly, the only one who could do that was Morris. And until he got what he needed to fix the guy's car and get him on the road, he was powerless.

Livi checked the time on the big clock hanging on the wall. "Oh my, we need to get going on the main event. Let's get back to the stage," she said to Guy.

It looked like there was no more postponing the inevitable. "Kind of a short event if the judging starts this soon, isn't it?" he said as they made their way to the stage.

"Oh, not really. The judging takes longer than you might think. We bring up each contestant and have her or him talk about the recipe. And there are door prizes to give away in between. Then it takes a while for the judges to confer. While they're doing that, people mingle and finish up their silent auction bids. We announce those, then sing some carols, and then we present the awards to our fruitcake runners-up and first place winner."

She had mastered the art of drawing out a short affair into a marathon. Livi Berg was definitely good at what she did. "Then what happens?" In a perfect world, they'd go back to her house and he'd find a way to get another kiss. Or two. Or five.

But they weren't in a perfect world. He was the Grinch and she was Mrs. Claus. He was such a fake. It would serve him right if he choked on a piece of fruitcake.

"A lot of us unwind at Family Tree," she said. "They make the best pot roast."

Guy told himself he didn't need to be unwinding with Olivia Berg. He didn't need to be doing anything with her. But he didn't listen to himself. "Sounds like fun," he said.

Which was more than he could say for what he was about to do.

Going up those few steps to his judge's seat on the stage felt like climbing to the gallows.

The other two judges were already in place. "This will be a challenge," the little old lady named Tillie informed him. "We have some first-class bakers entered."

"And it's a big prize," put in Carol from the bakery. "That money will mean a lot to many people."

Her words put the pressure on. This was a fun event for the town but it meant groceries and the easing up on a tight budget to many of the entrants. It was hardly on a par with carrying a struggling company on his back but Guy still felt the weight of what he'd been asked to do and wished he'd never allowed himself to get talked into it.

Many people had already claimed seats. Others, seeing Livi settling in the final judge, left the booths and silent auction table and found seats, as well. She picked up the microphone, welcomed everyone and announced that the judging would now begin, bringing the rest of the crowd over.

"I'm so glad you could all join us for our third annual fruitcake competition," she said. She motioned to the table where the entries sat. "As you can see, we have a lot of entries this year. A big job for our judges."

"Shit," Guy muttered.

"You'll do fine," Tillie assured him.

Guy could feel beads of sweat decorating his brow. No sports competition, no business meeting had ever made him this nervous. He so didn't belong here.

"Our judges will be looking at each fruitcake's visual appeal," Livi informed the audience.

There was nothing appealing about fruitcake.

"They'll be checking entries for moistness, flavor and that something extra that says, 'I'm the best this year.'"

Guy's right leg began to jiggle up and down like it had done when he was in high school, waiting for a tennis match.

"And now, let me introduce our judges," Livi said, and went on to introduce the first two along with their credentials. "And we have a special guest judge joining us today. Please welcome Joe Ford from Seattle."

The fraud.

Everyone applauded. Well, almost everyone. Guy saw Morris Bentley out there in the crowd, sitting next to his mother, his beefy arms crossed over his chest, giving Guy the glare of death.

Only a few more hours, dude. That belt would come in the next day, Guy's Maserati would get fixed and then he'd get gone. Except part of him didn't want to get gone. Part of him wanted to stay inside this never-ending Christmas movie with Livi Berg and the good people of Pine River.

He reminded himself again that this wasn't his world, these weren't his people. This wasn't his life. He had a company to help run. He had a mom and a new family waiting for him in Coeur d'Alene.

"Our first entry is from Bernadette Bohn, our favorite middle school teacher," Livi said, and welcomed a petite brunette dressed in slacks and a red turtleneck to the stage. "Bernadette, can you tell us a little about this recipe?"

"It was my mother's recipe, and she kept it top secret for years. She finally gave me permission to share it."

"And what makes it special?" Livi asked, and held the mike to Bernadette.

"For one thing, the fact that it's my mother's," Bernadette said, beaming out at a little woman in the audience who looked like an older version of herself. "But I also like it because it's not your traditional fruitcake. It's a banana bread base, which makes it really flavorful."

"Well, let's see what our judges think," Livi said, and her assistant carried the plate over to the judge's table.

What were they supposed to do now? Guy stared at it.

"Make notes about its appearance," Carol coached him, pointing her pencil at the notepad lying in front of him."

Guy pulled it to him and wrote, *Looks like...* Then he faltered. It looked like fruitcake. He peered over at Tillie's page. She'd written, *Nice and high.* Okay, that looked good. He wrote the same thing.

Bettina cut a piece of the cake and both judges scribbled more notes. *Good texture*, Tillie had written. He'd never copied anyone's work in school. Never needed to. He wrote down everything Tillie had.

Bettina now cut three bite-size pieces off the fruitcake and served them to the judges. Guy was surprised. It wasn't bad. There was actually some cake in there instead of the usual loaf of cheap fruit barely glued together with something that bore no resemblance to cake. *Not bad*, he wrote.

The next contestant was Jan Kragen, a pretty woman with long reddish hair, who was also a teacher. Hers was a chocolate fruitcake, elaborately decorated, that brought several oohs and aahs from the audience.

"Jan, you were our winner last year," Livi said. "And now you're back with something new. Tell us about this fruitcake."

"It's my own creation," Jan said, and as she described the various ingredients in it, Guy found his mouth watering.

He didn't have to copy anyone else's paper for this one. *Looks good*, he wrote. After they'd sampled it, the other two judges made notes about texture, flavors, moistness and quality of ingredients. He simply wrote, *Tastes good. I'd buy this.* And that was the best praise a businessman could offer.

He felt the same thing about the fruitcake submitted by Becky Grimes, a local Realtor, and an apricot one that had been made by Mrs. Newton, the little old lady with the so-called watchdog. That also rated an *I'd buy this.* Maybe fruitcake wasn't so bad after all.

The entries kept coming—some with frosting, some plain, many of them so soaked in booze he was sure the judges would be staggering by the time they left the table. Even with the palate cleansers Bettina kept giving them, he felt like his taste buds were going numb. Guess there'd been no need for that whiskey he'd wished for.

"It's all starting to blur in my mouth," he whispered to his fellow judges as Livi gave away another door prize, this one a bottle of wine from a vineyard on the other side of the Cascades.

"Hang in there," Carol encouraged him. "We're almost done."

Two more fruitcakes, one so bad it was all Guy could do not to spit it out and another that hadn't quite gotten done in the middle, and then they were finished. People went to check out their silent auction bids and the judges went to work.

"Shall we see if we can agree on our top three?" Tillie suggested. "Carol?"

"For appearance, texture and taste I have to say Jan's makes my top three easily."

"Mine, too," said Tillie, and looked at Guy.

"I hate fruitcake," he reminded them, "but I'd buy that one."

"All right. Jan's goes into the top three," Tillie said, and made a note.

Two more fruitcakes made the top three. Then it was time to vote.

"How about Mrs. Newton's apricot fruitcake?" said Carol.

"That was wonderful but I think I liked Bernadette's a little better. Not your traditional fruitcake. What about you, Guy?"

"I liked the chocolate one but you guys are the experts."

Tillie turned to Carol. "What do you think?"

"The chocolate fruitcake is spectacular," said Carol.

"I'd buy that one," Guy repeated.

"Me, too," said Tillie. "But Mrs. Newton could really use that grocery store gift card."

Carol nodded and chewed her lip.

"Yeah, but which one do we like the best?" asked Guy.

"Oh, the chocolate," Tillie said easily. Then turned to Carol. "So, first place to Mrs. Newton for her apricot fruitcake?"

"Yes."

Guy blinked. "Huh?"

"Sometimes we fudge a little," Tillie explained. "All for a good cause."

"What's the point of entering if the judges aren't going to be honest?" Guy protested.

"The point is to help people," Tillie said. "Believe me, if Jan were in straitened circumstances we'd have awarded her first place. But she's won before and she'll be happy with her second-place winnings. And Bernadette will be equally happy with hers. And if they were sitting here with us right now and knew that Mrs. Newton was barely able to pay her electric bill last month they'd insist we give her the first-place prize. This will help her without hurting her pride."

"And she may not be around next year to enter," added Carol. "Cancer."

That shut Guy up. But he couldn't help marveling at the dif-

ference between men and women. In Man Land you won fair
and square, and if you lost, you lost.

The crowd was called back to their seats and the winners of
the various silent auctions were announced. Jenny Lind let out
a whoop when Livi announced that she'd won the giant cake
tree and Livi blushed when she announced that Joe Ford had
won the basket of books.

Once more Morris was glaring at him, longing to crush him
like an empty beer can. Well, too bad. Morris could deal with
it. If the man had any brains he'd have known to bid on those
books.

Finally, it was time to announce the winners of the fruitcake competition. All the entrants were called up on stage and
given certificates of appreciation. Bernadette, the third-place
winner, was happy with her fifty-dollar gift card, and Jan gra-
ciously accepted second place. Mrs. Newton was announced the
grand winner for the year and burst into tears and all the other
women gathered around her for a group hug. Next to Guy, the
two judges smiled, satisfied with the outcome.

A couple of men wearing Santa hats and carrying guitars took
over for a community sing, and finally, the event was at an end.
Guy went to collect his winnings, and Morris, who was helping take down chairs, stopped to growl, "She can't be bought."

"I'm not buying anyone," Guy snarled, and walked away with
his prize. Except maybe he was. If he threw around enough
money, could he endear himself to Olivia Berg and get himself
off Santa's naughty list? He hoped so.

Meanwhile, he helped with cleanup and taking down booths.
Finally, with everything done, Livi and her volunteers were
ready to hit the local restaurant to unwind. Her dad passed,
claiming he was tired, but her assistant, Bettina, and another
friend named Kate, who Livi introduced as her bookkeeper,
were both eager to go out and celebrate.

"You have to come with us," Kate told Guy. "I mean, how

would it look if the fruitcake judge refused to hang out with the little people?"

Oh boy, celebrating with the assistant and the bookkeeper. That would be fun. And then Morris Bentley promised to join them after he'd dropped off his mom—who wasn't smiling at Guy now that she'd failed to place in the competition. Oh boy. More fun.

As they walked to the car with her father, Guy handed over the gift basket of books, saying, "This should be enough reading to keep you busy for a while."

"Oh, you shouldn't have done that," she protested, but her eyes were shining as she took it.

"Consider it a thank-you for letting me stay with you," said Guy. Andrew Berg nodded in approval and Guy smiled. He'd scored points with both father and daughter.

They dropped off her dad, who took her gift basket in the house for her, then drove on to Family Tree. Built to look like—surprise, surprise—a log cabin, the place had colored lights running along its roofline and, inside, tinsel garlands strung across every window. Christmas carols were playing an accompaniment to the sound of laughter and conversation. Guy could smell onions grilling.

Most of the booths and tables were filled, and he spotted several people from the fruitcake competition. The winner of the Christmas tree cake sat at a large table with her family. The creator of the chocolate fruitcake sat at a booth with her husband, a studious-looking type with dark hair and glasses. Carol, the owner of the bakery, was at another table with a couple of other women.

Bettina had arrived now, along with a husband and baby in tow, and Kate the bookkeeper with a tall man named Tom, who was wearing jeans and a jacket hanging open over a dark sweater. He had an easy smile and was happy to shake hands and congratulate Guy on being brave enough to get sucked into judging fruitcake.

"The things we do for our women," said Bettina's husband, Danny, with a shake of the head, and winked at his wife.

Guy didn't bother to correct him but Livi said, "Oh, I'm not, we're not..." Then she blushed. "We only just met."

Funny, Guy felt like he'd known her for years.

"Really?" Tom looked surprised. "Oh. Well, anyway, cool that you stepped in."

"It was kind of fun, actually," Guy admitted.

"Are you a fruitcake convert now?" Livi asked him.

"Maybe. That chocolate one was awesome."

Now here came Bentley. Too bad he hadn't stayed home. Everyone else greeted him warmly and he had a smile and a handshake for the other men. He didn't bother with Guy.

The maître d' sat them all at a table across from the Christmas cake winner and her gang, and their waitress, a woman named Coral, appeared shortly after to take drink orders.

"I'll take a Hale's," said Tom.

"Me, too," said Bettina's husband, and Guy made that a third.

A very un-merry Morris went right for the hard stuff, ordering Scotch on the rocks. Livi and Kate decided on peppermint shakes and Bettina ordered a soft drink. The baby, settled in a portable high chair, got a bottle.

So there they all were, a happy band of revelers and one Grinch. And this time it wasn't Guy. Drinks came and Tom asked Guy where he was from and how he wound up in Pine River.

"Just our bad luck," Bentley muttered, and Livi stepped in to quickly explain how she and Guy had met.

"I hope that belt comes in tomorrow so you can get to your mom's in time for Christmas," said Tom.

"It will," Bentley said in a tone of voice that dared the parts supplier to screw up. Guy strongly suspected that if it didn't arrive Bentley would drive him to the nearest bus station and personally escort him onto the first bus out of town.

The women chatted and the guys talked sports. Coral arrived to take their food orders and hamburgers were ordered all around. Bentley scowled at his empty glass and asked for another Scotch and Livi frowned at him.

"What?" he demanded.

Obviously, they were all old friends because Kate stepped in and said, "If you keep drinking like that you're going to be celebrating Christmas on your lips."

"I'll be fine," he said, and when his drink came, tossed it back like it was pop.

"Morris," Livi scolded. "What's the matter with you? Take it easy on that stuff."

He held up a hand. "Okay, okay."

Their food arrived and everyone dug in and conversation turned to the event and how successful it had been. "I couldn't have done it without all of you," Livi said.

"You know we'd do anything for you, Liv," Bentley said, and Guy couldn't help feeling sorry for him until he added, "The people you can count on the most are your old friends."

"Friends are important," she said diplomatically.

Everyone but Bentley, the two-legged wet blanket, kept the conversation going, making sure to include Guy. The main course came and went and Bettina and her husband ordered dessert. Tom and Kate decided to split a piece of cheesecake. Livi passed, claiming cookie overload, and Guy declined as well, claiming fruitcake overload, which made almost everyone smile. Except Bentley. He passed on dessert and ordered a third drink.

Meanwhile, all around them, other diners were visiting, laughing, enjoying themselves. Much like Livi's party would have done if the boyfriend wannabe hadn't joined them. He wasn't winning any points with her with his great Sphinx imitation, but Guy wouldn't be the one to tell him that.

Finally, the check came. Guy picked up the tab, paying cash. No way was he going to let Livi get a glimpse of his credit card. Everyone thanked him, except Bentley who muttered that he could pay for his own food.

"Don't be an ass, Morris," Kate told him in disgust.

Then it was time to leave, the assistant and her family in the lead and the accountant and her boyfriend following. Livi stood and grabbed her coat.

Guy moved to help her with it, but he'd barely gotten a hand on it when Bentley said, "I can help her," and gave him a shove.

It caught Guy off balance and he stumbled backward just as a wired little boy came running past. Guy managed to not take down the kid but he wasn't able to avoid colliding with someone from the table next door who'd just stood up. The someone who'd won the Christmas tree cake.

The family had begun to sing "Happy Birthday" to Grandma, and she was moving toward the old woman, her prize held in front of her. Her collision with Guy sent her stumbling and the cake went flying.

Oh no, Guy thought. *Please don't let it...* Too late. It did.

12

Jenny Lind let out a cry of horror as the Christmas tree cake catapulted out of her hands.

"Wow," breathed the kid, stopping in mid-run.

Yeah, wow. The cake landed in Grandma's lap and she, too, let out a cry and threw up her hands as if a bomb had just hit her. The other women at the table ran to help clean Grandma up, one of them bumping into Guy and bouncing him off Bentley, who gave him a second shove, which bounced him off a waiter passing by with a tray of food. That sent two hamburgers, one serving of pot roast complete with mashed potatoes and gravy, an order of fish and chips, and a plate of spaghetti crashing to the floor and got the attention of every diner in the place.

Livi had forgotten about putting on her coat and rushed to help with Grandma, as did her friends.

"Watch out for the spaghetti," someone called. Too late. Down went an unsuspecting diner.

"You Neanderthal," Guy snapped at Bentley. "If we weren't in a restaurant..."

"You'd what?" Bentley stepped up to Guy, invading his space.

"This is not the time or the place," Guy said through clenched jaws.

"Yeah? There's never a time or place for gutless wimps like you," Bentley snarled.

Okay, that did it. Guy's temper was now officially boiling over. "You want to take this outside?"

"Damn straight I do."

"Good idea," said the restaurant manager, who had joined them. "Get out."

Meanwhile, Jenny Lind was crying over spilled cake, and Grandma was whimpering and brushing at her frosting-coated chest as the women hovered around her, trying to mop her off with napkins.

This should not have happened. Guy dug his wallet out of his back pocket.

"You gonna try to pay me off?" Bentley taunted.

"No, I'm going to try to clean up the mess you made," Guy said, disgusted. He turned to the upset cake winner and gave her a fifty. "I'm really sorry."

Still crying, she nodded and took it and thanked him.

"That's all you rich boys do is buy people off," sniped Bentley.

"Out!" roared the manager, his face the color of the spilled spaghetti sauce. He pointed to the door and Guy and Morris Bentley marched out of the restaurant, the rest of their party trailing after.

They barely made it outside before Bentley rushed him, sending them flying out into the snow, landing on the ground. He was bigger and a bruiser, but Guy had indulged in some cage fighting when he was younger and he was fit. And pissed, and he came up swinging.

Legs, fists, kicks and punches—it quickly became a bloody

battle and the most excitement some people had seen in a while. He got Bentley in the gut and the chin and Bentley socked him in the eye. Of course, he and Bentley had drawn a crowd, and now the locals were hooting and cheering and calling instructions to both Bentley and Guy.

"Come on, fruitcake, fight like a man," someone called.

"I've got ten bucks on Bentley," someone else said.

"You'll lose it," Guy snarled, and threw a good, solid punch.

Bentley staggered back but then returned like an angry bear. Small town brawling, a new way to enjoy the holidays.

Suddenly, in the middle of everything a new body entered, just as Guy was aiming to take Bentley down. "Stop it right—" She got no farther. Guy was already in mid-kick, and she ran into his leg, getting scooped off her feet. Bentley had been ready to lunge at Guy. Instead, he wound up completing what Guy had started. Livi went down, Bentley falling on top of her and the two of them taking Guy with them. They crashed into the snow in a pile worthy of an NFL game.

"Livi, are you all right?" Bentley asked, scrambling off her.

At the same time Guy was saying, "I'm so sorry. Are you hurt?"

She rubbed her leg and glared at Bentley. "Morris Bentley, you should be ashamed of yourself. What is the matter with you?"

"It's not me, it's him," Bentley said, pointing at Guy. "He's all flash, Liv. He doesn't deserve you."

It was true, but Guy couldn't help pointing out, "I'm not the one who made a scene in the restaurant."

"Good fight, men," said Tom, giving Bentley a friendly slap on the arm before Kate hauled him away.

Yeah, great entertainment for the locals. Guy rubbed his throbbing hand. What the hell was he doing here?

"And right before Christmas," Livi continued as if that elevated the fight to a cardinal sin. She rubbed her thigh again. Poor woman would probably have a bruise come morning.

"I'm sorry, Liv. I'll make it up to you when we do our deliveries Christmas Eve," Bentley said, penitent.

"Morris, I think it would be good if we took a break from hanging out."

Now he looked panicked as well as remorseful. "You need help delivering stockings and turkeys."

"Joe can help me," she said, her voice frosty.

Bentley was in deep shit. In spite of being pissed at the idiot, Guy couldn't help feeling sorry for him.

"He's leaving town," Bentley pointed out.

"Did the part come in?" she demanded.

"Not yet. But it's supposed to be in tomorrow. And as soon as it is I'll have that fancy toy fixed and ready to roll. He'll be out of here before Christmas Eve," Morris added, glaring at Guy.

Guy almost asked if Bentley thought he could manage it, then decided to keep his mouth shut. No sense antagonizing him. "Fine with me," he said.

"Well, you just concentrate on that. I can handle making deliveries fine without you," Livi said. The look in her eyes was as arctic as her voice.

"Where will you get a truck?" Bentley demanded.

"You're not the only man in town with a truck," she reminded him, then whirled and started for her car. "Come on, Joe."

"He may have money but money isn't everything," Bentley called after them.

That was what losers like Bentley always said. Class envy. Just how did that tool think nonprofits survived? It wasn't on good wishes. It was thanks to people with money.

Livi was making such fast tracks for her car she slipped in the snow. Guy caught her arm to steady her. She looked up at him and the expression in her eyes said it all. *I'm falling for you.*

The anger he'd felt only a moment before melted into a puddle of shame. *Don't. You don't know me.*

"Look, that was as much my fault back there as it was his," Guy said.

Sure, Bentley had started it, but Guy had been more than willing to go along for the ride and burn some testosterone. Much as Guy disliked the other man, it wasn't right to let him take all the blame for what happened in the parking lot.

"He was the one who pushed you in the restaurant. It's Morris's fault the cake Jenny won got ruined." She shook her head. "There's no excuse for what he did."

Yeah, there was. Men in love did stupid things.

But Livi had made up her mind. Bentley was stuck in a time-out.

"So, will you help us?" she asked Guy. "If you're still here?"

"Of course I will." Although with Bentley anxious to run him out of town, Guy would probably be on the road long before it was time to make deliveries.

Anyway, would driving around with her handing out turkeys and Christmas stockings full of trinkets transform him into a man she could respect? The sooner he got out of this town and forgot about Olivia Berg the better.

Except she was unforgettable.

"I hope you'll attend our volunteer appreciation lunch tomorrow," she said as they drove away from the scene of the Christmas cake murder.

"I'm not a volunteer."

"No one paid you to help us out today. I really did appreciate it, and I'd love to have you come."

So he could be reminded of what a two-faced liar he was. "No problem," he said, careful not to commit.

The one she should have been inviting was Bentley. It sounded like he did a lot to help her.

Maybe she had invited him. If she had, it was as good as canceled.

Poor schlub. Morris Bentley smelled a rat. He was simply trying to run Guy off and protect Livi, and yet he was the one in deep shit. Guy should run himself off.

Starting that evening. He'd make some excuse, go up to his room and hide for the rest of the night. He'd find a reason to miss her volunteer lunch the next day and then scram as soon as his car was fixed. Bentley would be back on turkey patrol and he and Livi would patch things up. She'd return to her life, marry the big doofus and live happily ever after.

And never see the Eiffel Tower. Guy frowned. He didn't deserve her, but neither did Bentley.

Livi noticed him rubbing his hand, which felt like he'd pounded a cement wall with it. "Does it hurt a lot?"

"It'll be fine," he said, and stopped rubbing.

"I'm so sorry. I don't know what got into him."

"Sure you do. He's in love with you." As if she couldn't see that.

She nodded and bit her lip. "I know. And I love Morris, too, but as a friend."

The *F* word. "It's important to be able to see yourself spending a lifetime with someone." Guy sure couldn't see Livi spending her life with Bentley. But then, what did he know?

"I do want to get married and have a family." She paused. "There aren't exactly a lot of choices here in Pine River. Morris and I are the best of friends. Maybe that's enough." She stole another look at Guy. Waiting for him to offer her an alternative?

He was a fake, which made him a pretty crummy alternative. "There's a whole big world out there, Olivia."

"But maybe I'm meant to stay in this corner of it. You know, brighten the corner where you are."

"You're doing a good job of that."

She murmured her thanks and they both fell silent. If they knew each other better, if she knew who he really was, and that he wanted to be more than he was… What would he say to her? *Don't commit to anybody just yet. Give me time to grow. I could change.*

He didn't say anything. He simply couldn't spit out what he needed to, couldn't tell her what she should know about him. He had to get out there and do something to earn her respect.

Of course, being the CFO of a large company like Hightower Enterprises would have been more than enough to earn the respect of most people. Sadly for him, Olivia Berg wasn't most people.

They turned onto her street. "I was going to watch a Christmas movie," she said. "Maybe you'd like to join me."

Of course he would, because he'd been drugged with fruitcake. *Don't be stupid*, he told himself.

Too late. "Sure." He was making a bad habit of not listening to himself.

Back at the house they hung up their coats, then she disappeared into the kitchen to fetch cookies. Guy caught sight of the gift basket he'd gotten her sitting on the living room coffee table, all gussied up in cellophane and a big red bow. He'd bought it because he knew she'd like it. And maybe because he hoped she'd still like him when she learned his true identity? Could a gift basket erase a bad first impression? If only they hadn't gotten off on the wrong foot.

Ha! There was an understatement. He'd kicked her with the wrong foot.

He went upstairs to wash up. The man in the bathroom mirror had a banged-up face and a dribble of dried blood under his nose.

"You are such a fool," Guy told him.

Livi was just coming out of the kitchen bearing a plate of cookies when he came back downstairs. "I thought my dad might join us," she said, "but he opted not to."

"Not into having company?" Guy asked as they settled on the couch.

"More like recovering from politeness overload. He still misses my mom, and getting out there with people and pretending to enjoy the season tends to drain him. Christmas was her favorite holiday," she added, and Guy noticed that some of the joy had dropped out of her voice.

He understood. "I get it. The holidays weren't the same after my dad died."

"How did your family cope?" she asked, setting the cookie plate on the coffee table.

"I'm not sure we ever really did," Guy said with a shrug. "We don't get together much as a family anymore. My oldest brother's on his third divorce. My mom's remarried. We're still trying to do Thanksgiving but..."

It was difficult to put into words how their lives had changed over the years, especially during the holidays. They still made a point of doing Thanksgiving—ate turkey and stuffing, had some laughs, played with the kids, but it always felt to Guy as if their hearts weren't in it. This year had been especially hard with Michael's latest marriage mess leaving him far from being good company.

As for mixing with Del's family? Well, they'd never be the Brady Bunch. "I'm the only one going to see my mom for Christmas this year." And even though he wanted to see her, he wasn't sure how that visit was going to turn out.

"I so miss having my mom with us. She made the holidays special."

"It looks like you're doing a pretty good job of that yourself," Guy said.

"Not like her. There are times when I wish I could go back in time."

Him, too. He'd have made sure a big chunk of money got given to Christmas from the Heart. How different this all would be without that fateful decision hanging over him.

"But since I can't, I'm determined to continue living the best way I can and to try to keep our family together," Livi said. "I want my mom to be proud of me."

"How could she not?" Guy couldn't help wondering how proud his dad would have been of some of his choices. Would he have cared that Guy had told his CSR director to sever old ties with this small charity?

Maybe not. But would he have been disappointed with his son's cowardly duplicity? For sure.

Guy remembered one of the last pieces of advice his dad ever gave him. "Sometimes you have to make hard decisions, son. Once you make one, stand by it and don't be ashamed. And always be honest in all your dealings, no matter how hard that is. Nothing pays as high a dividend as honesty."

And nothing cost so much as dishonesty. Guy was seeing the truth of that now.

Meanwhile, here was Livi, smiling at him as if his opinion mattered. "I'm sure trying to keep the joy in our lives," she said. "I just wish my dad could try a little harder. I'm sure when my brother and sister-in-law come tomorrow, though, that will perk him up. Meanwhile, we have a movie to watch and Christmas cookies to eat. Would you like some milk to go with them?"

Cookies and milk, like when he was a kid. "Sure." Keep the holiday movie playing.

She motioned to the gift basket. "Or we could have some champagne."

"Milk will do it for me."

She nodded. "All right then. I'll be right back."

What are you doing here? Make some excuse and leave before this goes any further. Hide in the guest room until the car's ready.

Guy not only stayed put, he settled on the couch in the hopes that she'd join him there.

She did, after putting in a DVD. She didn't cuddle up right next to him—Livi Berg was too classy to get pushy unless it was for a good cause—but she did sit close enough to tell him it was at the back of her mind.

Her phone pinged, signaling a text. She picked it up, looked

at it, then turned off the phone and set it on the coffee table.
Guy could guess who it was from by the irritated expression on
her face. Bentley was still stuck on the outside looking in while
Guy was snug in the living room, eating cookies and watching
a movie with Livi. How long could his luck hold out?

Out of the corner of his eye, he could see a couple of nut-
cracker Hessian soldiers on the end table on his side of the couch.
He'd never liked nutcrackers, always thought they were creepy.
These two seemed to be glaring at him, like characters from a
Stephen King novel. It would serve him right if they came to
life in the night and stabbed him with their bayonets.

"I love this old movie," Livi said, aiming the remote at the
DVD player. "I watch it every Christmas."

Not *It's a Wonderful Life*. That was his mom's favorite and
she'd made him and his brothers watch it with her every year—
until they got old enough to make an excuse and escape. Corny
and stupid. No man was poor who had friends, or something
like that.

Or maybe she was about to show him *A Christmas Carol*. The
evil businessman. That would be even worse. He braced himself.

The screen showed him *The Family Man* with Nicolas Cage.
It was *A Christmas Carol* and *It's a Wonderful Life* melded together
and wrapped up in modern clothes. He'd seen the movie once,
years ago, with a girlfriend. He'd found it pretty entertaining.
This time he wasn't so sure he'd be able to watch it.

Go now. Take a cookie and scram. He took a cookie and stayed
put.

And watched Jack Campbell, investment broker, learn a thing
or two about life. Well, sort of watched. Between thinking
about how much he'd like to pull Livi next to him and wishing
he was the kind of man who deserved to do that, it was hard
to concentrate on the plot. Not that it needed much concentra-
tion. The story was the same one writers brought out in some
form or other every Christmas.

"Wasn't that wonderful?" she asked when the ending credits finally rolled, tears in her eyes.

"It was okay."

"Just okay?" She looked shocked.

"Well, it's kind of the same old story told over and over again—man with no heart grows one."

"That's a classic theme," she pointed out.

"Yeah, the theme that every businessman is a hard-hearted bastard."

"Some are," she argued, and he knew exactly who she was thinking of.

So he'd screwed up. But he wasn't all bad. "You know, Livi, most businessmen are trying to do something good in their own way, trying to make something of themselves, provide a better life for their family and their employees." That was what his dad had done.

"I know," she said softly. "And without those businesses, Christmas from the Heart wouldn't be able to do what it does. I guess I like these movies because they remind us that life is about priorities. All the success in the world doesn't mean much if you lose the people in your life while you're pursuing it, especially when that's why you want the success in the first place. And I think all of us were put here on this earth to share. Did you ever see the old movie *Hello, Dolly!*?"

Conversational whiplash. Where were they going now? He shook his head.

"I watched it on TV with my mom and grandma when I was a little girl. It's all about this widow who's a matchmaker and she's always talking to her dead husband."

"So, she's a medium?"

Livi smiled and shook her head. "No, she just likes to keep his memory alive. Anyway, she has this line in the movie where she talks about money being fertilizer, meant to be spread around to make things grow. I think that's a good attitude to have, no matter what your business. Don't you?"

Livi Berg was exactly the kind of woman Guy's mom would approve of. "You are something else," he said, and slipped an arm around her and drew her toward him. She came willingly and she kissed him back willingly. And, oh man, life was good for that one moment.

If only he could find a way to make it last.

A shower, some aspirin and a bag of frozen peas to his aching chin hadn't left Morris feeling any better. He'd been an ass—there was no getting around it. And now Joe Ford, who'd done nothing more than eat some fruitcake and put away some chairs, was Liv's new hero. And Morris's moment of madness hadn't helped.

He had no excuse for his behavior other than… Okay, there was no excuse.

He texted an apology to her, which she ignored, then tossed aside his phone and grabbed the TV remote in an effort to distract himself. Nothing worked, not even streaming *Die Hard*, one of his all-time favorite holiday movies. Instead of seeing Bruce Willis taking down bad guys, all he could see was himself, shoving Ford and starting that nightmare chain of disaster in the restaurant. He never got mad like that. Of all the times to start. He was an idiot.

An idiot who'd been in love with Liv ever since he turned twelve and came to the realization that girls didn't have cooties. From then on he'd done everything to win her heart from tugging on her hair or snitching her lunch sack from her and making her chase him to putting cheap Valentine candy on her porch on Valentine's Day—yeah, he got smoother as he got older—and then running away so she wouldn't catch him in the act. *Okay, not that smooth.* It had taken him clear until their junior year in high school to get up his nerve to ask her out, and then it had taken him three dates to get up his nerve to kiss her. But after that they'd been a couple. He'd hated it when she left for college and it had killed him when she broke up with him when she came home for Thanksgiving. He'd been patient, though, and after she returned to Pine River for good he'd convinced her to try again. The second try hadn't worked and she'd relegated him to the friends corner. He hated the friends corner.

But even that was better than where he was now. Now he was in deep shit.

Okay, he may have been an idiot but Ford was... What? An interloper, a slick newcomer turning Livi's head with his fancy clothes and his fancy car.

It was more than that. There was something else about the guy, something Morris couldn't put his finger on, but he sensed it in his gut.

He grabbed his phone again, got on the internet and typed in *Joe Ford*. Up came a singer, a football coach, a funeral home and an insurance agent. Last up was a former CEO of a global communication company in another part of the country who had graduated from college before this Joe was even born. Morris searched Facebook, too, and didn't find anybody who looked like Joe Ford.

"You're a fake," he muttered. Whoever this man was, whatever he was hiding, Morris hoped he could find out before it was too late and Liv got her heart broken.

We Wish You
a Merry Christmas

13

The next morning Livi had eggnog coffee cake waiting for her father and Guy. Guy had hoped not to see her dad. His face was a mess and he wasn't sure Mr. Berg would be impressed on hearing about his brawl with Bentley outside Family Tree.

The man was sitting at the vintage kitchen table with his paper, sipping his morning coffee. He said nothing about Guy's face, instead giving him a friendly nod and informing him that the weatherman was predicting clear skies for the next couple of days.

"Should make things easier when you get on the road."

Either Mr. Berg was the most unobservant man on the planet or the most diplomatic. Either way, Guy was grateful he didn't say anything about the purple swelling under one eye and his swollen nose.

"It looks that way," he said, and helped himself to a piece of coffee cake. "This looks good," he said to Livi.

"It's one of my specialties. I hope you enjoy it," she said, and laid a platter of bacon on the table, as well.

"I will," Guy said. He was enjoying everything about being with the Bergs.

Except for the pressure his guilty secret was putting on his conscience. That was taking on glacial proportions.

"I wish you'd come home for the volunteer luncheon," Livi said to her father as he stood to leave.

"You'll have enough people to feed without adding your old man to the list."

She shook her head. "You need to be thanked, too."

"No need to thank me for putting out a few chairs." He stood and kissed the top of her head. "I'm sure Joe won't mind standing in for me."

"If I'm still here," Guy said, and noticed that Livi didn't look as happy as she had a moment ago. Maybe the belt wouldn't come in.

What was he saying? That part needed to get in and he needed to get gone.

Mr. Berg shook hands with him. "You're welcome to stay as long as you need. If you do get your car going, have a safe trip and feel free to come visit anytime you're on your way through town."

Olivia's father was a nice man. Nice to Joe Ford, anyway. But Guy Hightower, the creep who'd insulted his daughter and left her charity hanging in the wind? The man would be fighting Bentley for the privilege of ripping off Guy's head and using it for a bowling ball.

Her father left and then it was just the three of them, Olivia, Guy and the glacier. "I'll help you," he said, grabbing a plate.

"No need," she assured him.

Yeah, there was. He needed to prove he was no Christmas monster. As if clearing the table and helping load the dishwasher would do it.

He did anyway. Then he left her to get ready for her party and went to his room to call Bob's Auto Repair. If his car was ready, he could leave while everybody still liked him. Then, once he got to Idaho, he'd get his mom to advise him on how to proceed with Livi. That was the smart thing to do. Still, part of him hated to leave.

He got Morris. Where was good old Bob, anyway? "It's Joe Ford. Did that belt come in?"

"Not yet," Morris growled.

"Are you going to get it today?"

"We should. The sooner you're out of town the better."

Sadly, truer words were never spoken.

He'd barely ended the call when his phone announced a text from Mike. You at Mom's? Call me. We've got a situation.

Guy much preferred to deal with a million situations at work rather than the awkward one in Pine River. Any business-related problem would be a piece of cake in comparison.

Cake. The great flying cake incident at the restaurant, the fight in the parking lot. Good Lord. He wasn't in a holiday movie anymore. He was in a reality show.

He called Mike. "What's up?"

"Hey, I know Mom's gonna be pissed if you're doing business down there instead of family stuff but we've got a major fire that needs to be put out," Mike said.

Guy didn't bother to tell his brother that he wasn't at their mother's house yet, that he was stuck in a small town, the resident Grinch incognito as a man with a heart. No sense going into all that. Mike had problems of his own. Besides, Guy wasn't sure his big brother would understand what he was feeling.

"Breville wants to back out of buying the business park on Aurora."

"He's a real estate broker. He should know what a sweet deal this is."

"He's got cold feet for some reason. Bry and I have finessed him all we can. I think you need to talk numbers with him again."

"Okay, I'm on it."

Guy spent the rest of the morning dealing with Hightower issues. It was a relief to focus on something other than his personal life.

The problem was on its way to being resolved when voices began to drift upstairs. Soon Livi was tapping on his bedroom door.

He opened it, ready to give her some excuse for why he couldn't come down, but seeing her, the words mutinied and ran away. She was wearing a green sweater over black leggings and some little red shoes that made her look like a ballerina. She looked so happy, he wanted to be with her and let that happiness spill over onto him. He followed her downstairs.

On the way down he noticed a new holiday decoration had been added—a jewel-shaped acrylic crystal topped with gold-glittered mistletoe hung from the hall chandelier.

"A new decoration?" he asked.

"I always put up mistletoe," she said in an obvious attempt to sound casual. "I almost forgot this year."

Until they started getting close. He could easily envision himself kissing her under it.

He could also envision her slapping his face when he said, "By the way, my real name is Guy Hightower."

He had to tell her.

But not yet.

The dining room table was laden with plates bearing fussy little sandwiches and cookies and a bowl of fruit salad. Christmassy plates and napkins sat on one end of the table and a teapot and more Christmas china on another, along with a bowl of punch. Her friends Bettina and Kate were there, along with an older woman named Jean, who, he learned, was one of the daughters of Tillie, his fellow fruitcake judge.

"Mom was a little tired," she explained, "and one of our waitresses called in sick, so Annette's holding down the fort." She looked Guy over speculatively as Livi made the introductions. *New boyfriend?*

Probably never.

The doorbell rang and more people flooded in, all bringing good cheer and laughter. It was a small, simple gathering, nothing as extravagant as what Hightower Enterprises would put on. No free booze, no fancy ice sculptures.

No pretention, no hidden agendas. Not a single fake.

And no leeches. The glacier got bigger and as soon as he could, Guy claimed the need to make some phone calls and slipped away.

"I see you hung the mistletoe," Kate said to Livi as she and Kate and Bettina put away the luncheon leftovers. "I wonder what prompted that," she teased.

"I put up mistletoe every year," Livi said.

"I didn't see it when I came over the other night," Bettina said.

"Quit playing dumb and tell us about this man," Kate commanded. "Is he as fabulous as he seems?"

"Yes," Livi said, and put the last of the mini quiches in a plastic container. "He's smart and fun and kind." And a wonderful kisser. If she'd had more on hand, she'd have hung mistletoe in every room in the house.

"And not bad on the eyes, either," said Kate. "Although I bet he looks a little banged up today."

"That was some fight," put in Bettina. "I can't blame Morris for being jealous, though. Joe is in a class all by himself."

"It looks like Santa was listening when Annette made her request. He's coming through with the perfect man for you."

It sure looked like it.

★ ★ ★

By four o'clock, the last of the deliveries had been made to
Bob's Auto Repair and there was still no sign of that serpentine belt for the Maserati. Morris was ready to put a fist through
the wall.

He called Foreign Auto Parts and got Gustav, the manager.
"So where's that serpentine belt? You promised me we'd have
it by today."

"We got behind," said Gustav.

More like somebody screwed up. Morris swore. "I need it,
Gustav. I've got a guy trying to get to Idaho for Christmas."

"What's he doing way up there?" Gustav demanded.

Messing up my life. "Never mind that. What are you doing
down there? Are you gonna get that belt to me or not?"

"I'll get it to you already."

"No more screwing around. Overnight it."

"Okay, okay."

"I mean it. I want that thing tomorrow." Joe Ford, whoever
he was, had messed up enough stuff. No way was Morris going
to let him hang around to mess up Christmas.

Dinner at the Berg house wasn't much easier for Guy than
the luncheon had been.

"Looks like you're still stuck with us," Mr. Berg said.

Stuck. If only Guy could get out that confession that was stuck
in his throat.

In spite of the guilt, he wound up hanging around after dinner, playing cards again, this time with both Livi and her father.

"Really?" she'd said eagerly when her dad had suggested a
game of hearts.

"The least we can do for this poor man is keep him enter-
tained," said Mr. Berg. "I'm sorry that part didn't come in today,
Joe."

"We'll have to help you make the best of it," Livi said.

"You've both been more than generous. I appreciate all you're doing for me," Guy said. Was he ever going to find the right time to tell Livi who he was?

Not now, he decided. *For sure not now*, he concluded later when it was only the two of them, sitting at the table drinking hot chocolate, then when it was the two of them kissing under the mistletoe. *Not tonight.*

The next morning was Christmas Eve, good deed day. And it looked like Guy would be around to be part of it all. That should help melt the glacier. Maybe it was a good thing his car still wasn't fixed. It bought him time to improve his image.

"Where are you getting a truck today if Morris can't help you?" Mr. Berg asked his daughter as they ate breakfast.

Can't help her? So that was the story she was giving. Guy wondered what she'd told her dad about his bruises and skinned knuckles. That he walked into a wall? With his face and his fist?

"Bettina's husband is off from school and they've got a minivan. Some of our other volunteers have trucks. We'll be fine."

It looked like Guy was going to have to share distribution duties and Livi's attention with another man. *Darn.*

It turned out to be his lucky day, though. Bettina wasn't feeling good and her husband, Danny, had baby duty. "Sorry, I can't help," he told Livi when they came over to pick up the minivan.

"It's okay," she said to him. "Joe and I can handle it."

"Don't be surprised if you get every woman in town wanting to give you ice for your face or a cookie to make you feel better," Danny said to Guy. "You'll probably get some pointers on your fighting technique if any of the guys are home. Old man Jones will give you some, for sure."

He could hardly wait.

"It is a small town," Livi explained.

And if word of who he was got out they'd all probably tie him to a tree somewhere with nothing but a Santa hat on his head and let him freeze to death.

Meanwhile, though, he'd get to spend the morning with Livi. He half wished that belt would come in too late to fix the car that day. Then he'd have to spend Christmas Eve with the Berg family, one last happy holiday movie scene before going back to the real world.

They said goodbye to Danny, then headed for Christmas from the Heart headquarters to pick up Christmas stockings, Livi in her car, Guy following behind in the minivan. A minivan. He was in a minivan. Good Lord. He thought of the movie they'd watched the other night. Was this how all men ended up, driving minivans, following wherever the woman they loved led?

Not that he loved Livi. He wasn't that far gone yet. He'd just met her. He was fascinated, infatuated, wanted to be with her and be part of her life. Who was he kidding? He wasn't at the edge of the love pool anymore. He was wading right on in, heading for the deep end as fast as he could.

Livi's office was above Tillie's tearoom, so naturally, they had to stop in and say hi. "It's so good to see you again, Joe," gushed Tillie, giving his arm a friendly pat. Then she took in his bruised face. "Oh my. What happened to you?"

"I fell," he said quickly before Livi could go into detail. No lie. He had fallen, more than once, making a complete fool of himself.

"I have just the thing for you." Tillie moved to a long shelf behind the checkout counter that was lined with glass jars filled with loose tea. "I call it Tillie's Healing Comfort," she said over her shoulder as she took down a jar. "It has comfrey, hops and white oak bark in it, and it's very good for bruising." She spooned some into a lavender-colored net bag, then handed it over. "Steep this, then put it on the bruise. You should drink it, also."

"Thanks," he said.

"I think I'll take some of that, too," said Livi, and he thought about her bruised thigh. He was hazardous to this woman's health. On so many levels.

Tillie stocked Livi up on chocolate mint tea as well, and then they proceeded upstairs to her office, where boxes filled with stuffed red felt Christmas stockings occupied every inch of space. The boxes were labeled: family with girls, family with boys, girls and boys, single.

One box was filled with cat toys and dog chews. "We add those at the last minute," Livi explained. "For homes where people have pets. You never know when someone's gotten a puppy for Christmas," she added happily.

Guy wondered if he'd ever get a dog again. Maybe he would. A golden retriever. Or a cockapoo.

"After we load these we'll load our turkeys and hams from Tillie's cooler, where she's been thawing them for us," Livi explained.

Looking at all the boxes of Christmas stockings he wondered if she was being realistic about how many deliveries they'd be able to make in a morning. Until, a moment later, the older woman he'd met the day before walked in along with another woman he assumed was her sister, Annette.

"So, you're the new man in town," Annette said after they'd been introduced, and she, too, eyed him speculatively.

"Only for a while longer," he said. And if Bentley had anything to do with it, that while would be as short as possible.

More volunteers arrived—a couple of older men with trucks and two couples that he'd also met at the luncheon—and everyone got to work. They'd carried most of the boxes to the waiting vehicles, bumping shoulders on their way in and out, when Kate and her boyfriend arrived in a truck.

"Did we miss all the heavy lifting?" Tom joked as he got out.

"Hardly. We still have turkeys and hams to load," Livi informed him.

Once he saw what was in the walk-in cooler, Guy did a men-

SHEILA ROBERTS

tal count of Christmas stockings versus meat. "Looks like you're not going to have enough for everyone."

"Not this year," Livi said with a scowl, and he knew why.

"Well, I guess we'd better get started," he said before she could say anything. "But first, I need to swing by the grocery store. You go ahead and start loading these in the trucks. I'll be right back." No way did he want her next to him when he pulled out his charge card.

Guy drove the minivan to the local Safeway where he bought out an entire case worth of fresh turkeys and two dozen hams. It was a load and he enlisted a couple of baggers to help him.

"Wow," said the checker when they started unloading the meat. "Are you buying turkeys for everyone in town?"

"Something like that," he said. "It's for Christmas from the Heart."

"Aww." She smiled at him. "Say, I saw you Sunday at the fruitcake competition. You were one of the judges."

He had a moment of panic. Had she entered a cake? He knew she hadn't been one of the winners. He remembered who they were.

"Uh, yeah," he said warily. "And you are...?"

"I'm Suz. I didn't enter," she said, and he breathed a sigh of relief. "I suck in the kitchen." Then she frowned, taking in his face. "You need ice for those bruises. Alex, get some party ice for the man. On me," she added.

He thanked her and wondered how she thought he was going to drive with a giant bag of ice on his face.

"And, Billy, grab me a box of plastic gallon freezer bags. Put some in a bag and hold it to your face when you're driving," she instructed Guy.

Again, he thanked her, then pulled out his credit card.

She took it, looked at it and frowned. "I thought your name was Joe."

"That's my middle name," he improvised, and she nodded and rang up the sale.

The baggers helped him rearrange the boxes in the van and squeeze in the mountain of meat. Following Suz the checker's instructions, they put some ice in a baggie for him, then tossed the rest—assuring him they wouldn't tell Suz—and sent him on his way, the minivan stuffed with turkeys... The biggest one of all behind the wheel.

"That part's not here yet," Morris snarled into the phone. "How'd you send it, by mule?"

"Lighten up, Morris," said Gustav. "It should be there by two."

"It better be," Morris said. Joe Ford was out with Livi, doing what he should have been doing. If he didn't get Ford out of town soon, what else would he be doing with Livi that Morris should have been doing with her?

Guy got back to Christmas from the Heart headquarters as everyone was loading up the last of the meat from Tillie's cooler. "I've got more if you can fit some in your truck," he said to Tom.

"Sure," Tom said.

Guy got out and slid open the door.

Tom blinked. "What the hell?"

"I stopped by the store."

"Whoa. I guess you did. Hey, Livi," he called, "Santa just came to town."

She joined them at the minivan and gaped. "Where did all these come from?"

Guy was aware of Tom's assessing gaze on him. *Trying to get lucky, huh?*

He shrugged, feeling embarrassingly aware of his sizzling face. "It looked like you were pretty short on turkeys. There's ham, too."

Livi put a hand to her mouth and let out a little sob. "How can I ever thank you?"

Don't hate me.

"I bet he can think of something," Tom said with a smirk.

"You can thank him later. Let's divide these up and get this show on the road," Kate said.

They did, and then they were off, turkeys and hams equally distributed between the volunteers and everyone heading to a different location. Several went to the nearby towns, leaving Livi and Guy and the sisters in charge of Pine River.

"I'm glad you're still here," Livi said to him. "Now you'll be able to meet some of the townspeople."

And maybe earn some points. *Maybe.*

Their first stop was the Williams family residence. Three boys, looking like they ranged from ten on down to five, had been watching at the living room window of the little cracker box of a house. Seeing Livi and Guy coming up the walk they disappeared and a moment later were at the door, the littlest one jumping up and down like an excited puppy. They reminded Guy of his brothers and himself when they were kids, wound up and raring for Santa to come. He caught sight of a mangy tree in the corner, probably one bought from a tree lot as a last-minute bargain. But it had been decorated with paper chains and popcorn strings. A few small ornaments shaped like cars and trucks hung on the boughs but most of the ornaments looked handmade by kids. A small collection of presents sat under the tree. Looking at the boxes, Guy doubted any of them contained an iPad or a Nintendo Switch. Still, these kids were all smiles.

"Hi, Miss Berg!" sang the little one. "Have you got a stocking for us?"

"I sure do," Livi said, handing him one she'd taken from the box marked *Family, boys.*

The mother appeared in the hallway, wiping her hands on a dishcloth. "Thanks, Livi. The boys live for this stocking."

An older man was right behind her. The grandpa figure. "Hello there, Livi. Did you bring my girl a turkey?"

"I sure did," she said, and Guy handed it over.

"Good," the old man said, taking it. "I'm making mashed potatoes and my famous biscuits to go with it."

"And tonight we're making cookies for Santa," said the older boy. His brothers had run off to the living room to plunder the stocking, but he lowered his voice all the same. "I know there's no Santa, but I like the cookies."

"Don't we all," Livi said, and mussed his hair.

"Saw you the other night at Family Tree, son," the older man said to Guy. "You got to remember to keep your hands up, protect your face. Never mind all that Kung Fu shit. All somebody has to do is grab your foot and you're down for the count."

Oh yeah, everyone was an expert. Guy thanked him. "I'll keep that in mind."

Livi sighed as they made their way back down the walk. "Everyone's going to be talking about that fight for the next six weeks."

Guy shrugged. "Or until they find something new to talk about." Okay, he didn't want to go there.

"Yes, that's the nature of small town life, I guess."

"Yeah, small minds," Guy muttered.

"We don't all have small minds," she said, sounding a little huffy.

"I hope not. Sometimes, it's easy to only see your corner of the world, though, Livi, and not the bigger picture." Which was what you had to see when you ran a company.

Was he making excuses for himself? *Maybe.* But maybe he'd been being hard on himself, too. When a man was hot for a woman it tended to scramble his thinking.

So did seeing so many people in need and so grateful for something as simple as a turkey and a stocking stuffed with trinkets.

"Thank you so much," said Mrs. Newton, peeping inside her

stocking when they dropped it off. "I love these little scented soaps." She pulled out a chew toy and showed it to her little dog. "Look here, Juniper. Here's something for you, too." The dog rose on its hindquarters, pawing the air and barking. "Not until Christmas morning," she said, then told Guy, "I always like to wait until morning to open presents. It makes the fun last so much longer."

Like the Williamses, she didn't have much under her tree. He couldn't help wondering how long her fun would last. The house looked festive, though, with candles and little angel figurines scattered around the living room. He caught a whiff of cinnamon. It sure smelled like Christmas.

"Are you coming to the community Christmas dinner?" Livi asked her.

"Oh yes, I'm looking forward to it."

"Don't forget, dinner's at two," Livi said.

"I won't, dear," Mrs. Newton said. "I'm making a pie to bring."

"That sounds wonderful," Livi said.

It did. Well, his mom was making shortbread for him. His Christmas would be good, too. He hoped.

The day rushed by as they visited homes in town. Guy met more single moms and widows, families where the dad was temporarily out of work, a family or two where Guy suspected the dad had given up on ever having work again. What did that feel like, not having a job? Sometimes Guy resented the long hours he put in, but now he found himself grateful that he had work and a purpose. Men needed a purpose. And a project.

And men and women alike needed to feel like they were making a difference.

Which was exactly the way Guy felt right then. He'd never realized how like a puzzle with a missing piece his life had become. Yes, he'd been keeping his eye on the big picture, but big pictures were made up of many small pieces. And each piece was important. This piece, this bit of heart and humanity which business needed to serve, had been missing. He'd focused on strategies and figures, seeing his family's company as a giant entity that kept everyone involved with it going. But the faces that made up that nebulous everyone had never really come into focus.

Guy still wanted to be a businessman, but he wanted to run his company differently, to really see the people who worked for his family. He wanted to find that balance in his life that he and Livi had talked about. He wanted to be George Bailey living again. He wanted to be the new and improved Jack Campbell. He wanted to be a Scrooge who knew how to keep Christmas well. A good woman, a good life, being a good neighbor—he wanted to mix that all into his holidays. And every day.

He was on a holiday high when they returned the minivan and he climbed into Livi's car. "That was cool." There was an understatement.

"It's so heartwarming to see how much such small kindnesses mean to people," she said. "I think it reassures them that we're all in this together."

In a Christmas movie. Why didn't it seem at all corny anymore?

His cell phone rang. It was his mother, wanting to know the status of his car. "We're all anxious for you to get here," she said. "How much longer do you think you'll have to wait?"

"I don't know, but it's supposed to be done today," he assured her. "I'll call you when I'm on the road."

"Okay," she said. "The sooner the better. Christmas is no time to be stranded alone in a strange town."

Except he didn't feel stranded, and he was far from alone.

"Was that your mother?" Livi guessed as he ended the call.

He nodded.

"She's probably anxious for you to get there."

"As long as I'm there for dinner tomorrow it will be fine," he said. He could linger a little longer here. Maybe he could even come back for New Year's Eve. He'd bring a nice fat check with him when he came, promise to double what Hightower had given in the past. Then he could finally tell Livi who he really was. Money smoothed every bump in the road.

They pulled up in front of her house to see a new car parked at the curb. "Oh, my brother's here. You'll get to meet him," Livi said, excited.

Another family member to meet, another man in Livi's life who would happily beat the crap out of him if he knew Guy was the evil lord of the Hightower empire. A storm of nervousness swirled inside him, but he nodded gamely and followed her inside the house.

There in the living room, sprawled on the couch, visiting with Livi's dad, sat a fit-looking man around Guy's age, his arm casually draped around a cute brunette who was wearing an ugly Christmas sweater and a Santa hat. Guy could instantly see the resemblance between Livi and her brother. Same eyes, similar hair color, and even though the brother kept his hair short, the same curls his sister sported were present.

The woman in the Santa hat smiled at him. The brother half smiled. *Heard about you. Maybe I'll give you a chance. Not sure yet.*

Guy half smiled back and nodded a greeting. *I'm not a shit.*

"Did we miss all the action?" asked the sister-in-law.

"Afraid so," Livi said as the woman hurried over to hug her.

The brother followed and gave Livi a hug, as well. "Merry Christmas, sis." To Guy he said, "I'm David," and held out a hand.

Guy shook it, smiled and nodded. Couldn't get out the fake "I'm Joe Ford."

"This is Joe Ford," Livi said, extending the lie. "His car broke down and he's been staying with us and helping out."

"So Dad says." Brother David looked Guy up and down, assessing him. The man had only a couple of inches on Guy, but at the moment, it felt like two feet.

"I'm Terryl," said the sister-in-law, "David's wife." Unlike her husband, she looked fully prepared to become pals.

"Still waiting for your car to get fixed?" David asked Guy.

"Still waiting."

"You may be stuck here for Christmas Eve," Livi said, sounding hopeful.

Christmas Eve with the Berg family, eating ham dinner and enjoying eggnog and Christmas cookies.

Or not. Guy's cell phone popped the bubble. He saw the caller ID and answered reluctantly.

"Your car's ready," Bentley said, and hung up.

"Who was that?" Livi asked.

"The garage. My car's ready," Guy said.

Her smile faltered. "Oh. Well, that's good. It looks like you'll be able to make it to your mom's for Christmas."

"Looks like it." And yes, that was good. He wanted to see his mom. He just hated to leave Livi. Hated to leave the possibilities he'd found here in Pine River.

But he could come back. And he would, new and improved.

"I'll run you to the garage," offered Livi's brother. "My sister probably has to get working on dinner. At least I hope you're gonna," he said to her. "I'm starving."

Was that disappointment Guy saw in her eyes? Had she been hoping to drive him to the garage, hoping for more time together? It was what he'd wanted.

But he nodded and thanked David. Then he got his belongings from the guest room.

When he came back downstairs, brother David already had his coat on and was ready and waiting to escort him on his way. The rest of the family was standing in the front hallway, Terryl, the sis-in-law, and Mr. Berg both smiling at him, Livi smiling wistfully.

"Thanks for putting me up," he said to Mr. Berg, shaking his hand. Then, to Livi, "And for teaching me to like fruitcake. I hope you'll let me come back and see you again."

Her smile got brighter. "Please do."

"Okay, taxi's leaving," said her brother, and started down the front porch steps. The party was over.

"Joe," Livi called after him as he followed David down the steps.

Guy turned. There she stood, the porchlight framing her like a nimbus, Little Miss Helpful, his Christmas angel.

"If you want a quick bite to eat before you hit the road, come on back."

He could fit in dinner and get to Coeur d'Alene later that night. A win-win situation. "Thanks. I'd like that."

"So, you're from Seattle, huh?" David said as they got in his car.

Even though it was nothing special, Guy felt inferior climbing in. "Yeah."

"Family business, dad says."

"Yeah."

"Keeps you pretty busy?"

"It does."

"You one of those sixty-hours-a-week types?"

"Sometimes," Guy answered cautiously. Where were they going with this?

"Not much time for a personal life," David observed. "Guess you won't get up to Pine River much then."

"I don't know. I kind of like the town."

"Kind of like my sister, too, huh? Sounds like you two have been getting pretty friendly."

No point denying it. "I do like her. A lot. I'd like to see more of her."

"She's pretty amazing. Deserves somebody amazing, somebody who's in it for the long haul, not just a sightseer looking for a good time."

Guy frowned. "Somebody like Bentley?" Was that what he was getting at? *Stay away. My sister already has someone I know and trust.*

"Not necessarily. Bentley's okay, but Livi's looking for something more. I don't want to see her get hurt in the process." David shot him a look, his eyes suddenly like granite.

"I'm not out to hurt your sister," Guy said.

"A lot of men say shit like that."

"Some men mean it."

"I hope you do," David said, and pulled up in front of Bob's Auto Repair. "If you don't, don't bother to come back. Have a good trip."

No beating around the bush from brother David. If Livi was his sister, Guy would have felt the same.

"I'll be back," he said, and went inside the garage to rescue his car. It would be nice to have his own wheels again, no more bumming rides from protective brothers.

Morris Bentley was waiting for him at the customer service counter. Guy hadn't been expecting a welcoming smile. Bentley didn't disappoint him.

"Your ride's ready," he said, and shoved an invoice across the counter.

Guy took it and frowned. It was double what he'd expected. He cocked an eyebrow at his rival.

"I don't do the billing," Bentley snapped. "You gonna pay with cash or plastic?"

Guy could have paid with cash if he hadn't been throwing around hundreds and fifties right and left. He'd drained his reserves making sure Livi didn't see his identity so there was no help for it now. He'd have to use a credit card. He pulled out his Visa and handed it over, hoping Bentley wouldn't look at it too closely.

Bentley took it and glared at it. Then his brows pulled together. Then he looked at Guy.

Shit. "What?" Guy demanded. The best defense was a good
offense.

Bentley merely shrugged. "Nothing."

Except it was something. Morris Bentley, the ever-loyal side-
kick had to have heard about the rotten Guy Hightower who'd
failed to come through for Christmas from the Heart. *Shit. Shit,
shit, shit, shit, shit.*

Bentley rang up the sale, Guy signed the damning merchant
receipt, then took his copy along with his car keys, picked up
his overnight bag and computer, and scrammed. Once in his car,
he roared off down the road, hoping to outrun Bentley. Maybe
Livi was on the phone and Bentley wouldn't get through to her.
Maybe a customer would come in.

Or maybe the gremlins were out to get him.

So, Joe Ford was a fake. "I knew it," Morris crowed, and
reached for his cell phone.

14

"Hotness," Terryl said as she and Livi moved into the kitchen to work on Christmas Eve dinner. "Total hotness."

"Not just hot. He's smart and funny and generous," said Livi.

"Single, I assume? I mean, it would be a dirty trick if Santa dropped such a man on your doorstep and he turned out to be married."

"He's not married."

"Girlfriend?"

"No," Livi said with a grin. She put the ham in the oven to heat, and she and Terryl started scrubbing potatoes.

"Not yet, you mean," Terryl said. "I saw the way he looked at you."

The way he'd looked at her before he left, like she was something special, had warmed her through and through. She could already picture them engaged, sitting before a roaring fire and planning their wedding. Of course, that was way premature. But a girl could dream. And dreams could come true, especially this one because everything about this romantic beginning with Joe Ford felt so right.

"Is he rich?" Terryl wanted to know. "Not that it matters, but considering the fact that you run a nonprofit it would be a nice bonus."

"I'd say so. He drives an expensive foreign car and throws around fifty-and hundred-dollar bills like they're fives." *And he knows how to melt a woman with a kiss.*

"What is he, an Amazonian or Microsoft millionaire?"

"No. He's part of his family's business."

"If he's driving a fancy car the business must be doing okay. I wonder what it is. Not that it matters," Terryl added with a shrug. "Did he donate to Christmas from the Heart?"

"Oh yes, starting with the fruitcake competition. In fact, he wound up stepping in for one of our judges who got sick, which was really sweet considering the fact that he doesn't like fruitcake."

"That had to be interesting," Terryl said with a snicker.

"It's been interesting the whole time he's been here," Livi said, and put the potatoes in the oven. Including an extra one in case Joe decided to come back. "And he's been such a help."

"He sounds like a great guy. And any man who's willing to eat fruitcake for you has got to be a keeper. Pretty cool that his car just happened to break down in Pine River. Maybe this is Santa's way of making up for your losing Hightower as a donor."

"Maybe," Livi agreed. "I hope he comes back for dinner before he starts for his mom's."

"Me, too. I want to get to know this potential...donor better," Terryl added with a grin. She leaned on the counter and watched as Livi pulled out the ingredients to make red velvet cake. "So, give me deets. What was the moment when you knew he was the most amazing man ever? Well, second most amazing, right after your brother."

"I know it's going to sound silly," Livi said as she cracked eggs into the mixing bowl, "but the minute he got in my car, I almost felt this déjà vu thing, like we'd met before." *And when he kissed me.* That kiss they'd shared at the kitchen table—it had been delicious. And then, the encores.

Good grief, she was like a tween with her first crush. She focused on measuring sugar into the bowl.

"That is so romantic," Terryl said with a sigh. "So, what was it about him that attracted you in the first place? Was it his smile?"

"That certainly got my attention." Livi added the last of the ingredients and began to mix up the batter. "He was just...so nice. You know? I mean, there he was stranded and not wanting to put me to any trouble. I really had to do some fast talking to convince him to stay with us. But you know what's most important, he's generous. I think what really did it for me was when he went out and bought all those turkeys."

Terryl pulled out the cake pans. "Oh well, yeah. If a man bought me a turkey I'd be all over him."

"We couldn't buy as many this year thanks to Hightower letting us down. And Joe saw how few we had to give and went to the store and bought them out. He bought two dozen hams, too. It was so kind."

"Okay, that makes it official. He is the perfect man for you."

Livi remembered the wish she'd made when she first hung the mistletoe. Joe was everything she'd ever wanted in a man, Livi was sure. But she was half-afraid to get her hopes up. What they'd been enjoying was almost too good to be true.

"It's probably too soon to know," she said.

"I knew right away with your brother. I hope this works out for you. You deserve to be happy."

"I don't know about what I deserve," Livi said as she put the cake in the oven. "But I can tell you, right now I'm pretty happy."

The landline rang. She picked up the kitchen extension to

find Morris on the other end. "Livi, I just learned something about Joe Ford."

His tone of voice made it sound like he'd discovered Joe was a serial killer. Livi frowned. What was Morris up to now? "Morris," she began, her voice stern.

"You need to hear this. Are you sitting down?"

Who was Guy kidding? He wasn't going to outrun a phone call. And he knew as surely as he knew there was no Santa that Bentley was already on the phone with Livi, leaking his true identity. He had to go back to the house and face her, explain his changed outlook on life. But how was he going to get her to even listen to him?

He couldn't show up empty-handed. He'd dated enough women to know that was a strategic error. If you showed up empty-handed, your apology came across equally empty. He needed a peace offering, an olive branch.

He pulled into the downtown and began to cruise the slushy streets, looking for a flower shop. Flowers 4 You. It had a number of nice-looking floral arrangements in the window. *Perfect.*

Except the owner of the shop was turning the sign in the window to Closed. *No! Don't do that!*

Guy jumped out of his car and raced to the door. He could see the woman moving toward the back of the shop. He banged on the door.

She was somewhere in her fifties, pudgy with dark hair and thin lips. She turned and looked at him, the lips getting thinner.

He gesticulated wildly, begging for her to come let him in.

She shook her head, and even though he wasn't good at reading lips it wasn't hard to figure out what she was saying. "We're closed."

The store hours said ten to five. It was all of one minute after five. "Oh, come on," he groaned, and banged again. "Have a heart."

She glared.

He held out his hands, beseeching mercy.

She shook her head and turned and disappeared. What ever happened to good customer service?

"Oh yeah. Thanks. And Merry Christmas to you, too," he growled.

He got back in his car and roared off for the grocery store. They had a floral department, and they understood the importance of being open late in the afternoon on Christmas Eve.

The grocery store was busier than Santa's workshop, with people buying last-minute grocery items and salt for their driveways. The floral department was busy, too. A woman passed Guy bearing a bouquet of red roses, baby's breath and ferns. Another was making a selection from a bucket filled with red-and-white carnations. Carnations wouldn't do. Not expensive enough. Roses were nice but trite. Guy moved to where the floral arrangements sat. He saw a big, impressive one and reached for it just as an older man snagged it. Full of Christmas spirit, Guy swore under his breath.

But lo and behold. What was this? There sat a miniature red wooden sleigh with all manner of greens and red-and-white flowers sticking out of it. And a candy cane to boot. Oh yeah. Livi would love that.

Someone else thought it looked good, too—a teen boy wearing a stocking cap and a collection of zits on his nose. Guy snatched it away as the kid reached for it.

"Hey," the kid protested. "I was gonna buy that for my girl-friend."

"You gotta be fast, kid," Guy said. "Get her some carnations and chocolate."

Poor kid. He was probably hoping he'd get lucky with this cutesy little offering. Well, there was getting lucky and there was desperation. Guy was desperate.

He hurried to find the fastest checkout line. There was no

such thing. Every checker was busy and the lines stretched clear to the North Pole. Even the express lane was clogged. Guy's blood pressure was going to go through the roof.

He got in line behind an old man with a cart that was practically overflowing. Eggnog, boxed dressing, enough onions to make an entire kitchen crew cry while peeling them, spuds, lettuce, turnips and carrots, canned soups, canned green beans, some kind of rolled-up white lump of meat, whipping cream, little colored marshmallows, canned pineapple and other cans of fruit. Butter, eggs, milk. Pop, beer. Red paper plates and napkins, tinfoil. Was there any shelf in the store the old man hadn't hit? Antacid. Guy could have used some of that. His stomach was churning.

"It's a fifteen-item limit in this line," he pointed out to the old man.

The man was stooped and skinny. He had bushy eyebrows and hair growing out his ears. The wedding band on his left hand suggested that he'd been given a list and checked it twice. And the downturned mouth suggested he was in no mood to be messed with.

"Close enough," he said, daring Guy to contradict him.

"Can I at least go in front of you?" Guy asked. "I have to be somewhere." *I'm late to my execution.*

"No, you can't," the man snapped. "My wife needs this stuff for dinner."

"Oh, come on."

"Wait your turn."

The old man not only had too many items, he had coupons. The same woman who had rung up Guy's purchase only the day before was working the register. She gave Guy an apologetic look.

"Oh for crying out loud," Guy said in disgust, and shoved a twenty at the man. "Here. Take this. It's worth more than your damned coupons anyway."

The man looked ready to give him a verbal lashing until he saw the bill. "You young pups are always in such a hurry," he grumbled. But he took the money and pocketed his coupons and let the checker finish up without any more delays. Then he shuffled away.

"Sorry," Suz the checker said to Guy as she rang up his purchase. "I'm not allowed to say anything to people when they get in line with too many items. I'd get in trouble."

"It's okay," Guy said, and paid her. He was already in deep shit so, really, what was his hurry? Oh yeah, anxious to explain, anxious to try to fix this mess. To know how his story was going to end. The suspense was killing him.

Or maybe it was guilt.

"Merry Christmas," Suz said to him, handing him his receipt.

It would be anything but merry if he couldn't make things right with Livi. He wished Suz a merry Christmas and made his way back to the car.

Darkness was taking over and as he drove to Livi's house he tried rehearsing different openings. "Livi, I know what you must think of me… I know I should have told you who I was right from the start… Give me a chance to explain…"

He kept stalling out after that last opening. He had no idea how to explain.

He drove down Livi's street. Porch lights were winking on and Christmas lights coming to life. A group of people dressed in winter garb stood in front of a house singing a Christmas carol. Everything looked greeting card perfect. The churning in Guy's stomach picked up speed.

The white icicle lights were on at the Bergs' house, and so was the porch light, inviting visitors to stop by for hot cocoa and a chat. This was going to be some chat. Inside his fleece-lined leather gloves, Guy's hands were sweating as he clutched the floral arrangement. He forced himself to go onto the front porch and ring the front doorbell. He was fearless on the slopes, zipping down double black diamond trails, but he stood on Livi Berg's front porch with his mouth dry and his heart hammering.

The door yanked open so quickly and forcefully, he found himself taking a step back. There stood her brother, looking ready to pull off Guy's head and drink his blood.

"I need to see Livi," Guy said, keeping his voice even.

"She doesn't need to see you," said brother David.

He was about to close the door when Livi appeared behind him, her parka in hand. "It's okay, David," she said, and slipped past her brother onto the porch, shutting the door behind her.

The expression on her face was a hundred times worse than her brother's. She was disgusted, and Guy felt every bit of that disgust. He hadn't felt like that since he got hauled into the principal's office when he was twelve for blowing up a hair spray bottle in the girls' bathroom.

"I'm surprised you had the nerve to come back," she said. The words came out like chips of ice.

"I had to. I couldn't leave letting you think…" Here he skidded to a stop, unsure where to go next. This was already coming out badly.

"Letting me think what? That you're a stingy, sneaky fake? How dare you pretend to be a decent human being."

"I am a decent human being," he protested.

"No, you're not. You're… Guy Hightower." She spat out his name as if it were a dirty word.

Well, it wasn't. Maybe this latest generation of Hightowers weren't the most perfect men on the planet, but they weren't crooks or scoundrels, either. They were men trying to run a company under the mighty shadow of a father who had been larger than life. They were trying to keep things going and not screw up. Okay, so they made some less than stellar choices along the way. Did that make them a pack of Scrooges?

"Yeah, I'm Hightower," he said. "That means I'm responsible

for the finances of an entire company and hundreds of jobs. I do the best I can, make the best decisions I can."

"Oh really? And was the way you treated Christmas from the Heart the best decision you could make?"

"Well, excuse me for giving money to other charities. That's what really made you mad, wasn't it? You didn't rate as high and it rankled."

"No, that's not it," she shot back, her voice rising.

"Oh? Really? Then what?"

"You...deceived me."

"Well, can you blame me? If I'd told you who I really was, you'd have run me over instead of giving me a lift into town." She'd been more than willing to help a stranger. He flashed back to how she'd grilled him about his business as she drove him into town. It hadn't hurt that he was a rich stranger. "As it was, you took one look at my car and couldn't wait to help me out. Why was that, Livi?"

"You were stranded!"

"Yeah, a rich dude stranded right here in Pine River," he said. "You know, I thought when you first picked me up that you were being nice. That you were into me. Were you into me or my money, Livi? Did you really see a man stranded by the side of the road or a rich sucker to hit up?"

Her eyes flew open as if he'd just slapped her.

Okay, that was a low blow and totally unfair. Why was he turning the tables when he should be on his knees, begging her to forgive him?

"I thought I saw a knight in shining armor," she said, her voice trembling. "I thought I'd met a nice man with a good sense of humor and a generous heart, but really all I met was a fake. You lied to me, Joe. Guy. Whoever you are."

"I told you why I lied."

"Were you ever going to tell me the truth?"

He held out the floral arrangement. "Yeah. Right now. It's why I came back."

His gift didn't have the desired effect. She looked at it in disgust. "Are you trying to buy my forgiveness?"

"No. This is a peace offering." She was making this so difficult. He swore. "Come on, Livi," he urged. "We got off to a bad start months ago. I was a jerk. I admit it and I'm sorry. But I was stressed. Our company's been going through some hard times."

"A lot of people are going through hard times," she said and her gaze rested on his Maserati parked at the curb. Judging him because of his car?

"Come on. Seriously? You're going to judge my business decisions by the car I drive?"

Her only response was to lift her chin to a holier-than-thou angle.

"You know, you're not the only nonprofit out there. I'm a CFO trying to keep my company alive and well. Every decision I make is for the good of the company. And just because I drive a nice car it doesn't mean I'm made of money." Now his voice was rising.

"Poor, poverty-stricken Guy Hightower and his expensive foreign car," she mocked. "You were on your way somewhere when I first met you, weren't you? I'd better let you get going. I hope you'll forgive me if I don't invite you in for dinner after all. I'm sure you can find something to eat on your way. Oh gosh, I hope you can afford it. Times are tough."

There it was, that same adder's bite he'd seen in her email. His own chin lifted. "Nice speech. Sweet little Olivia Berg, the darling of Pine River. Until you cross her. Maybe I'm not the only fake around here."

The rosy hue disappeared from her cheeks and her face suddenly looked pale as snow. *Crap.* He was a tool.

He opened his mouth to say so, and, once more, ask to start again, to remind her of everything he'd done for Christmas from the Heart since he came to town, but she cut him off. "I'm sure your mother will love those flowers," she said, and yanked the front door back open.

"Livi, don't!" he protested as she slammed it shut.

"Come on, we're bigger than this," he pleaded, banging on the door. It didn't open.

And now here came the carolers, singing "Joy to the World."

All the joy had sure been sucked out of Guy's world.

He left the floral arrangement on the porch, then slumped to his car. He drove away, going back over every word he'd said on Livi's front porch, analyzing where he'd gone wrong, trying to figure out what it would take to climb out of the deep, dark Grinch hole he'd dug for himself.

He should turn around, go back. Pound on Livi's door until she opened it. Promise her anything. Tell her that he wanted the life she had, that he wanted her.

But he didn't have the life she had. He never would. And he sure wouldn't have her.

He called his mom. "I'm on my way."

"Good. I can hardly wait to see you."

Somebody would be glad to see him. A little way out of town he found a fast-food burger joint and pulled into the drive-through. A burger and a shake, Christmas Eve dinner of champions. Yeah, merry Christmas.

15

Livi sat at the kitchen table, crying, dinner preparation long forgotten.

Terryl sat next to her, an arm around her shoulder. "I'm sorry, Livi," she finally said.

"Don't be. I'm glad he's gone. He's a fake and a creep, and I wish I'd never met him," Livi finished on a sob.

"Do you? Really?" Terryl asked softly.

"Yes," Livi insisted. "I had this silly fantasy that I'd met a man who was everything I'd ever wanted, that maybe something could happen between us. It was all so romantic—kisses and walks in the snow and working side by side distributing turkeys and hams and Christmas stockings. And…it was like Disneyland. All pretend. Nothing was real."

"Except maybe the way you both felt."

"I could never love a man like that."

"A man who helped you do all those good things?"

"Don't you see? It was all a cover, a facade. An act. His heart wasn't really in any of it. He was just putting on a show."

Terryl sighed and moved to fill the electric teapot. "I think you need some tea."

She needed more than tea.

Her father finally braved the storm of female emotions and joined them, David at his heels. He took the chair Terryl had vacated and put an arm around her. "I'm sorry, Snowflake."

Her dad's gentle comfort really turned on the tears.

"What a gutless wonder," David said. "He should have told you who he was."

"If he had, she'd never have given him the time of day," said Dad. "I probably wouldn't have, either. But maybe the man wanted to make a new start. It looked like he was doing a pretty good job while he was here."

"Yeah, well, a man will do a lot to get into a woman's pants," David muttered.

"You are not helping," his wife scolded.

"She's better off without him," David said in his own defense.

Yes, she was. Joe Ford was a fictional creation. He'd come to town, painted a nice story and then, like Frosty the Snowman, melted away. And, unlike Frosty, he wouldn't be back again someday.

It was almost midnight when Guy's Maserati finally purred down the snowy driveway to his mom and stepdad's house on the shores of Lake Coeur d'Alene. He grabbed his overnight and computer bags and the box with the chocolate pot that had started his whole ugly Christmas adventure and went to the door.

His mom threw it open before he could even ring the doorbell. She looked like an ad for a high-end clothing magazine. Tasteful slacks and sweater, fancy scarf knotted at her neck, pearl earrings, hair carefully colored to hide the gray.

"You're here," she sang, and drew him to her for a hug. As always, she smelled like Chanel. It was her signature perfume and Dad had gotten it for her every year. Guy had ordered some and had it shipped.

Behind her stood her husband, Del, looking natty in wool slacks and a red cashmere sweater, holding a highball glass in his hand. "Glad you finally made it, Guy. How about something to chase away the cold," he offered as he and Guy shook hands.

Guy needed to chase away more than the cold. He doubted a drink would get rid of all the depressing thoughts that had been riding with him ever since he left Pine River, but he nodded, dumped his overnight bag and laptop case, and followed them into the enormous living room, carrying the family treasure he'd been commissioned to deliver under his arm.

The decorators had been busy. Fir garlands and gold ribbons hung from the stair railing leading to a second-floor landing, and a tree decorated in gold and red stood guard in the front hall. As he'd predicted, there were the greens and the Mercury glass and candles on the mantelpiece over the mammoth stone fireplace, and there stood the twelve-foot tree lighting up a far corner of the room with enough presents piled beneath it to keep an entire third-world nation busy opening them.

And there sat his stepsisters, Lizbeth and Melianna, both as skinny and fashionable as the last time he'd seen them. He had the same mixed feelings about each one.

Lizbeth had hated his mom on sight, which hadn't endeared her to Guy. She'd done everything she could to sabotage the relationship, but she'd lost that battle and consoled herself by getting drunk and making a scene at the wedding. Mom had forgiven her and they'd eventually called a truce. They didn't go shopping or do all those girl things Mom had hoped for once she had daughters, but at least Lizbeth got past making scenes. She'd made a small effort to be nice to Guy and his brothers, giving the impression that she was trying to make up for her earlier tacky behavior, and he was polite in return, but he still couldn't forgive her for not falling in love with his mom.

Unlike her older sister, Melianna could be bought, and she'd taken advantage of Mom's generosity early on. She'd made a play for Guy at the wedding and had been both shocked and insulted when he hadn't jumped at the chance to sleep with her. She still considered him a challenge and loved flirting with him whenever they met—even if she did have a man in tow. Tonight, it looked like she didn't. She was a spoiled brat but at least she was a fun-loving spoiled brat.

She slid out of her chair and flitted across the room to give him a not so sisterly hug. "Brother dear, about time you got here."

"Yeah, I'm sure you missed me," he said, disengaging himself.

"You should have flown in," Del told him.

"I would have if it wasn't for this," he said, and handed over the chocolate pot.

"Thank you, dear," gushed Mom. "We'll have to make hot chocolate for Kimmy in it tomorrow," she said as she opened the box.

"She wanted to stay up and see you," Lizbeth told Guy, "but it was getting late so I sent her to bed." Her tone of voice implied it was all Guy's fault her daughter had been banished from the party.

Just as well. Kimmy was a high-energy kid, who loved being the center of attention, and Guy wasn't sure he had the emotional energy to deal with her at the moment. She would have been all over him. He'd won her devotion when he danced with her at the wedding, swinging her around until she was helpless with giggles and she'd been his Mini-Me ever since. Yeah, he had that effect on women.

Most of them.

Mom pulled out the china pot from its nest of packing. "Great-grandma's chocolate pot," she said happily. "Limoges."

Melianna looked over Mom's shoulder. "Nice," she said. "What a cool thing to pass on to one of your daughters." Hint, hint.

Mom didn't take the hint. "It has a lot of sentimental value," she said, setting it on the coffee table. "How was your drive?" she asked Guy as she pulled out the tiny cups and saucers that went with it.

Miserable, filled with regret. "Long and boring," he lied, and accepted a drink from Del.

"We'll make sure your time here isn't boring," Melianna said with a wink.

Melianna making sure he didn't get bored. Oh joy.

Another man joined them now—Lizbeth's husband, a short, loud man addicted to working out at the gym and playing tennis. He and Guy had played once when Guy and Bryan came out for the Fourth of July. Guy had won two straight sets in a row, 6-0 and 6-1, and they'd never played again.

He gave Guy a clap on the shoulder. "Glad you could make it."

No, he wasn't. Not really. And his wife sure didn't care one way or the other. As for Melianna, she'd entertain herself flirting with him but she'd tire of that game before his visit was over. And Kimmy would adore him until it was time to open presents. Del liked him well enough and enjoyed talking business with him but was well aware of the fact that he'd come on the scene too late to be a father figure. They were friends by marriage. Sort of. Other than his mom, none of these people had cared one way or another whether Guy showed up. He was an extra body at a table that wasn't his. He sighed inwardly and prepared for a long Christmas Day.

The day started early, with Kimmy up before the birds. He heard footsteps running down the hall past his guest room at five, along with excited squealing, and figured any minute he'd be summoned downstairs to open presents. Her mom must have sent her back to bed though because there was no summons and the squeals turned to whining and then to silence.

Until six. Then the entire household gave up and got up.

"I don't know why she can't stay in bed and play with the things in her Christmas stocking," Lizbeth complained as she filled her mug of coffee to take out to the living room, where her daughter was already gleefully exclaiming over the new bike Santa had brought her.

"I never could wait," Guy said, helping himself to a pastry. He and his brothers always got up at the first hint of sunrise. "Go back to bed" were words that were never uttered on Christmas morning in their house.

"Boys are little beasts," Lizbeth said, putting him in his place. "Thank God we had a girl."

Who would hopefully not grow up to be like her mom.

Although it looked like she was going to grow up to be like her aunt. Both Melianna and little Kimmy appeared to special-ize in greed. Melianna tore through her presents almost as fast as Kimmy, who was going at it like a frenzied terrier, barely ac-knowledging one before grabbing the next and pulling off the wrapping. Hair chalk, the present Guy had shipped to her, had been a big hit, earning cries of delight and a quick hug, and he was glad Mom had given him the suggestion.

"She's going to be as vain as her aunt," Lizbeth said, rolling her eyes as Kimmy ripped open the next package.

"I'm not vain," Melianna insisted. "I'm simply honest about my assets and believe in maintaining them." She, too, was happy with the present Guy had given her. "You can never go wrong with jewelry," she said, thanking him. "Well, unless it's cheap," she added.

That necklace hadn't been.

Lizbeth's husband had gotten her jewelry, also. "Wrong color," she murmured with a toss of her well-styled golden hair. "But I'll exchange it."

"Next year I'll just give you a check," her husband grumbled.

"Good idea," she said, and kissed him on the cheek.

Guy couldn't help it. He found himself comparing his step-sisters to Olivia Berg. Would she have sneered at a diamond bracelet because it was the wrong color?

Was the Berg family awake yet? Opening presents?

"Come on, sis, quit screwing around," David called as Livi loaded pastries on her favorite holiday platter.

"Coming," she called back. She picked up the plate and her mug with her eggnog latte in it and hurried out to the living room.

Even though there were no little kids in the house, they'd all gotten up at seven, thanks to David racing up and down the hall-way, announcing it was Christmas morning and time to get up. Who needed kids when they had David, the biggest kid of all?

While Livi made coffee, he'd turned on the tree lights and found Christmas music for them to listen to. Now he sat on the couch holding his mug, with his arm around Terryl, both wear-ing matching hooded holiday footie pajamas. Dad wore the bath-robe Livi had given him the year before over his pajamas and was in his favorite chair. Livi, too, was in crazy pajamas, ones that Terryl had given her the night before, insisting she had to wear them when opening presents. All part of the holiday fun.

Livi wished she was in the mood for fun. She reminded her-self that Christmas morning was no place for unhappiness and regret. This was the season for joy and kindness and gratitude. So what if her holiday fantasy had fizzled? She still had her fam-ily and that was what counted.

"Okay, let's get to it," said David. He grabbed himself a pas-try and knelt in front of the tree, digging among the packages. "Here's one for Dad." He pulled out a flat package wrapped in silver paper and decorated with a red bow, and handed it over. "Man to man," he added.

"Thanks, son." Dad opened it to discover a framed picture that Livi had taken of them fishing at the river a few summers back. "I'll have to hang this someplace special," he said.

It was so good to see her father smiling at Christmas. It edged away a little of the sadness, and Livi couldn't help but smile, too.

"And for you from us, sis," David said, handing her a gift bag with a heft that hinted at a book inside.

Sure enough, it was a fat treasury of holiday recipes. "I love it," she said, hugging it to her.

"Terryl said you would," her brother told her. "Although I thought you could find any recipe you wanted online these days."

You could and she did. She was addicted to Pinterest and haunted foodie websites on a regular basis. "But there's something special about a cookbook."

"We expect great things of you next Christmas," Terryl said to her. "Speaking of expecting, open that one to you," she said to David.

He pulled a small box out from under the tree. "All right, a signed baseball," he joked.

"Aw, you guessed," said his wife.

He pulled off the wrapping and opened the box. His easy smile turned to wonder as he pulled out a baby rattle. "Whoa, what's this?"

"My present to you, babe. I just took the test a couple days ago. We're pregnant."

"No way. Oh, Terryl, wow."

"That's the best Christmas present ever," said Dad as David hugged her.

"It sure is," David said.

"I can hardly wait for us to tell my family later today," she said.

"I can hardly wait for us to have the kid," David said. "Man, this is the best Christmas ever."

"Congratulations, you two," Livi said, and hugged them. "What do you want, a girl or a boy?"

"A girl," said David.

"A boy," said Terryl. "Girls are a pain," she told her husband. "All that drama."

"I like drama," David assured her.

"I have to admit, little girl clothes are so cute," said Terryl.

"And if it's a girl we can bake together," put in Livi.

"And if it's a boy Dad and I can take him fishing," David said.

"Or if it's a girl," Livi corrected him.

"So, really, it doesn't matter what we have as long as the baby's healthy," said Terryl.

"And as good-looking as my wife," David said, and kissed her.

Livi raised her coffee mug in salute. "Well, then, here's to a healthy baby."

"To a healthy baby," everyone echoed.

Their family was growing, and this time next year they'd have a baby in the living room with them. It was exciting news and Livi was happy for her brother and sister-in-law.

But, she realized, she was also a little bit jealous. The best Christmas ever, her brother had said. She wished she could say the same for herself.

Okay, so not the best Christmas ever but not the worst, either. The worst had been their first one without Mom. What was losing a potential dream man compared to that?

And that whole thing with Joe… Guy…whatever, had been a silly, impractical dream. Middle-class girl on limited income meets Prince Charming in a Santa suit and lives happily ever after. Really? So silly. But she was back in the real world now, with real people. And that was where she was going to stay from now on.

The family finished opening their presents—silly holiday socks from Livi to David as well as his favorite old-fashioned hard candy, a pretty snowflake ornament for her from her father to hang on the tree, the crossword puzzle book for Dad, which he said he loved. Terryl was delighted with the scarf Livi had knit and Livi was equally delighted with the Starbucks gift card from her and David.

Then that was it. After hanging around for another couple of hours, Terryl and David packed up their things and went on to the next family gathering to share their good news.

On the way out the door, David almost tripped over something. "What the heck?"

There sat the floral arrangement Guy had showed up with the night before, mocking Livi.

"Toss that thing," David instructed her.

He didn't have to tell her. As soon as she and Dad had waved them away, she marched to the kitchen and threw it in the garbage.

She'd barely gotten rid of it when Morris called. "Do you want a ride to the hall?" His voice sounded unsure. Underlying message: *Are you speaking to me?*

Part of her wanted to stay home and feel sorry for herself, but Christmas from the Heart had a community dinner to put on. "Sure," she said, trying to inject some enthusiasm into her voice.

"Okay, I'll be there in an hour."

True to his word, he arrived right on time. He looked leery as she climbed into his truck, as if bracing for a scold.

But it wasn't his fault he'd been the bearer of bad news. How ironic that she'd been so mad at him for the way he'd treated Joe, no, Guy, when really Guy had deserved every bit of that bad treatment and then some.

"Are you doin' okay?" he asked.

"I'm fine," she said to both him and herself.

She handed over the calendar she'd gotten him and his eyes widened. "You got me something?"

"I always get you something."

"Yeah, but this year, after... I didn't think..."

"Just open it."

He did and smiled at the red Corvette on the cover. "This is awesome. I got something for you, too," he said, looking suddenly self-conscious. "I wasn't sure you'd want anything from me." He handed her an oversize card envelope.

"Oh, Morris," she said sadly. "How could you think that?"

"You were pretty pissed after the restaurant. And I deserved it," he hurried on.

Yes, he had. He'd acted stupidly.

But then, who was she to talk. She'd been pretty stupid herself.

"Open it," he urged.

She did. The card pictured a nativity scene. Printed beneath it in gold script were the words "Good news, Good cheer." She opened it and out fell a necklace with a small heart pendant and a check for fifty dollars. She picked up the check and saw it was made out to Christmas from the Heart.

"Oh, Morris," she said, tears filling her eyes.

"I didn't do that because of anything that happened," he hurried to explain. "I had it planned long before...for a while."

"Thank you," Livi said, smiling at him. "It's a wonderful present. And I love the necklace."

He nodded, satisfied with her gratitude, and put the truck in Drive. "I know I should say I'm sorry about how things turned out, Livi, but I can't. Yeah, I was jealous, but all along I thought he wasn't good enough for you. Not that I am," he hurried to add.

Morris was honest and trustworthy, which put him head and shoulders above Guy Hightower. "Don't say that, Morris. In fact, don't say anything. Let's not talk about this, okay?"

He nodded. "Okay."

They rode the rest of the way in silence, Livi brooding and Morris probably wondering when she was ever going to appreciate him.

Right now, she told herself later as he helped her and the other Christmas from the Heart volunteers serve ham and turkey, mashed potatoes and green beans to the people in the community who were in need.

Morris really was the whole package: kind, caring, responsible. Honest. She'd be a fool to look further.

"Another successful meal completed," Tillie said later as she dried her hands on a dish towel.

"Thanks for coming in early to cook," Livi said to her.

"Cooking a couple of turkeys, heating ham—nothing to it," Tillie said, waving away her thanks as if that had been all there was to it. "I guess that nice young Joe Ford had to get going to be with his family."

Livi nodded and left it at that. He'd had to get going, all right. And now he needed to stay gone.

Christmas dinner with Mom and Del and the gang featured caramelized onion tarts, standing rib roast, cider-roasted vegetables, Brussels sprouts with pecans, and yams drizzled with maple syrup. At one point Guy found himself thinking how much his mother would have liked Livi Berg. They'd have enjoyed being in the kitchen together, getting creative.

He found his mother studying him. "How is everything?" she asked.

"Delicious," he said, bringing out a smile and forking up some yams.

It was a *Bon Appétit* worthy menu; everything was washed down with the finest of wine. The table centerpiece was an elaborate display of greens and candles set in red Mercury glass that carried out the theme Mom's decorators had used throughout the house. Everything was perfect except for the fact that Guy was with the wrong people.

Kimmy had indulged in too much candy and could barely sit still in her seat. She'd begged to sit by Guy, the only one besides his mom who'd paid much attention to her, and she'd bombarded him with ceaseless chatter until her mother snapped, "Enough talk. Eat your dinner."

Kimmy got that hurt look kids wore when they'd been unjustly scolded and pushed a Brussels sprout around her plate.

"Mother of the year," murmured Melianna.

"Next year when she wakes up at five we'll send her in with you," Lizbeth threatened.

"Or you can come in with your grandpa and me," Mom said. "We'll have a no-slumber party."

Kimmy liked the sound of that and her sunny mood returned.

"Guy, I thought for sure you'd have someone with you this year," Melianna said to him. "Still can't decide what you want?" she teased. Underlying message: *You could still have me.*

Guy knew exactly what he wanted now. Too late.

"How about you?" he asked, turning the tables on her. "How many hearts have you broken since I saw you last?"

"None," she replied lightly. "At least not on purpose."

"You're both young," Mom said. "You have time to find someone special."

The hourglass had run out for Guy. He poured himself more wine.

Dessert was Mom's traditional chocolate yule log. It was spectacular. Guy ate it and thought of sugar cookies.

After dessert, the family moved into the living room for coffee and brandy and more conversation.

"I'm bored," Kimmy announced.

Del frowned. "You just got an entire pile of toys. Play with some of them."

Kimmy fell into a sulk and kicked at the box containing all manner of arts and crafts supplies.

"Here, dear," Mom said easily. "Bring over your hair chalk and let's make your hair pretty."

"So tacky," Lizbeth muttered.

No, tacky was setting aside the costly present your husband gave you without so much as a thank-you. Guy vowed to find a way to spend time with his mom alone in the future. Once again, he wondered what was going on at the Berg house. They were probably entertaining the neighbors now, not sniping over who hadn't gotten what they wanted for Christmas. Or maybe Olivia was already off, feeding the world.

Guy left the living room and wandered out to the kitchen in search of more of the holiday shortbread his mom had made for him. On the way, he stopped at the liquor cabinet in the dining room and poured himself a drink. Milk would have gone better with the cookies, but booze went better with the stepfamily.

His mom found him lounging at the kitchen table later, nursing his drink, a couple of cookies on a plate in front of him. Sounds drifted in from another part of the house—a raised male voice, a child bursting into tears.

"Are you having fun yet?" she teased.

"Oh yeah, tons." He shook his head. "How do you stand these people, Mom?"

"Easy. I do it for Del's sake. I'm afraid his wife spoiled the girls and he wasn't around much when they were little, so now he spoils them, too. But really, we don't see that much of them. A couple of days at Christmas, a week during the summer. I can live with that."

"Are you happy?"

She shrugged. "As happy as someone can be who lost the love of her life. Del's a good man," she hurried to add.

"Yeah, he is," Guy acknowledged, and downed the last of his drink.

"Speaking of happy, what's wrong?"

"Nothing."

"Guy Jamison Hightower, don't lie to me. I can always tell when something's bothering you."

He shrugged. "Just life, I guess."

"The business?"

He shrugged again. That was as good a reason to not be happy as any.

She studied him. "Did something happen in Pine River I don't know about?"

A lot had happened in Pine River she didn't know about. "I met someone."

"And?" she prompted.

"And it's not going to work out."

"Why on earth not? Why wouldn't any woman in her mind want my wonderful son?"

"Because he's not that wonderful."

"Nonsense," she said crisply. "Now, tell me about this someone."

He did. He spilled the whole ugly tale, ending with his and Livi's parting words on her front porch.

"You should have been up front from the beginning," Mom said, telling him what he already knew.

"Yeah, I should have. But she was so nice and so happy to give me a lift into town. And then, the more time I spent with her the harder it got. I wanted to say something, wanted to explain why we didn't give to Christmas from the Heart this year."

"And why didn't we?"

"Because we didn't have as much to give and went with other nonprofits. What's so wrong with that?" Nope, not defensive. Not him.

"Nothing, if your motives were pure. Who were you trying to help the most, those nonprofits or Hightower's public image?"

"Both," he said.

She didn't say anything, just cocked her head and studied him.

"Why does everyone have to make business owners out to be shits?" he demanded in exasperation. "I'd like to see Olivia Berg step in and run the finances of a company. Then maybe she'd see the big picture."

"She is running a company," his mother pointed out. "And maybe she saw more than made you comfortable."

"Thanks, Mom. You're really helping," he said bitterly.

She laid a hand over his. "You know I think you're wonderful. But, like all of us, you're not perfect."

"I never said I was."

He didn't claim to be a saint. He sure hadn't made any such claim to Livi. He'd only claimed not to be a shit.

"But you do tend to get your back up when criticized. Do you think you might have gotten a little defensive when you two had that last conversation?"

Conversation? It had been an argument, and a heated one at that.

"You're right," he said, and pushed away his glass. That so-called apology on Livi's porch had been a disaster.

"No one likes humble pie, but a wise man knows when to eat it," his mother said gently.

Too late for that. He'd already consumed a double helping of high horse.

"This woman sounds special, worth getting to know better."

"That won't be happening now," Guy muttered. He shook his head. "I really blew it."

"People do change their minds, Guy. When there's a reason to. Sounds to me like you have to give her a reason."

Easier said than done, but he nodded.

"You'll find a way to work things out," she said, giving his arm one final pat. "Now, come on out in the living room and be sociable. We're going to play Christmas twenty questions with Kimmy."

Twenty questions, great. Animal, mineral or vegetable. He knew what he was: mineral, a walking lump of coal. And nobody ever wanted a lump of coal in her stocking.

He did his best to be sociable but the evening stretched on forever. First thing the next morning he was ready to leave.

"I hate to see you go so soon," his mom said when he told her. "You just got here." Once more, it was only the two of them at the kitchen table.

"I can't take any more," he said, and took a final swig from his coffee mug. "I'll come back when it's just you and Del."

She nodded her understanding. "I don't blame you. You didn't marry them. I did. And that's how it goes when you say yes to someone. You say yes to all the people who come with that person."

Guy thought of all the people who came with Livi. He'd happily say yes to all of them. Well, all except Bentley.

The rest of the household was still asleep when he slipped down the stairs with his duffel bag and computer, even little Kimmy, who'd finally gotten worn-out from her holiday high. His mom was waiting at the front door with a thermos of coffee to keep him going, and something else, as well.

"You have some repair work ahead of you. Maybe this will help," she said, and gave him a check for five thousand dollars made out to Christmas from the Heart. "But when you go back to that girl, make sure you bring her more than a check."

He wasn't going to go back. She wouldn't want to see him. She would be happy to see the check, though. He'd mail it as soon as he got home.

And wish he had the guts to take a chance on delivering it in person.

Really, though, what good would it do? Money could buy a lot of things. But respect wasn't one of them.

16

Livi took down all the inside Christmas decorations the day after Christmas. It was what her mother had always done. "They're never as much fun after the holiday celebrating is done," Mom used to say. "They're like guests who nobody told the party's over."

Livi agreed. It always seemed to her that the tree never knew what to do without presents under it, as if it had lost its purpose. All that festive gaudiness had seemed to mock her anyway. Especially the mistletoe. She threw that in the garbage.

It seemed almost wrong to throw away a Christmas decoration, but this one was something she'd purchased back when she was young and silly. It had no sentimental value and the memories attached to it hurt her heart.

The rest of the holiday treasures she packed up with loving care. "Until next year," she said, as she stuffed the last one in its box.

What did the new year hold? A new baby in the family, that was for sure. And maybe a new beginning for her, too.

"Have you heard from Joe yet?" Bettina asked when they were in the office a couple of days later.

Livi shook her head. "There is no Joe."

"What? I don't understand."

"That man we all thought was so nice? His name isn't Joe Ford. It's Guy Hightower."

"Guy Hightower," Bettina stuttered, and stared at her. "That nice man was Guy Hightower?"

"That man pretending to be nice was Guy Hightower," Livi corrected her.

"I don't believe it."

"Believe what?" asked Kate, walking into the office.

"We've been had," Bettina informed her, and shared the shocking news.

"OMG," said Kate. "That is just too weird. Of all the people in all the world…"

Livi scowled at her. "Don't go quoting old movie lines to me."

"Sorry," Kate muttered. "I just can't believe it. And he seemed like such a great guy, er, man. Talk about a holiday Jekyll and Hyde."

"He's worse. Hyde experimented on himself and took something that made him evil. Guy didn't have to take anything."

"No, and he still managed to be good while he was here," Bettina argued. "For such a Scrooge, he sure did a lot of nice things."

"Only because he didn't want to be found out," Livi insisted.

"Maybe he wanted to make a good impression on you," said Bettina. "Maybe he wanted to change."

"Or maybe he just wanted to get laid." Kate shook her head. "Men are such farts. Well, except for yours and mine," she said to Bettina.

"And Morris," said Bettina, looking to Livi. "At least you know where you stand with him."

"Are you arguing for Morris?" Kate demanded. "After what a jerk he was that night at Family Tree?"

"Cut him some slack," Bettina said. "He's a nice man. And there's nothing he wouldn't do for you, Livi. He's got a good heart and he's loyal."

"So's a dog, for heaven's sake," said Kate. "Were you not present when we were talking about the perfect man for Livi?"

"I thought I'd found one," Livi said, "and look what I got."

Kate settled in front of the computer where she worked on the books. "You don't want to settle."

"Well, she doesn't want to go through life alone, either," Bettina argued.

No, she didn't.

"But Kate's right," Bettina said. "You shouldn't settle. Love's too important and life's too short."

It seemed everywhere Livi went people wanted to talk about Joe Ford. Suz at the grocery store said, "Hey, your friend was in here on Christmas Eve."

"Oh?" *Which friend?*

"He bought an awful pretty floral arrangement for someone," Suz said with a sly grin.

"It must have been for someone else," Livi said shortly.

Suz blinked in surprise. "Oh. Well, uh, whoever he got them for, it sure was nice."

Yeah, nice. There was nothing nice about Guy Hightower. He only pretended to be nice.

Still, no one had twisted his arm to buy all those extra turkeys and hams. Was he a holiday Jekyll and Hyde, the corporate Guy ready to act one way while Joe, his nobler version, kept trying to be generous? She had his email. She could ask.

He had hers. He could grovel.

Morris called just as she was depositing her groceries in the car trunk. "Want to grab a burger and see a movie? That new musical's playing at Pine Cinema."

Morris was not crazy about musicals. It spoke—or rather sang—volumes that he was willing to sit through one with her.

"Sure," she said. She certainly wasn't going to mope around over someone who'd come into her life for such a short time. "That sounds fun."

And it would be. She and Morris always had fun together.

They didn't go to Family Tree, which had the best burgers in town. Instead they wound up at a popular chain. After the scene Morris had created in Family Tree she couldn't blame him for not being in a hurry to venture back yet.

How had he known Guy wasn't who he said he was? And what had been wrong with her woman's intuition that she hadn't sensed something was off? Did she have a faulty intuition?

They finished their burgers and were dredging the last of their fries through ketchup when he brought up the subject they'd been avoiding. "Liv, I'm sorry about Hightower. Are you okay?"

She focused on a french fry. Was she? "I'm still mad. I feel like an idiot." And she was disappointed. It didn't seem right to share that with Morris.

"He was smooth." Morris shoved away the last of his fries, a very un-Morris thing to do. "Look, I know I'm not rich. I can't compete with someone like that."

"You don't have to. You're honest. And kind."

"I acted like an ass." He made a face. "But damn it all, Liv, I was so jealous. Look, I can't give you a mansion in Seattle."

"I don't need a mansion in Seattle," she said firmly.

"I can't give you a ton of money and trips around the world."

"Travel is overrated."

"It is. You know what they say, Liv, there's no place like home."

Of course, he was right.

"I'll be there for you whenever you need me. We could have a good life."

Here was where she should say, "Let's do it then. Let's start planning a future together."

He rushed on before she could speak. "I just want you to think about it. Okay?"

She nodded. "Okay." Then added, "I don't know what my problem was, Morris."

"Me, either," he said with a half smile. "Are you over it?"

"I'm working on it."

The half smile turned into a whole one. "Hey, maybe there really is a Santa," he joked.

Later that night, after he'd walked her to her door, she let him kiss her. And she kissed him back, really putting herself into it. This wasn't so bad. She could get used to this. And she and Morris could be happy together. Morris would never lie to her or break her heart. He may not have been as smooth and charming as *some* men, but charm was deceitful. He also didn't come with any fancy trappings, but fancy trappings were overrated. Very overrated.

Guy Hightower had turned her head, but thank God she had it on straight again.

"How was the fam-damnly?" Mike asked Guy as the three brothers settled around the conference table with their morning coffee. Neither brother knew about Guy having been stranded in a small town in the shadow of the Cascades and he wasn't about to share his experience with them. They'd be bound to mock his attacks of altruism, writing them off as a case of a man trying to get a woman into bed.

"The same as always," he said. "It's somebody else's turn to do Christmas with the steps next year," he added, putting them on notice.

"Oh yeah, sign me up," said Mike.

"Now that you're about to be single, Melianna will be more than happy to see you," Guy teased.

"Like I said," Mike retorted. "So, how's Mom?"

"She's good."

"I'm glad somebody's good," Bryan said with a scowl. "Gina wants a divorce. Counseling didn't work. She says I'm not making her a priority."

"Saw that coming," muttered big brother Mike.

"She's gonna take me to the cleaners," Bryan predicted miserably.

"Of course she is," Mike said. "Women are not worth it. They steal your money and eat your soul."

Was that what had happened to Guy in Pine River? He'd felt like crap ever since he got home. Had Livi Berg eaten his soul?

No. First he had to have a soul to eat. The only problem with Livi, not to mention his brothers' wives, was that they wanted more from their men than success.

Guy went through the motions during the meeting, went through the motions at his desk, went through the motions the rest of the week, running on autopilot. Was this what he wanted the rest of his life to look like?

Every night he came home and saw the check from his mom sitting on his bedroom dresser. He'd planned to send it off right away. Then he'd hesitated, trying to think of some grand gesture he could couple it with. No grand gesture had come to mind. The year was almost at a close and he was miserable. What to do? What to do?

Go out on New Year's Eve with a couple of pals he sometimes went snowboarding with. Drinks, pretty girls, dancing.
Boring.

"So, who's making a new year's resolution?" asked Jessica, his date.

"Not me," said one of his pals. "Too much work."

"I am," said one of the women.

To be more organized? To get fit? Give more to charity? *I can recommend a nonprofit.*

"I'm going to lose ten pounds," she announced.

She didn't look like she could spare ten pounds. Guy said as much.

"You haven't seen me naked," she replied, and giggled.

He didn't think he wanted to.

"I've got a resolution," said his date. "I'm going to ask for a raise. No way am I getting paid what I'm worth."

Neither was Olivia Berg. What was she doing tonight, and who was she doing it with? As if he couldn't guess.

Livi and Morris were at Family Tree, ringing in the new year with Kate and Tom and Bettina and Danny, who were trusting their baby—barely—to the care of Danny's sister, who had two kids of her own. Morris had survived some light razzing when they came in, a sure sign that his earlier brawling was forgiven. Livi was dressed up in a clingy black dress she'd ordered online and a vintage silver sequined jacket that had been her mom's and wearing the requisite New Year's Eve party hat. After dinner, they'd move into the lounge and dance in the new year.

They sat squeezed into a booth, Morris's arm draped possessively over her. She smiled and he beamed. They looked like the perfect couple.

"This is the best way to ring in the new year, with friends," Livi said. Unbidden, the memory of sitting at that very table with Joe, no, Guy the deceiver, came to mind. She'd liked him so much when he was Joe.

Who was she kidding? It had been more than like. Much more. It had been love, budding and waiting to bloom.

The bloom is dead. Forget it.

Good advice. She needed to listen to herself. In only a few hours it would be a new year and she wasn't going to waste so much as one minute on thinking about Joe. No, Guy. Mr. Two

Face. She'd gotten carried away with silly fantasies. She was done with that now, over her Belle complex. There was nothing at all wrong with her provincial life. It was a nice life with good people in it. And a good man who was crazy about her.

People said you could always tell what kind of a husband a man would make by watching how he treated his mother. Morris was definitely husband material. He was a great son, always doing handyman chores for his mom and taking her to church every Sunday. Who knew how Joe/Guy Two Face treated his mom? He probably lied to her all the time.

"It's going to be a great year," Kate predicted, grinning at her fiancé.

"It sure is," Tom said, and they kissed.

"Yep," agreed Morris, and gave Livi a one-armed hug.

Of course, he, too, expected a kiss and Livi obliged. Yes, indeed. It was going to be a great year.

After dinner they all moved to the lounge, where the band was tuning up. They grabbed a table and ordered drinks, confetti cocktails for the girls—champagne served in glasses rimmed with Pop Rocks candy—beer and Scotch for the men.

As soon as the music started, they all got up to dance, and Livi was the first one on the dance floor. She was having fun. Yes, she was!

Until the band slowed the music down and started singing the Great Lake Swimmers song, "Gonna Make it Through This Year." What a downer song. Whose idea had it been to play this?

Morris was perfectly happy slow dancing to it. Livi pretended to be, but after the song she headed for their table and her drink. Confetti cocktails. Party on.

It was the night for songs about the new year. The band dug one out she'd never heard before, assuring her that "this will be our year."

"I want it to be," Morris said as he moved her around the floor.

New year, new beginning. She was ready now. Morris had waited long enough for her. And she'd waited long enough for love.

"Morris, you're the best," she said. And she meant it. She'd never find a man who was a better fit for her than him.

Once she thought she had. But she'd been wrong.

They danced on and laughed and drank and ate bar munchies. And then the countdown to the new year began.

"Ten, nine, eight…" everyone chanted.

Almost there. A new year, a new beginning.

"Seven, six, five…!" Out with the old, in with the new.

"Four, three, two…" Livi chanted along with everyone else. "One. Happy New Year!" Morris pulled her into his arms and they kissed. She was enjoying those kisses more and more. They'd make this work and they'd be happy. Very happy.

As for Guy Hightower, well, Livi pitied whoever he was with.

Happy New Year

17

A snowy January hurried by, full of cross-country skiing and cozy nights watching movies with Morris along with Sunday dinners either at home with her dad or out with his mom. It was a quiet life, the kind of life everyone settled into sooner or later.

Livi kept busy. And she stopped watching episodes of *House Hunters International* online. Really, she had better things to do with her time.

Like sending out thank-you notes to their Christmas from the Heart donors. She labored long and hard over the one to Guy Hightower. Ugh. What to say? Thanks for lying to me? For making a fool of me? Thanks for breaking my heart?

Except that had been a two-person project. She'd put her stupid heart out there to get broken.

She settled for pretending he was simply another donor and kept her handwritten note on a professional yet properly grateful level.

Dear Mr. Hightower, on behalf of Christmas from the Heart I'd like to thank you for your donation this past year. Please know that it made a difference in many lives.

She signed it with *sincerely*. There. Done.

Come February it was time to think about Valentines and love. She baked Morris's favorite sugar cookies for the big day, cut out in the shape of hearts and frosted with pink frosting and he made reservations for them at Family Tree. She was surprised to learn that he'd invited Kate and Bettina and their men along.

"Thought you might want to make it a party," he said.

A party. On Valentine's Day? At the same restaurant they'd been to a million times. Actually, if he'd asked her she'd have said she would have loved to have gone someplace special, maybe over to Schwangau, the fancy restaurant in the nearby Bavarian town of Icicle Falls. But oh well.

The restaurant was running a surf and turf special. That explained it, thought Livi.

"No offense or anything," Kate said to her, "but I hadn't planned on spending Valentine's Day with you. I thought it would just be Tom and me and he'd be taking me into Seattle or at least as far as Everett. Someplace special."

"You should insist," Livi said.

"I did. He told me he's got something special planned for the next night. So what do you think the guys are up to?"

"Who knows? At least they're up to something."

And so what if she wasn't going to be at a fancy restaurant? Who cared if Morris hadn't planned anything glamorous and exotic? She hadn't exactly made big plans for him, either. All she'd done was bake him cookies.

At least he was doing something and that was what counted. It wasn't about where you went but about who you were with.

Livi decided to make the night special with her red dress and red heels. And red lipstick—Red Razzle, brand-new from the drugstore's cosmetics section. And perfume.

"Wow, you look great," Morris said when she opened the door.

So did he. Morris, who only dressed up for funerals and weddings, was in his suit. And he had a bouquet of red carnations for her.

"You look pretty special yourself," she said, taking the flowers. "Let me put them in a vase before we go. Your present's in the living room."

"Awesome," he said with a grin. "I hope it's what I think it is."

"Try to act surprised."

She came back out into the living room to find he'd already opened the box of cookies and was sampling one. "I love your cookies, Liv. These are the best. You made these just for me?"

"I did."

"Thanks," he said, and beamed as if she'd given him a new truck.

And there, she thought, was the difference between men and women. Women liked candlelight dinners and flowers, bling and trips to romantic locales. Men were happy with cookies.

Okay, not all men. Some men drove fancy cars and took ski trips to Vail.

Never mind some men, she told herself firmly. They're shallow and selfish and they don't matter.

The men who stuck with you through thick and thin, who really, truly gave of themselves, and who were honest, those were the men who mattered.

Out the door they went and off to the restaurant. It had been hung with shiny red and pink valentines and silver tinsel and, like Livi, their hostess was wearing a red dress.

"Happy Valentine's Day," she greeted them.

"Happy Valentine's Day," Livi murmured in return. She was so lucky to have someone special to go out with.

The rest of the gang was already at the table and had started on a bottle of champagne.

"Thanks, Morris," Danny said, raising his glass to Morris.

"Champagne. You went all out," Livi said to him.

"Of course. It's Valentine's Day," he said.

They settled in at the table, good friends, solid, happy couples, all celebrating love. The perfect way to keep Livi's new and improved new year going. Surf and turf for one and all.

"Who's for dessert?" asked Coral, their waitress, after she'd cleared their plates.

"I'm stuffed," Livi said. Steak and lobster, a baked potato and salad—Livi was going to explode.

"Live it up," Morris encouraged her. "Order the cheesecake. You know you want to."

Livi loved cheesecake. Still, she didn't want to overindulge. And this meal was costing Morris a fortune.

"I'll help you eat it," he said.

That decided it. "Okay. Why not?"

"Yes, why not?" agreed Kate. "I'll take the brownie sundae. And no, you can't help me eat it," she said to Tom.

Bettina and Danny opted for pie and that rounded out the order.

"I think this would be a good time to do the group trip to the bathroom," said Kate.

"Good idea," said Bettina. "Pregnancy killed my bladder."

"I'll join you," Livi said, and they left the men to enjoy their coffee and talk sports.

"You and Morris look pretty happy," Kate said a few minutes later as the three women stood in front of the mirror, freshening up.

"We are," Livi said.

Kate's easy expression was replaced by one of concern. "Are you really, Livi?"

"Of course I am," Livi insisted. "I've finally realized what a treasure he is."

"Yes, but is he your treasure?" Kate persisted. She frowned at their reflections. So did Bettina.

"What?" Livi said defensively.

"We want you to be really happy," Bettina said.

"I am. I'm getting on with my life and that feels good." She was aware of the look her two friends exchanged. "I love Morris," she insisted.

"I know," Kate said. "But there's love and then there's love."

"And there's smart and there's stupid. I'm done being stupid," Livi said.

"It's not stupid to refuse to settle," Kate told her.

"I'm not settling. I'm being practical. I'm tired of waiting." Tired of waiting for a certain two-faced man to contact her. He wasn't going to. And she didn't want him to.

But maybe he was afraid to. Maybe he was just waiting for her to email him and ask for a donation in the new year. She could write a simple business email. She needed donations for Christmas from the Heart. She'd only be doing her job.

The idea of contacting Guy Hightower made her feel almost ill. After everything she'd said to him... No, she couldn't do it. She'd have to find new donors somewhere.

The women returned to the table to find their waitress had delivered everyone's desserts but Livi's.

"That's weird," Bettina said. "Coral never messes up an order."

"She didn't this time, either," Morris said.

Sure enough, there she came, bearing Livi's dessert. Cheesecake with raspberry sauce swirled over it.

And something glinting from on top of it. "Looks like we're gonna have another scene here in the restaurant," she joked as she set it down in front of Livi.

Livi stared at it, her stomach doing somersaults. If she took that ring, she swung the gate open and walked into the next phase of her life. With a very good man.

"What do you say, Livi?" Morris asked. He was looking at her with such hope in his eyes. If he hadn't spoken she'd have sworn he was holding his breath.

It seemed like everyone at the table was holding their breath. Even Livi. This was it. Now or never. Choose to get on with your life or hang in limbo. The diamond in the ring winked at her.

"I know it's kind of soon after...uh, that is..."

An image of Guy Hightower floated into her mind like one of Scrooge's Christmas ghosts. The Ghost of Christmas Past.

"But I'm here for you."

And Guy Hightower wasn't.

"I love you," Morris finished.

That decided it. The ghost from Christmas Past hadn't said he loved her, hadn't made an appearance since their fight on her front porch. She could hang in limbo forever like Miss Havisham in Dickens's famous novel, surrounded by cobweb-shrouded mistletoe, or she could get on with her life. She chose to get on with her life.

"I say yes," she said, and slipped her arms around Morris's neck and kissed him.

"She said yes!" Coral announced, and everyone at the neighboring tables applauded.

Yep, she'd made the right decision. No doubt about it.

By Valentine's Day Guy had seen all the heart-shaped candy boxes he could stand. He'd worked ten hours and was craving steak, but a restaurant was definitely out of the question. He never liked to eat in a restaurant alone anyway. So he was picking up something at the grocery store. He knew if he went in there to snag a top sirloin that those stupid candy boxes would be everywhere, mocking him.

Just like that check his mom had given him. He should pop the thing in the mail and be done with it, maybe even include a handwritten note saying how sorry he was for everything he'd said and done. For being himself.

She'd written him. A stilted thank you that had been anything but from the heart. That had been the final nail in the coffin.

Even though the check was for no small amount, it didn't seem like a big enough gesture. As for writing her, *I'm sorry* really wasn't enough. He'd tried that and look where it had gotten him.

Of course, apologies mixed with defensiveness and angry words weren't really apologies. He'd blown it, pure and simple.

He went straight home, called out for pizza delivery and grabbed a beer from the fridge. In a perfect world he'd have been up in Pine River, taking Livi to dinner. No, not dinner in Pine River. He'd have had her here in Seattle with him, and they'd have been eating at the Space Needle.

He needed a plan. *Come on, Cupid, you little shit. Help me think of something.*

The diamond in the ring was a modest stone, nothing pretentious. And that was fine with Livi. She didn't need wealth and pretension.

She pulled the ring out of the cheesecake, wiped it off with her napkin and slipped it on her finger. A perfect fit. See?

She held out her hand and admired her new acquisition. That was preferable to looking at her friends' faces. Oh, she knew they were smiling, but she also knew they were concerned that she was making a misstep. She'd surely see it in their eyes.

"It's not much," Morris said, obviously worried.

"It's beautiful and I love it," she told him.

"And I love you, Liv. We're gonna have a good life together. You wait and see."

He'd said that so many times now that she simply had to believe him. "We're already having a good life together," she told him.

"Bathroom break," Kate said in commanding tones.

"Yes," said Bettina, scooting out of the booth.

"You guys just went," said Tom, perplexed.

"So we're going again," Kate said. "Come on, Livi."

"You guys go. I'm fine," Livi said, knowing full well what was coming.

"Oh no. You need more lipstick," Kate said, tugging on her arm.

It would be childish to resist and make a scene. It hadn't been that long since her party had made a scene in the restaurant and they didn't need to provide the night's entertainment for the other diners again so soon. She gave up and followed her friends to the women's room.

They were barely through the door before Kate demanded, "What are you thinking? I don't care if Morris did put you on the spot by getting us all here for this. You don't have to say yes just because he asked."

"She's right," said Bettina. "It's only been a couple of months since... I mean you're not really over..."

Livi held up a hand to shut them up. "I certainly am, so don't even mention his name. This is a new year and my new life and I'm getting married and that's that."

"Liv, are you sure?" Bettina asked. "Morris is a good guy, but are you sure?"

"Of course I'm sure. Otherwise I wouldn't have said yes."

"You said yes because you're not thinking clearly," Kate insisted.

"I am thinking clearly, and I want to get married," Livi said with a scowl. "To Morris," she quickly added.

Kate gave up. "Okay. It's your funeral."

"No, it's my wedding," Livi snapped. And she and Morris were going to be very happy together. Very happy!

And to prove it, she danced until she was a sweaty mess, drank too much champagne and hung all over him like a girl with her first boyfriend. Ha! Funny, considering the fact that he had been her first boyfriend way back when she'd been a girl. So there you had it. She'd come full circle, back together with her high school sweetheart.

The night flew by. Yes, time really did fly when you were having fun. And drinking too much.

"You made my life," Morris said as they stood on her front porch.

Making someone's life, that was a big responsibility. For a moment Livi's smile faltered.

But then Morris wrapped his big, strong arms around her and kissed her again and bolstered that smile back up.

"See you tomorrow," he said. "I'm gonna come over and watch the basketball game with your dad."

The guys would watch the game on TV and Livi would make chili and cheese bread. While they watched the game, she'd hang out on the couch and finish her book or check out stuff on Pinterest. Either way, it would be a nice day. Her dad would be glad to see her happy. He'd always liked Morris.

He was already in bed when she entered the house. She half wished he was awake so she could show off her ring and hear him say how happy he was for her, what a great guy Morris was and what a good decision she'd made in accepting him.

She reminded herself that she didn't need her father to tell her she'd made a smart decision. She already knew she had.

He was at the kitchen table when she came down the next morning, reading the paper and drinking his morning coffee. "Did you have fun last night?" he greeted her.

"I did." She sat down opposite him and held out her hand to show off the ring.

Her father's brows knit as he stared at it. "Well, this doesn't surprise me. But are you sure, Snowflake?"

Of course she was sure. "Yes. Why shouldn't I be?"

"It seems a little soon after..." He cleared his throat. "I hate to see you rush into something."

"Dad, Morris and I have known each other for years."

"I know. Marriage is a big commitment and I want you to be sure. I don't want to see you make a mistake."

The mistake would be to keep moping around over someone not worth moping over. "I'm not."

"Well, then, I'm happy for you. Morris is a decent man."

Yes, he was.

Later that morning, while the men watched the ball game, she slipped into the kitchen and called her sister-in-law to share the news that she was engaged.

"Wow! Did Guy come back?"

"Guy? No. I'm engaged to Morris."

"Oh."

"Your enthusiasm is underwhelming," Livi said.

"Sorry. It's just that I didn't think you felt that way about him."

"I was wrong. I do."

"Livi, are you sure? I want you to be ecstatically happy."

"I am," Livi assured her. "I'm really excited." Yes, she was. Well, as excited as a woman who was marrying a man she'd known for years could be.

"Because you don't have to rush into anything, you know."

"Who's rushing? It's past time," Livi said.

"Okay, so give me deets. When did it happen and how?"

"Just last night. He had the waitress stick the ring in my cheesecake." Maybe not the most original idea in the world, but it had been cute.

"Good thing you didn't swallow it," Terryl joked. "I always wonder with those kinds of proposals how it is the woman doesn't crack a tooth or choke to death. So, have you set a date?"

"Not yet."

"Well, let me know when you do. Just don't set it in August. I'm pretty sure we'll be busy having a kid then."

"I'll make sure we work around the baby," Livi promised.

"Get married, then hurry up and get pregnant so our kids can play together," Terryl said.

Marriage, kids—it was all going to be so perfect.

And she and Morris were already comfortable together, already like an old married couple, she thought later as he and her father watched the game and devoured salsa and chips while she surfed the internet. Yep, a nice homey life. Perfect.

Of course, Morris stayed all day. They ate chili with her father, they watched a movie on TV in the evening. And, after her father went to bed, they went at it on the living room couch. She put a halt to things before they could start shedding clothes.

"Not here in the living room with my dad right upstairs," she scolded. "Anyway, I want to wait until our wedding night."

He heaved a sigh. "Jeez, Liv, I've been waiting for years."

"So a little longer won't hurt."

He frowned. "Okay, then let's set a date right now. What about next month?"

"Morris, I can't plan a wedding that fast."

He looked disappointed. "Oh. Okay, then, spring."

"That's still too soon."

"Summer."

"David and Terryl are having a baby in the summer."

"They're not taking all summer to have it," Morris said. "How about June?"

"The weather's so iffy in June. Christmas might be nice," she mused.

"Christmas! That's almost a year away. You're killin' me here, Liv."

"Okay, not Christmas. Anyway, we'd be too busy with Christmas from the Heart. How about September? Our weather's always nice then. We can have fall colors."

"I don't care if we have polka dots. I just want you to pick a date."

"Okay, September," she said. "The weekend after Labor Day."

"Weekend after Labor Day," he repeated, happy she'd made a decision. "I hate to wait that long but if that's how long you need, I will. Man, this is gonna be great," he said, and kissed her.

Yes, it was, and she could hardly wait to start planning her wedding.

She walked him to the door and sent him off with one last kiss, then went upstairs to bed. She snuggled under the covers and let her thoughts spin in whatever happy direction they chose. Location. Well, the wedding at church for sure. They could have the reception at the community hall. Or maybe they could have a destination wedding. Hawaii. What would Morris think of that? He wasn't big into traveling, but who didn't like Hawaii? No, they'd better stick to the hall so everyone on the guest list could afford to come. They could fix it up cute. And there was plenty of room there. Cake. They had to have a traditional cake. But maybe a cookie bar, too. What could her colors be? She preferred spring colors to fall, but oh well. White roses were available any time of year. And her bridesmaids didn't have to dress in fall colors. They could wear any color they wanted. It was going to be a beautiful wedding. Beautiful...

Her eyes drifted shut and the dream began. There she was in her wedding dress, ready to walk down the aisle. But she wasn't in church. She was in some small wedding chapel in Vegas. Bettina had already gone down the aisle and so had Terryl, and Kate was making her way down.

"All right," said the wedding planner, who was dressed like a showgirl, complete with a fancy headdress. "It's your turn now."

"I'm so happy," Livi said, and sneezed.

"I think you're allergic to chrysanthemums," said the wedding planner.

"I hate mums," she said. "Why am I carrying these?"

"Because you're having a fall wedding and these are what your groom wanted. Go on, now, get down there. We've got another wedding here in half an hour."

And so down she went. Morris stood at the altar waiting for her with Tom and Danny and Livi's brother, David, standing next to him. And there was the minister, an Elvis impersonator. "Love me tender," he crooned as she made her way toward her groom.

"Look how pretty she is," someone whispered. That was when Livi realized that all the guests weren't people—they were giant frozen turkeys wearing dresses and black tuxedos. "Wouldn't Guy love this?" one of them whispered.

"Yeah," his turkey friend whispered back. "But she was smart to dump him. I don't care how many of us he bought. He just wanted to get in her pants."

On the other side of the aisle another turkey asked his companion, "Where are they spending their honeymoon?"

"Paris Las Vegas, of course. She always wanted to see the Eiffel Tower."

Livi whirled around and yelled, "You turkeys shut up!"

She blinked awake with a start, then scowled. What was that about?

Her subconscious, needling her, of course. Maybe her subconscious hadn't noticed that she'd heard nothing from Guy Hightower since his ignoble departure from Pine River. Christmas past. She had her future to think about.

"Thanks, Jack," Guy said as he slipped his Visa card into the leather sleeve sitting on the table next to him at Cutters. "Glad you could work this into your schedule."

The view and the food, not to mention the price, which proclaimed, "You're worth spending money on," made it the perfect restaurant for business lunches. Not that this lunch with the owner of a high-end clothing chain had anything to do with

Hightower business. It was about the business of life, and it was one of many Guy had scheduled over the last couple of weeks.

The other man smiled. "This is the most expensive free lunch I've had in a while."

"Yeah, but it'll get you off Santa's naughty list," Guy teased. Maybe if he hosted enough of these lunches it would get him off, too.

He left the restaurant and walked back to the Hightower building. The rest of his schedule bulged with phone conferences and meetings, the most difficult one looming at the end of the day. He kept everything compartmentalized, though, maintaining his focus.

Finally his last spreadsheet was in order, his report finished. He left his office and walked down the hall to Mike's office, where he and Bryan were waiting. They weren't going to like this.

Tillie and her daughters, who had been informed of Joe Ford's perfidy, were happy to offer Livi congratulations on her engagement when she popped in to purchase some of Tillie's fancy chocolate strawberry tea.

"Sometimes the best man is right there under your nose all along," Tillie said.

She was right.

"He's a good guy," said Jean.

Yes, he was.

"I'm so excited for you," Carol Klaussen said when Livi stopped by the bakery on her lunch break to check out cakes. "When are you getting married?"

"The weekend after Labor Day," said Livi.

"Oh, all those pretty fall colors."

"I was thinking maybe white and crimson for the cake."

"Or, since we're surrounded by forest, what about a woodland design? I saw something online I'm dying to try." Carol opened her laptop and brought up a page with a three-tiered cake with a hand-painted wooden design in the frosting. It came complete with a heart carved into the wood and inside the heart the couple's initials. Purple wildflowers and petite birds finished the look.

"I love it," said Livi. Simple and sweet, like her love for Morris. "I think he'll like it, too. I'll bring him in later to check it out."

She ran by the grocery store on her way home from work to pick up a few items, and Suz, the checker, was quick to spot her ring. "Ooh, congratulations. Who's the lucky man?"

"Morris Bentley."

"Aww, Morris. He's a sweetie."

"Yes, he is," Livi agreed.

At least her personal life was on track. "You have to find some more big donors," Kate informed her as they went over the Christmas from the Heart books.

"I know," Livi said with a sigh. "I sure don't move in the right circles."

"You know someone who does, and he owes you. Big-time."

Kate didn't have to drop the name. Livi knew exactly who she was talking about. "Oh no. I don't want to ever talk to that man again." And he obviously didn't want to talk to her, either.

"I'm not saying you have to call his office and have a heart-to-heart. But you could shoot off a professional email. In fact, why don't you send it to the CSR director. She can be the middle person. He'll still get the request and the guilt trip, and we'll get money." When Livi hesitated, she added, "You know, it doesn't matter how you feel about the man. You love this nonprofit and we need money."

"You're right," Livi said with a sigh. And that afternoon, before leaving the office, she drafted an email.

From: Olivia Berg, Director, Christmas from the Heart
Date: 1-8-20
To: Ms. Marla Thompson, CSR Director, Hightower Enterprises
Subject: A New Year and New Needs

Dear Ms. Thompson,
I'm sure everyone at Hightower Enterprises is looking forward
to a banner year. We here at Christmas from the Heart are also
looking forward to a good year, and hoping to help even more
people than we have in the past. Even though your company
wasn't able to give last year I'm hoping we can count on you for
this coming one.
Best,
Olivia Berg
Christmas from the Heart
Giving from the heart makes all the difference

There. Done. At least Guy Hightower had met some of the
people they helped. He now knew the work they were doing. He
may have been a cowardly liar but he wasn't completely heartless.

Morris came over for dinner that night and convinced her
father to play cards with them. Oh yes, Morris had so been the
right choice. And later, when he kissed her—okay, so it wasn't
the kind of set-your-panties-on-fire kiss she'd experienced with
a certain deceiver, but it was filled with love—she knew she'd
made a wise decision to get practical and get engaged to Morris.

Her dream that night confirmed it. There she was, in the
church, floating down the aisle, surrounded by friends and family, not a turkey in the bunch. Kate and Terryl and Bettina, her
bridesmaids, were all up at the altar, smiling fondly at her as she
came forward on her father's arm. She was in a gorgeous gown
fit for a Disney Princess's wedding and it swished and rustled as
she walked. The church was filled with roses and gardenias and
pink satin ribbons and candles. The music sounded like an angel

choir singing. And there went Carol Klaussen, staggering under the weight of her wedding cake. It wasn't the one she'd fallen in love with when she'd stopped in at the bakery. No, this was an edifice of a cake, and it was shaped to look like the Eiffel Tower.

"He's taking her there on their honeymoon," whispered Tillie to Suz, the grocery checker. "She always wanted to see the world."

"She made the right decision," Suz whispered back.

"Yes, she did," agreed Tillie's daughter Jean, who was sitting on the other side of Tillie along with Annette.

A voice called down from heaven, "I'm so happy for you, daughter. You're going to have a wonderful life."

The heavens opened and light streamed down on her. She stopped and twirled around in delight, the skirt of her wedding gown billowing out around her. "Everything's perfect."

Yes, it was, and she awoke with a smile on her face.

"I had the best dream," she greeted Bettina when she walked into the office the next day. "I was at my wedding and it was gorgeous."

"What did your gown look like?" Bettina asked.

"Pearls and sequins and gobs of lace. And a long train, removable for dancing."

"Of course."

"And you all looked so beautiful in your dresses."

"Of course," Bettina said again with a grin. "And what were the guys wearing?"

"The guys?"

"Morris and the groomsmen?"

"Morris?" Livi blinked. "I…didn't see him."

"He wasn't at the altar?"

Livi shook her head. Where had Morris been? Everyone else in town had been there, even the grocery checker.

"Well, it was only a dream."

"With no groom. What would someone who interpreted dreams have to say about that?"

"That in a wedding it's all about the bride. You're already planning it and you're playing it out in your head, seeing how you like the flowers and the gown."

Of course. That was it. "You're probably right," Livi said.

"Or else it means," Bettina began with a worried expression.

"I'm sure it means just what you said it did," Livi said before Bettina could complete her thought, and settled at her computer to check her emails.

Here was one from Marla Thompson at Hightower Enterprises. Livi read it, her brows pulling together.

Thanks for getting in touch with me. I trust that you, also, had a great holiday. I hope we'll be able to contribute to your worthy cause this year. The company is still doing some restructuring but I will certainly make our new CFO aware of your organization once we have one in place.

New CFO? Where was the old one?
Livi quickly emailed back.

Guy Hightower is no longer your CFO?

The reply came a couple of hours later.

Mr. Hightower has moved on.

Moved on? Moved where? What happened to him?

As if it mattered. Who cared where Guy Hightower had gone? Not her. She was moving on, herself. Yes, she had definitely made the right decision when she said she'd marry Morris.

Where had Guy Hightower gone?

18

Livi checked a number of wedding venues to see if she could find something that might feel a little more special than the community center. She did find a place in Icicle Falls. Primrose Haus was a charming old Victorian with beautiful grounds. It was a little pricey but it looked worth every penny.

Except she didn't have that many pennies to spend.

"Don't worry about the cost," her father said. "If that's what you want, that's what we'll do. I have some money put by."

"I don't want to eat up your savings," she protested.

"I only have one daughter," he replied. "I want this to be special for you, Snowflake."

"Hey, it's your day. Do what you want," Morris said when she showed him the pictures online.

"You don't sound all that enthused," she said.

He shrugged. "I don't get why the reception has to be so fancy."

"There's nothing wrong with wanting something fancy," she argued.

"I guess."

"Honestly, Morris. You could show a little more enthusiasm."

"I am enthusiastic. About marrying you. The rest is just trimmings. Why does everything have to be such a big deal with you, Liv?"

"Everything? This is our wedding, Morris. It should be a big deal."

"Okay, I didn't mean it that way. I just meant why do we have to pretend we're rich? Who do we need to impress?"

"You think I'm trying to impress people?" Livi asked in a small voice. He made her sound so shallow when all she wanted was to have a pretty storybook wedding. Surely it wasn't wrong to want one special moment in her life.

"Are you? I'm trying to be practical here. The community center is easy for everyone to get to and plenty big."

That it was. A drafty old lodge that had been around for generations. Nothing special.

"But do what you want," Morris finished. *Be shallow and superficial.*

Livi decided to be practical. Streamers and balloons and some flowers and the community center could be spruced up.

It also wouldn't cost an arm and a leg. In fact, Elsa Olsen, who ran the Pine River Park Department, had offered it to her for free. "Anything for you, Livi, you know that," she said.

"It was the smartest decision," she said the next day when she and Kate sat at their usual table in Tillie's Teapot.

"You should have the reception where you really want it," Kate argued. "Don't just settle."

"I'm not settling. I'm being practical."

"Are you sure you're not settling...for everything?"

Livi didn't bother to pretend she didn't know what her friend was talking about. They'd had this conversation more than once since she got engaged.

"I'm happy, Kate. I really am." In the end, it had turned out that Morris was the man for her.

"Where are you going on your honeymoon?"

"We haven't decided yet."

"You can bet it won't be Paris."

No, it wouldn't. She'd be lucky if she could talk Morris out of his idea to go camping. "I don't need to go to Paris. I don't need to go anywhere. I'm happy right here in Pine River."

"I know. I'd just like to see you happier."

This was getting old. "I couldn't get any happier, so you can stop worrying," Livi said firmly, closing the subject.

It was true. She was finally getting married and her biological clock could stop ticking like a time bomb. She was going to have a great life helping people and raising a family. She and Morris were already looking at houses and they had their eye on a cute little Craftsman with a double car garage and a small backyard with an apple tree in it. They'd be married and moved in in time to harvest the apples. And maybe by the next fall they'd have a baby. They were going to start working on having a family right away. The man, the house, the kid—her future was picture-perfect.

And her life was great. So there.

March blew in, along with Livi's birthday. Morris was taking her out for dinner, this time just the two of them.

"Where's he taking you?" Bettina asked as they put their computers to sleep for the day. "Oh, wait. Don't tell me. Family Tree."

"There's nothing wrong with Family Tree," Livi was quick to say, although she'd love to have gone somewhere a little more special. But oh well. This would be special because it would always be their place, the place where they got engaged.

Livi went home and showered and lotioned and perfumed up and put on a simple black dress, which she accented with a green scarf and black stilettos. She checked out her reflection when she was done. Yes, she looked good. Happy. Fulfilled.

The doorbell rang and she slipped off the shoes and hurried downstairs to let Morris in. She was hopping into a shoe when she opened the door and saw Guy Hightower standing on her front porch.

"Don't shut the door," he said, holding out a hand to keep it open.

As if she could. She couldn't move. She stared at him, one shoe on, one in her hand, sure he was a hallucination.

He waved a hand in front of her face. "Livi?"

That snapped her out of it. "You've got a lot of nerve coming back here," she said as she leaned against the doorway and slipped on her other shoe.

"It took all the nerve I had. Nice shoes, by the way. They show off your legs."

"Never mind my shoes. Where have you been? You're no longer at Hightower."

"You were looking for me?"

"For a donation," she snapped. He frowned and she continued, "I figured under the circumstances perhaps Hightower would like to reconsider its position on charitable donations to our organization." There. That sounded better. Nice and professional.

"That's the only reason?"

"What other reason should I have?"

"Missing me? Wanting to talk things out?"

"There was nothing to talk out," she said stiffly.

"Really?"

"Really."

"Then I guess it didn't matter that you couldn't find me at Hightower. Want to know why I left?"

"Not particularly," she lied. "Why did you leave?"

"Because I realized it wasn't a fit for me anymore."

"What are you doing now then?" she asked, the anger sliding out of her.

"Trying to figure out where I go from here. I've got enough investments to live on for a while. I can take my time sorting things out."

Sorting things out. What did that mean? And why was she so interested? She shouldn't be interested. She'd moved on. She was getting married.

"What are you sorting out?" she asked.

"Who I am, for starters. Who I want to be. I'm thinking of turning my hand to fund-raising. God knows I've got the connections."

"Fund-raising," she repeated, trying to frame the picture of this new Guy Hightower in her mind. She didn't know what to say, didn't know what to think even. All she knew was that her heart was racing.

"You look good, Livi," he said softly.

The race got swifter. He looked good, too. He was wearing an expensive overcoat over equally expensive slacks. She looked behind him for his expensive car.

"I don't have it anymore," he said, reading her mind.

"What happened to it?"

"I sold it."

"You sold it?"

He nodded to the humble-looking model sitting out by the parking strip. "That's my new ride. Gets good gas mileage."

"Not very impressive."

"I'm not out to impress. Anyway, I thought the money I got for it could be put to good use somewhere." He held out a manila envelope. "I have something for you. Take it," he urged when she stood there staring at it.

She took it and switched to staring at him.

"Open it."

She did and saw what looked like several checks inside.

"One's from my mom," he said. "I meant to mail it but that seemed cowardly. If a man's going to eat humble pie, he should have a witness. I hope this will help Christmas from the Heart."

She pulled out a check and gasped. Then she stared at him again.

"Just trying my hand at this to see how good I am."

She pulled out another check. He was good. "Why are you doing this?"

"Because I need to. I got pretty pissed when you lit into me."

"I shouldn't have." He'd been a man trying to make up for a bad decision. She hadn't let him, not once she learned who he was.

She'd been so focused on noble deeds that she'd failed to see how ignoble her grudge against him had been. Remorse set in. Why couldn't she have handled things differently? Why couldn't they?

"I could have allocated something for Christmas from the Heart. I went with the more high-profile nonprofits. It was all about Hightower's image. I've learned a lot about image since then, Livi."

"I wish we'd had this conversation earlier." If they had, what would her life look like now? It didn't matter. It was too late.

"I guess I had some lessons to learn. And, honestly, I couldn't come back without proof that I'm on a different path. I hope this proves it."

"Everything you did while you were here proved it." She'd been too humiliated to admit that.

"I'm trying to start a new life, Livi. I'm hoping maybe you'd be open to being part of it."

Too late. She was finding it difficult to get the words out.

"Even Scrooge got a second chance."

She held up her left hand. There was the ring and that said it all.

His smile fell. "Bentley?"

"Yes." Why did she want to cry when her life was so good?

"When?"

"This fall." It was hard to get her voice above a whisper.

"I guess what we'd started was…"

"A fantasy," she supplied.

And here came reality. Morris parked his truck and jumped out. Guy turned, and at the sight of him Morris's easy smile hardened into tightly pressed lips.

"I guess I'm too late," Guy said. "Are you happy?"

Livi felt tears stinging her eyes. She pressed a hand to her lips. Of course she was happy. She nodded. Why had she been so quick to rush on with her life?

Morris had reached the porch. "What are you doing here?" he demanded, glaring at Guy.

"Dropping off some donations for Christmas from the Heart. I hear congratulations are in order." Guy held out his hand.

Morris looked at him suspiciously but took it, and they shook.

"I'm glad for you, Livi. I didn't deserve you."

"Damn right you didn't," growled Morris.

"But I want you to know I'm working hard to become the kind of man you thought I was when you first met me. Wish I'd told you sooner."

Sooner was in the rearview mirror. She was moving on and Guy Hightower wasn't a central figure in that move.

Morris stepped to her side and put an arm around her. "How long you in town for?"

Guy looked at Livi. What was she seeing in his eyes? Longing? Disappointment? Maybe both. It just wasn't meant to be for them.

"Not long, I guess," he said.

"Where are you staying?" she asked, and felt Morris stiffen.

Guy gave a half smile. "The River's Bend. They had a vacancy. Can you believe it?"

Morris grunted. Livi stayed silent. There was nothing to say to that now. Nothing to say at all.

Guy backed down the steps. "Anyway, I hope those contributions help."

"Thank you," she said, and watched him walk away.

"Let's go," Morris said.

He was quiet all the way to the restaurant, and still quiet after he'd slid in next to her in their corner booth.

"Can I start you two lovebirds with drinks?" asked Coral.

Morris frowned at the little vase with the green carnation sitting on the table, announcing the fast approach of St. Patrick's Day. "Champagne."

Neither of them looked like two happy people out for a night of celebration. Coral raised her eyebrows at Livi. *What's going on?*

Livi shook her head.

"You didn't have to order champagne," Livi said as Coral left them.

"It's your birthday. I wanted it to be special," Morris said. He let out a sigh that made his big chest heave.

"Morris," she began, anxious to reassure him. To reassure herself.

"This isn't gonna work, is it?"

"Of course it is," she said. It was halfhearted. She heard it in her voice.

So did he. He shook his head. "We were the same back in high school, but we're not now. We haven't been for years, have we?"

"Morris, don't."

He went on. "I don't want to travel and I could care less about TV shows with people looking for a house on a beach somewhere on the other side of the world. I like it right here. I like my job and I like going out for pizza or watching a game or a movie on TV. That's enough for me. Is it for you?"

Of course it is. Say it. Livi sat mutely, staring at him.

"Give me your hand."

She held out her right hand. His somber expression was rattling her, almost as much as Guy's sudden appearance.

"No, your other hand."

No, this wasn't right. She couldn't hurt Morris this way. "Morris, I'm happy in Pine River."

"You could be happier." He reached over and took her left hand. She watched with both horror and relief as he wiggled the ring off her finger.

"Oh, Morris," she said sadly as he dropped it on the tablecloth.

"If we'd really been right for each other we'd have been married years ago. I love you, Liv, and I want you to be happy."

But she didn't feel happy. She felt awful. "Morris," she pleaded as he slid out of the booth.

He didn't say anything and the next thing she knew she was sitting alone, surrounded by couples.

Coral arrived with the champagne. "Where's Morris?"

"Gone."

There was no sense staying in Pine River. That story was finished. Guy went back to the motel for his things. He wouldn't have Livi Berg, but he'd have the gift she gave him, the desire to be a better man.

It didn't take long to pay his bill and grab his overnight bag. He was walking to his car when Morris Bentley pulled into the parking lot in his truck.

He parked it next to Guy's car and got out. "Going somewhere, Hightower?"

"Yeah. I'm leaving. What are you doing here?"

"Making sure you don't leave. She's at the restaurant."

Guy stared at him, not sure he was understanding.

"It's you she wants."

What man in his right mind would give up Olivia Berg?

Bentley scowled. "Go on. What are you waiting for?"

Nothing! Guy opened his car, threw in his overnight bag.

"Hightower."

He stopped, halfway in.

"If you ever make her cry I'll beat the shit out of you."

"Deal," Guy said. He got in, shut the door and peeled out.

Livi poured herself another glass of champagne. The first one had been for shock treatment. The second glass was for... She wasn't sure. Consolation. Not every woman could manage to lose two men in one night.

Morris she hadn't really lost. He'd always be her friend. But Guy, the new and improved Guy—he'd been on her porch and then he'd been gone. She shouldn't have let him go. He really was the man for her, the right man. She thought back to the simple pleasures they'd enjoyed—playing cards, walking in the snow, watching a movie. None of those things were glamorous, certainly not on a par with traveling the world. But that hadn't mattered. Morris had it right all along. It didn't matter where you were or where you went. It only mattered who you were with. And she knew who she needed to be with.

She had to find him, but now she was stranded at the restaurant without a car. She fumbled in her purse for her cell phone. She'd call her dad, get him to run her over to the motel.

What if Guy had decided to leave? Panicked, she dug faster. Where was her phone?

"Looking for something?" asked a deep voice.

She looked up and there was Guy. She could feel happiness rising in her, filling her chest, tears prickling her eyes. "Only you."

From the Heart

19

The second marriage proposal Livi received was very differ-ent from the first. There were no friends around to witness because the proposal took place in a limousine, an extravagance her sweetheart said he was not going to make a habit of in the future, because, "I'll have important investments to make, such as certain worthy nonprofits."

The big moment had come after dinner at the Space Needle on May 5—the one-year anniversary of that fateful day when she'd first heard the name Guy Hightower. There were no pre-dictions of what a good life she and Guy would have together. There was no need. She already knew.

The ring was a princess cut one-carat diamond with a rose gold band. "Do you like it?" Guy had asked.

"I love it. And I love you!"

The wedding still took place the weekend after Labor Day, as planned. The bride was beautiful as she stood under the arbor in the garden at Primrose Haus in Icicle Falls. And it was the best moment of Guy's life when the minister finally said the long awaited, "You may kiss your bride." And kiss her he did, to hoots and applause from the men and a chorus of sighs from every female present.

The reception was a catered affair with salmon and prawns, prime rib and Caesar salad—something the groom had insisted on paying for. The cake was an edifice, a miniature Eiffel Tower to signify the bride and groom's honeymoon destination.

"You two are going to be so happy," Livi's sister-in-law predicted, then said to Livi, "Now, hurry up and get pregnant so little David has a cousin to play with."

"We'll have fun working on that," Guy said, making his bride blush.

"Good luck," Morris Bentley said to them. He kissed Livi on the cheek and shook hands with Guy, giving his blessing—something that was easier to do now that he'd met a woman online. She was into monster truck racing and camping and action movies.

"A much better match for him than I ever was," Livi had said, although Morris wasn't quite ready to admit that yet.

Her father had welcomed Guy to the family and his mother was delighted to finally have an ideal daughter. And the stepsisters… Sent their regrets and place settings of Livi and Guy's china. Mom had brought a special gift for the couple: the Limoges chocolate pot. Which, had, of course, put Livi in tears and endeared her to his mother forever.

"I hope it works out," Guy's brother Mike said to him later as the couple made the rounds, visiting with their guests.

"It will," Guy said. "And thanks for the contribution."

Mike shook his head. "A goofy wedding present if you ask me. But then I think you've gone nuts. Leaving us, selling the Maserati and your digs in Seattle, moving to that Podunk town—dude, where is your head these days?"

"In a good place," Guy assured him.

"You've lost your edge."

"No, I'm just focusing in a new direction."

"You're gonna end up broke," Mike warned.

He looked to where his bride stood, visiting with Tillie and her daughters. "Never," he said. He was now a very rich man.

★ ★ ★ ★ ★

RECIPES

How to Make Your Christmas Special— Tips From Christmas from the Heart

- Buy or make a tree ornament every year to commemorate something happening in your life—a trip, an anniversary, new baby, or new friend.
- Get together with someone you care about and create something special to enjoy over the holidays, such as hand-crafted greeting cards, candy corn or fudge.
- Make decorating for the holidays a team event. It's much more fun to dress up the house together!
- Take an older relation out for lunch or a holiday latte and let that person reminisce about Christmases past.
- Be sure to hang some mistletoe!
- Go see Santa, no matter how old you are.
- Take cookies to your neighbor.
- Enter a fruitcake competition. You might win!
- Share a memory by passing on a family treasure to a younger family member.
- Give a little extra to your favorite charity. And always give from the heart.

From Our Kitchens to Yours

We couldn't let you leave town without sharing recipes for some of our favorite holiday treats. A heartfelt Merry Christmas from your Pine River friends.

Bernadette's Banana Bread Fruitcake
(makes one loaf)

Ingredients:

1 ¾ cups flour
2 ¼ teaspoon baking powder
½ teaspoon salt
⅓ cup butter
⅔ cup sugar
2 eggs
1 cup mashed banana
¾ cup golden raisins
¾ cup chopped candied cherries
¾ cup chopped dried apricots
¾ cup chopped walnuts

Directions:

Sift flour, baking powder and salt into a large mixing bowl. Add sugar, butter, eggs and bananas and mix well. Add the rest of the ingredients and pour into a greased loaf pan. Bake for 1 hour at 350°F. Remove when pan is cool and set on wire rack until completely cool.

Chocolate Cherry Chunk Fruitcake
Created by the real-life Janet Kragen

Ingredients:

One 16-ounce package candied cherries (about 2 rounded cups)
Bottle of crème de cacao

3 ½ cups all-purpose flour
1 ½ teaspoon baking powder
⅓ cup Ghirardelli ground chocolate/cocoa
1 teaspoon ground cardamom

1 ½ cups softened butter (no margarine!)
1 ¾ cups sugar
6 eggs
⅓ cup milk
1 teaspoon vanilla

One 10 oz. package of Ghirardelli 60% cacao bittersweet
chocolate chips
One 11 oz. package of Ghirardelli classic white chocolate chips
(Or buy the weights and chop the bars in order to have some irregularity in the chocolate pieces.)

1 to 1 ½ cup shelled roasted pistachios (green)

Directions:

Combine cherries and ⅓ cup crème de cacao in a bowl and soak several hours or overnight.

Preheat oven to 300°F. Grease and flour pans: one batch fills one large Bundt pan or 2 large bread loaf pans. Sift flour, baking powder, cocoa and cardamom on waxed paper. Beat butter and sugar in large bowl with electric mixer until smooth. Beat in eggs.

Stir in flour mixture alternately with milk and vanilla, beating until smooth after each addition.

Stir in fruit mixture, nuts and chocolate chunks with a spoon. Bake for two hours in a Bundt pan and for 1 hour and 45 minutes in two loaf pans. Test with a knife. Make sure the fruitcake is completely baked! Cool in pan on wire rack for 20 minutes. Remove from pan. Cool.

Wrap cooled cake in cheesecloth. Use pastry brush to coat whole cake liberally with crème de cacao. Wrap in foil.

Store 3 to 4 weeks—or much longer—in refrigerator or unheated garage in wintertime.

Check every week or so, and re-soak cloth if it dries out. Use a pastry brush to add more crème de cacao.

Heat before serving. Serve with whipped cream. Add a little crème de cacao to the cream before whipping it—don't add anything else!

Livi's Candy Cane Cookies
Courtesy of Pat Greco

Ingredients:

5 ½ cups flour
3 teaspoons baking powder
Dash of salt
3 eggs
½ pound butter
1 cup sugar
1 teaspoon vanilla
¾ cup milk

Directions:

Mix sugar and butter in large bowl. Add eggs, one at a time, beat well. Add vanilla and milk and mix again.

Sift dry ingredients and add to mixture. Dough will be stiff and sticky. Work the dough with well-floured hands and knead well. Roll each cookie in rope form about 4 inches long and tuck in end to form a rounded candy cane shape. Bake at 400°F for 12 to 14 minutes. When cool, frost with a thin icing and decorate with colored sprinkles.

Livi's Eggnog Coffee Cake

Ingredients:

1 ½ cups flour
2 tablespoons baking powder
½ teaspoon salt
¾ cup sugar
¼ cup butter
1 egg
½ cup eggnog
1 cup chopped candied cherries

For Streusel:
½ cup brown sugar
2 tablespoons flour
2 teaspoons cinnamon
2 tablespoons butter, melted
½ cup chopped walnuts

Directions:

Cream sugar, butter and egg. Sift in dry ingredients and add chopped cherries and eggnog. If the batter seems too dry you can add a little more eggnog. Spread half of the batter on a greased 9 by 9 square pan. Add half the streusel mixture, sprinkling evenly. Add remaining batter. Sprinkle top with remaining streusel and bake at 350°F for 30 minutes or until a toothpick inserted comes out clean.